Y0-EHI-306

How Comfortable Are Those Shoes?

Jack Connor

Balboa Press books may be ordered through booksellers or by contacting:

Balboa Press
A Division of Hay House
1663 Liberty Drive
Bloomington, IN 47403
www.balboapress.com
1 (877) 407-4847

Print information available on the last page.

ISBN: 978-1-9822-1826-3 (sc)
ISBN: 978-1-9822-1824-9 (hc)
ISBN: 978-1-9822-1825-6 (e)

Library of Congress Control Number: 2019900125

Balboa Press rev. date: 01/07/2019

To Bob

Although sometimes we aren't prepared for the things that happen in life, learning from others and the gifts they possess can show how special life really is. Taking enough time to process things in terms of the all instead of one is the only thing that can make it seem easier that you're gone. I'm grateful to have been a part of your life.

Contents

Preface

The idea for this book is simple: we are all the same—to a point. We are all here for different reasons. We are here to experience life in the forms we do and to learn, teach, grow, create, feel, give, receive, and do. Change can happen in ways we may or may not see or understand. Sometimes it is obvious, and other times it isn't. No one is perfect.

I've been blessed to have met some people both willingly and unwillingly who were necessary parts of my life. They allowed me to see life in a different way. Each entered my life at the right time, even though I didn't know it. They were all essential for multiple reasons.

The early chapters of this book include some basic information that I feel is necessary and sometimes overlooked. The other parts of the book are about how life has played out for me.

This is a true story. I've changed some of the names. There is no need to say where this took place because it could have been anywhere. It's life. Some things happen that we can't control. Sometimes we have to make choices. Some things happen that we don't or can't understand.

Maybe you can relate. Maybe you can understand the idea and reason behind this book. If not, that's okay. Maybe later you will.

Since we all are always changing, whether we like it or not, the shoes we stand in change too—that's just life. Finding out and being comfortable with who you are in whatever shoes you're in at certain times is what many are here to experience. Sometimes wearing no shoes is the best answer for everyone.

Acknowledgments

I would to thank my family, friends and all the persons mentioned in the book. I'd also to many others along the way whom I didn't. For the their help, kindness, the lessons and experiences. Some of which that may not have been realized at the time in which they did, they do today. Thank you.

Part 1

1

You Are Energy

You are energy. It's a simple concept. You have a heartbeat; you are alive. Since you are alive, you are living and existing and a part of life. The heartbeat is the first thing tested when we are born—and even well before that. Throughout a woman's pregnancy, a doctor checks the fetal heartbeat to see if things are progressing properly.

What is it that makes the heart beat, though, in scientific terms? I have no idea. I do know that in some cases, the heart needs help to sustain itself. This can and does happen at any time in living things. Usually, some type of trauma occurs, or something just is the way it is and requires some type of assistance.

As humans, we try to keep our hearts healthy—and all the other things inside us too. We've found ways to keep our hearts going even when they are failing or aren't working at all. We are encouraged to take optimal care of our bodies.

In many cases, how a person treats his or her body is up to the individual, but many things can affect any living body at different times, points, and places in life. The heart is what makes us go, though. It pumps the blood to the organs, muscles, tissues, cells, and all that other stuff to fuel the other parts of us to work.

The heart keeps our lungs breathing, which, as everyone is probably aware, is essential for the brain. Obviously, the brain is important for many reasons. That's where we learn; understand; process; develop; store; and have the capacity to function, grow, and, most of all, react.

Researchers have studied the brain throughout time and continually do so to this day. The brain and its ability to fully function are by far the most important things we could ever study. The brain is powerful. It's limitless.

Somewhere between the brain and the heart in every one of us is what brings it all together—something science hasn't found. It is the pure energy that allows us to be alive. People have different opinions about what to call it. It depends on numerous factors.

It is enough to say it is your soul. The soul is what allows all of us to exist. When we're born into this world, no matter where, when, or why, we all exist because of it. Each person, animal, and living thing has one. Anything that has a heart has a soul.

The energy we are can change depending on certain points, places, and events throughout the span of life. Anyone's energy or vibration can become higher or lower; it can go to the extremes of each. We are energy, and the energy comes from having a soul.

You can't sell your soul; that's impossible. Because we each have a soul, some see us—and we may see ourselves—as spiritual beings. Despite having souls or being spiritual, we can make what seem to be bad decisions—bad morally, ethically, and in other ways.

In certain cases, we can sense or feel the energy that we give off or that surrounds us. Animals have this sense, but anyone can have the ability to sense emotions from anything with a soul. We have the ability to sense vibrations also. We can both give and receive energy. It's possible to create it and lessen it.

You can't love or hate anything that doesn't have a soul—anything that isn't living or breathing. Things without souls are only to be experienced. Take swimming, for example. I love swimming, but it can't love me. I enjoy the experience. I can swim in a pool, lake, river, or ocean.

The depth of the water and the elements I swim in allow the experience to occur. If it's not safe to swim, I might not love swimming as much. I might need to swim out of necessity, though, so I love that I can.

The same can apply to places where anyone is or has been. Consider a church. You don't even need to know its religion. Empty or with people in it—it doesn't matter. Churches are usually places of worship of something greater than ourselves. Whether quiet or joyous, these places are usually respected, reserved places with nonaggressive feelings in them. The energy they give off is usually seen in a positive or nonthreatening way.

Consider a prison. The energy of the people and the place is probably completely different. The atmosphere is likely built on fear, hate, anger, and other negative energies that have grown within it. Some souls there never return to life outside the prison. There is a greater chance for negative energy to develop.

Those who can leave it might carry the energy out with them if they do. They might not be considered criminals either. Escaping that type of energy or anything like it can be difficult. Energy can attach itself to other things. It can inspire in either direction.

Energy is created everywhere a heart beats, whether in one person, a million, or even billions. History shows us that many have tried to inspire others to raise or lower the energy at a particular moment.

Even today we see people trying to control others' energy, whether or not they admit it. Sometimes we see that we're unable to control the energy we or others have created. The thing to remember is that we react to energy as much as we create it ourselves. Energy is a constant that has been going on for many billions of years now. How long the energy exists in each person is anyone's guess. The point is that we all have it; we are all the same.

When the energy of the soul ends, the soul returns to wherever it came from.

2

Why Are We Here?

This question has so many possible answers that it's almost unfair to ask it. It's pretty simple, though, if you get simple enough to answer it. We are all here to experience, and some are probably here to do a lot more than that. Experiences can be different for everyone. That's why we are all different in our own ways. It's that way for every person on this earth.

When we look at all things on a grand scale, there is so much to see that it's overwhelming to take in. However, by narrowing the view down to one person, one individual, either ourselves or anyone else throughout time, maybe we will be able to see the why, where, how, and what if we look deep enough. Sometimes it can be easy to see, and other times it isn't.

We all have some things in common. We are all born into this world the same way. We are either male or female. We all have some type of pigment that creates skin color. The sizes and weights of many are the same. The date and time of birth can be exactly the same for some. Some even have the same name.

After that, though, things change. All the factors of who we are and why we are here might not be as visible or logical, or there aren't enough words to explain those factors in terms we are capable of understanding. It just is. It's life.

For reasons of our own curiosity, as one or as a whole, we ask the same questions about everything until we process or prove plausible solutions. These can be for ourselves or others. They can be with people, places, and things throughout time. When we don't fully understand an issue, we can sometimes try to explain it so that it is understandable, and much of the time, we can do so without all the information regarding what, who, how, where, and why. The bottom line is this: we guess.

Because of what, how, and why things are, these things can force or create new experiences that one or many may or may not be prepared for. Oftentimes, just because something is new to one person, that doesn't mean it hasn't happened before to someone else. It usually has, with nearly seven billion people on Earth.

Some experiences can change a person, a few, many, or the world all together. Look at the history of almost everything. History is by far the greatest teacher in how we attempt to gauge or create the future, including all of the mistakes or advancements and what we learn from each. However, that doesn't mean we will not make more mistakes or guarantee future successes.

We can change through anything that causes us to see things differently, such as the development or concepts of any of the sciences, mathematics, religion, spiritual beliefs, or any beliefs in any part of the world. Experiences can also be for leisure or pleasure.

Experiences are in anything we can think of that can be considered good or bad. They exist in every relationship and all we encounter, learn from, or are inspired by—or not. Developing ideas can come from any experience.

All things have happened or are happening within different levels of technology, wisdom, and our development. From the beginning of time, our minds have been for our own growth or basic survival. Today it's much more than that, though. Depending on available outlets, resources are different for everyone. It means we're all here for different reasons.

Ask children in kindergarten in any place in the world what they want to be when they grow up. You might get some interesting replies. Ask the same kids at age ten and then at fifteen or twenty. Many of those answers will be nowhere near their original plans. Some of the individuals might not even be alive anymore. Some might have great impacts all over the world.

At any time, we can be misdirected from the path we assumed was correct or desired. Our own free will, the will of others, or an act of God can lead us to particular places or events. I'll discuss the God thing in another chapter.

The resources or events of life might be variables in why we are here. Parental influences, access to or lack of money, nourishment, physical and emotional well-being, spiritual beliefs, where we live and at what point in time, and more all play a part in creating the energy of why and for what we are here this time. Any life experience can change in a moment of time for everyone and everything.

Many people have the necessities to live normal and enjoyable lives. We can try to comprehend how and why others are led on another path to achieve what they are here to do, with or without certain variables available.

What anyone does or how someone finds a particular calling depends on many things. Some might be obvious, while others will never be fully understood.

In life, we'll encounter or learn of people who can do or accomplish things they are naturally gifted at. Others have to work harder to achieve the same.

Unfortunately, at times, certain influences can slow, alter, or stop us from one or more possible events we are here for. These influences may be mental, emotional, physical, or spiritual. Sometimes they affect how people see themselves or how others view them.

Some are less affected by the same or things close to the same that deter others. The determination for the experience is for a purpose that isn't to be denied. These realizations can happen to anyone at any time and usually do. It can be a passion or purpose.

They're also some who might have less or nothing and then somehow have all they want. They find happiness and gratitude for what they are to experience.

Some things we are here to experience or are led to experience aren't fun or desirable. They can be sad, difficult, draining, senseless, and dumbfounding.

No matter what emotions or feelings anyone's experiences create, with reason or none at all, those experiences are why we exist. It's why we are here: we are here to live, be, and do.

There is something we are all here for. We are here to do something for ourselves or with others or to be assisted by others. The experiences for each might be the same, close to the same, or not at all the same. It depends on many factors. We all can be affected by a number of combinations of factors too, because we are all the same.

3

Where You Come In

This concept might be the easiest of all. We are all born into this world the same way. Where exactly that is isn't the same for everyone. Place of birth can have an effect on how people are perceived or influence how they look at themselves or the place or places they exist in. It can effect one's view of others and even the entire world.

The world today has new life entering it in all places every moment. In the same way, lives are constantly ending. Predicting when life will enter is easier, though. We can predict a date of arrival. Obviously, the arrival can be earlier or later than the prediction too.

There can be great anticipation for a birth, and there can be concern about it for a multitude of possibilities. Many factors impact how a life can go. Upon entering the world, a newborn is completely defenseless. It is unable to survive by itself, unable to fully communicate with words, and sensitive to everything, and it relies on so much. It doesn't even know who or what it is before entering the world.

The amount love and dedication necessary to raise a child in any situation might be the most selfless thing to ask of anyone, but it is essential. Love and dedication are needed to survive. When a life begins, its immediate state of health and availability of life-sustaining resources play huge parts in its continuance.

Depending on what part of Earth it's born into, there are questions of health. To whom is it born? What are that person's view of life, age, personality, family, culture, financial status, and education? Physical, mental, and emotional issues exist or are created during maturity and growth.

Many more things can compound the who, what, why, and how questions that come along with any of us, but being born is step one. We all enter life the same way; you can't argue that. It seems we are all the same that way. We are also the same in that no physical body lives forever. All of our bodies eventually die.

4

Influences

Whether or not it's noticeable to a person as a child or an adult, the presence or lack of influences that surround each and every person can help create or allow what we are here to experience. They also can create beliefs regarding what we do or do not want to do or be at any point. Certain things introduced at particular moments can greatly effect life in every way to different extremes.

Development is based on the many people, places, and things we willingly or unwillingly allow or have happen to us or to others that have the ability to make us act or react in certain ways at different times in our lives. These, and our thoughts and actions toward them, can change at any time based on what happens throughout our lives.

In a way, what we do or don't do is based on the decisions we learn to make or how we feel internally toward particular moments or toward time and events that occur in life. We can accept decisions as either right or wrong. They can be educational, inspirational, recreational, or out of necessity and can lead us to or deter us from life's possibilities.

Outside influence can shape how a person sees the world, views creation, and, more importantly, sees him- or herself currently in it. It can affect a person's ability to relate to or communicate with others. It can affect how someone sees and develops him- or herself. Individual growth, maturity, and social skills may be advanced, slowed, or even crippled by a variety of circumstances.

What is considered a healthy environment to be in or grow up in? Some factors include differences in number of parents, types of love, types of discipline, financial resources, health-related issues, education, and positive or negative role models. There are many others. These can be a way to explain or even assign blame for circumstances in life. Anyone can use them as positives and negatives. Some factors might not even be noticed.

In the world today, different things are considered normal compared to how life was in years past. Look back twenty, fifty, a hundred, two hundred, or five hundred years ago or even further. Various influences have made major impacts on the world to benefit us all.

There are influences in all phases of life; they are a constant. Television and the internet have us connected to everything. We have local, state, national, and world news at our fingertips in an instant. The weather is an influence on how we approach the day.

How we see the world involves influences on multiple levels: social, economic, emotional, physical, and spiritual. Many things create our beliefs and views regarding governments, countries, religion, freedom, races, equality, and our feelings toward them.

In whatever time, place, and age group we fall into, we are always influenced by many factors. We have the ability to learn from and adjust to our surroundings. We are guided in some life choices and shielded from others that might not be the best thing for us. Still, an experience might be essential for how we handle or see other particular events later on in life. It might also show or teach us what is needed to take further action or leave moments, people, places, or events behind in life.

Some influences, or the lack thereof, can feel permanent, and they might be. They might also be inspirational or essential to have, or not, for the lives we are currently living or would like to create.

Influence can be as simple as looking in the mirror and deciding it's time to change one, some, or all the things we are experiencing at a particular point. The people, places, and things that influence one person might not do the same for another.

Influences of any type can motivate or inspire anyone in any direction. They can also slow or even stop people, places, and things. An influence might help one see, learn, or discover the answers to questions about everything or anyone. It might also show we are the same in some way.

5

Emotions and Feelings

Whatever we are born into, in one way or another, we develop emotions and feelings based on the influences surrounding us, including who, what, where, when, and what is or isn't available to us in life. Maybe some feelings are installed in us before we are born. Any or all of these factors can change in any way throughout life as one grows. They can also remain the same throughout life.

Those who experience issues due to mental, physical, or emotional situations might have different types of feelings compared to others in certain ways, but they're still inside.

Anything we can see, feel, touch, smell, hear, or sense can create a variety of reactions. Emotions come from reactions to feelings we encounter or perceive. They can be fairly obvious or can be held within without the knowledge of others surrounding us. We can hide them if need be for whatever reason.

Ideally, we usually try to do or experience things that make us feel good or comfortable. Some things we encounter won't make us feel that way, though. When certain things happen, we might wish we didn't have to experience them due to how they make us feel.

Our placement in the world and the circumstances surrounding our development can add to or lessen our emotions and feelings toward life and how we see it. These factors may be seen as good or bad, depending on personal beliefs. As we age, our feelings and emotions can change for many reasons.

Firsthand experiences usually are the best way to develop feelings toward encounters in life. We may or may not enjoy the experiences that create these reactions. We can be told or taught things too. These can be true, or they can be misleading, as one person's experiences and feelings might be completely different from another's.

Seeing individuals' emotions can also have an effect. It can create the same or enhanced versions of other emotions. It can also create opposite emotions. It also might have no effect either way.

We also have the capacity to imagine and place ourselves in others' situations. We might do so for reasons of enjoyment or necessity or to see how something affects others. These imaginings might help or harm, and we don't even know it. Emotions and feelings can create energy within us too.

Some emotions are based on beliefs or the influences around us. They can cause new ones, depending on the person, time, and event. Some we can learn from throughout the history of the world and the individuals in it. Emotions and feelings toward the moment we are in have inspired love and hate, healing and suffering, spiritual growth and multiple religions, necessity and leisure, independence and freedom, laws and rebellions.

Emotions and feelings can lead to or force change willingly or unwillingly. It is undeniable that emotions and feelings are the reason life has developed as it has. It's scary to see a person without feelings or emotions. Emotions make us seem as if we're all the same in some way.

6

Skills, Talents, Abilities, and Gifts

When born into this world, we are tested on a variety of different subjects early in life and as we grow and mature. Tests can be done to determine intellect, physical potential, or a multitude of other things, depending on the exact place or time.

Genetics or family heritage can influence abilities. There might also be no genetic explanation for why certain individuals are below average, average, or above average in any area.

Every person in some way, based on his or her own individual makeup, has some type of abilities, if not multiples of them. They allow us to participate in some way in life. Oftentimes, they can lead us in different directions in our lives.

In some, abilities appear to come easily or naturally. We might say their particular skill, talent, ability, or gift is God-given.

Some skills are found through testing in different varieties of ways. Sometimes tests can't prove them, though. Anyone can develop skills, enhance talents, and use abilities. A gift might involve the combination of all three and applying them with the intent with which they were meant to be applied. Some people have to work to achieve skills through experience and life.

Gifts can also create judgment regarding how we use them and what we use them for. Sometimes we use them, and others times we might not. Some might come at different times in a person's life.

Judgments can be either helpful or detrimental to anyone or anything, even a place. The feeling of being judged isn't necessarily fair in many cases. Self-judgment might not always be fair either. Judgment can hurt or mislead, depending on the factors of who, what, where, when, and how.

The development of skills, along with the reasons behind how people use them, can be different. Some skills, talents, abilities, and gifts might come easier for some. Two or more persons might take uniquely different paths to get to the same place. We can make different choices to achieve a necessity, goal, or passion or just to enjoy using our gifts.

Time has shown the ways in which many different people around the world throughout history have used their skills to enhance life for either themselves or others, even millions. We have been able to learn directly from others who inspire the use of certain skills, talents, abilities, or gifts. They might be essential or influential in our own personal lives. Stories of family sacrifice, enjoyment, or how people lived in certain parts of history can impact us. It could be anyone throughout history.

There are also people, places, and things that challenge us to push and dig further physically, educationally, or spiritually in our careers or leisure. The influences can happen at any time in any given life.

There is the possibility we might not enjoy the moment of learning or experiencing something new, but it might be helpful for moments later in life or allow us to create or perfect new skills, talents, abilities, and gifts within. We use our gifts to think, learn, participate, or compete. Sometimes we can avoid an experience, and other times it's inevitable.

Some use their own particular gifts in ways that may be viewed as negative or bad. Some of those individuals are obvious in history. The misuse of skills, talents, abilities, and gifts can do harm to ourselves and others. How we use them is up to each of us.

There are many obvious moments of such harm. People have committed horrible actions upon other people, places, and things for reasons we may or may not understand. Whether we do good or bad things with what we have, we have the potential to change, add to, or improve our skills, talents, and abilities.

When you realize these gifts, you can see or know the gifts that you or others have. They might also allow us to see the potential of why we are really here.

Whether we use our gifts in career choices, worldly enhancements, or just for fun, we as individuals all add to the world in some way with who we are. We might not realize we can change or shape the development of the world by who we are and what capabilities we have.

We may experience events at any time that sidetrack us. These can affect our or others' potential to achieve what we are here to accomplish. We might not have control over these events.

On a larger scale, people have used talents, abilities, and gifts since time began. They are in everything that we are today. We would be nothing without them. Who has what gift? How are skills used? Those are questions that most ask, and the answers aren't always agreed upon.

The progression and development of mathematics, science, astronomy, music, architecture, cooking, speaking, teaching, parenting, sports, the military, computers, different forms of communication, and anything else you can imagine are based on the use of them.

People influence history with their gifts every day. We can do great things with them and still make mistakes. We have imperfections and flaws too. This shows we are all the same.

7

Religion and Beliefs

I mean no offense to anyone in whatever religion or belief system he or she follows or adheres to in his or her own life. I have one of my own. There were times when I didn't. There have been times when I questioned it.

Throughout time, there have been roughly more than four thousand different religions or belief systems since the start of mankind. That's a big number. How these were totaled or who counted them I have no idea, but for the sake of giving a number, that's what I found.

Many people today have no religious belief at all. That's fine too; there's nothing wrong with that. The reasons for such beliefs might be different depending on whom you ask.

With the population of the planet pushing beyond seven billion, the top ten religions are roughly the following:

1) Christianity: 2.2 billion
2) Islam: 1.6 billion
3) Hinduism: 1.1 billion
4) Buddhism: 490 million
5) Shintoism: 100 million
6) Daoism: 90 million
7) Sikhism: 28 million

8) Judaism: 14 million
9) Muslim: 10 million
10) Cao Dai: 6 million

These are from all parts of the world. Various different beliefs can be found in the same religion. The many different forms of Christianity are an easy example.

If you do the math and add the figures above, you'll probably notice that the total doesn't add up to the world's population. There is a reason for that: you must add in the nonreligious factions. The combined total of secular, agnostic, and atheist individuals falls just behind Hinduism, in fourth place overall, at more than one billion.

Where one is born can have a direct influence on which religion, if any, is introduced into one's life. When people move to new locations from all parts of the world, their regions and religions travel with them.

People interpret religious beliefs all over the world in different ways. The definition of the same religion can be different. It will probably always be this way.

The way things are today, the world is crossing itself over from corner to corner. People from different countries move to different places for different reasons. They also bring their religious beliefs with them. It has been and can still be difficult for others to understand different religions.

Religions are simply stories that have been passed down through time. Belief in them is entirely up to an individual. No matter the religion, people believe for many different reasons. These beliefs can impact views on birth and death, healing and understanding, forgiveness and redemption, giving and receiving, and more. The list is too long to finish here.

Some religions define how time started. Some define how to live. Some define the idea of the connection we have as one with the divine or the universe and how we ideally should be. Some define miracles; some define destruction. Again, the list is too long.

Each religion has certain relics or pieces to show supposed proof of its existence. In many cases, there is no proof available today for many religions, so people act on faith.

Faith is basically trusting without seeing, or relying on an inner knowing. Sometimes things happen that we can't define and that test our belief system—unexplainable or undefinable events for which there are no plausible answers. There are silver linings in tragic moments. There are certain situations we can explain only as miracles.

Many religions are based on the principles of peace, love, kindness, and blessings from man to man. Many have some type of ruling individual, supreme being, or creator to whom believers pay homage in the form of rituals, celebrations, prayer, offerings, and other practices.

Are the stories passed down over time in any religion exactly the same as they were when those events happened? They can be described as stories of folk lore if you think about. That's how those who don't believe think. Some also change religions for various reasons. I have met people with both points of view. They want proof.

Many religions ask for belief in how things were, are, and will be. Some speak of certain people who have had one-on-one connections with a higher power or God. Many have archangels and angels, along with other subdivisions of celestial beings. Miracles have been performed in many religions.

Some religions refer to the same individuals who exist in other religions. Many of them share the same message; the story line is the only thing that differs.

Many of these beliefs differ in where we come from before we are born and where we go after our souls have expired. In between those times are who we become, what we learn, how we use it, where we use it, the purpose and reason for it, the value of it, and, most of all, how we do it with what we have available at different points throughout life's journey. Because of that, we are all the same despite whoever or whatever created us.

8

Relationships

We have a relationship with everything we encounter. Relationships can be mental, physical, and spiritual. Relationships start at birth or, for some people, even before that. Ask a pregnant woman how and what she is feeling, and you will see that her relationship with the unborn has already begun. Possibly it has for the father too. There might also be siblings, grandparents, and so on.

As we grow and develop and our communication skills come forth, we encounter more relationships, including with toys, books, other children, and even others' spiritual beliefs and influences. In some circumstances, these might not occur.

We are born into many factors. Parental presence, the time and place, elements of nature, financial availability or lack thereof, physical or emotional issues, and overall health issues are just a few. Gender and race can't be overlooked.

The ideas and beliefs inside us and installed in us as we grow can create or negate some of the relationships we encounter. How we are taught and influenced in multiple ways can determine how we react and why we do so.

The relationships in people's lives can change. They usually do. In many cases, change is essential, but sometimes it goes unnoticed. Other times it does not. As maturity levels develop at different times for everyone, a person's skills, talents, abilities, and gifts can influence certain relationships to grow, stagnate, or end. The addition or subtraction of people, places, and things has the ability to lead people to new or different relationships, including friendships at any age. Relationships may provide challenges essential to learning why or what we are here to experience. They can shape how we view ourselves or others, either in healthy or unhealthy ways.

Some might be strong bonds of either love or dislike for people, careers, or anything you can imagine. We have relationships with things we have no control over too, such as the weather outside. Our relationships with people, places, or things can be beautiful or negative. They can be life-altering.

We need many individuals in life to help us experience why we are here. The relationships can be as friends, competitors, children, siblings, parents, aunts, uncles, educators, students, healers, builders, leaders, mentors and mentees, and so on. We need these interactions to experience a variety of feelings and emotions, including love, freedom, happiness, joy, independence, inspiration, creativity, regret, anger, healing, forgiveness, and many others.

We obviously can't have a relationship with every person in the world. There are too many people for that to happen. With the technology we have today, we can better try to understand other people and cultures. By seeing the world and events going on in it and traveling all across the world for work and pleasure, we all have some level of a relationship with the world. It can affect us in physical, emotional, and sometimes financial ways.

Spiritual relationships tend to be different depending on the person. Spirituality can play a dramatic part in one's life. Spirituality is for the most part a feeling or belief. Spiritual relationships can be with cultures, religious beliefs, nature, or even like-minded or inspiring individuals in your current life or the past.

Some relationships are sudden or unpredictable and can produce effects that can advance and assist or harm and even end in a split second. Sometimes we have no understanding or comprehension of why they occur.

All the relationships we have allow us to experience something.

Since we are all born in different places at different times, everyone will have different ones. They can lead anyone anywhere. They can also stop us from realizing why we are here. Sometimes we need new relationships to help us get there. We can embrace them, or we can resist them. They might depend on the individual and his or her fear or desperation at a particular time.

Sometimes we take relationships for granted. Our perception of the relationship might also be different from that of whomever or whatever the relationship is with.

The most important of all relationships is the one with ourselves, including how we feel toward and treat ourselves.

Anyone at any time can go through highs and lows with any relationship, including the one with him- or herself. Being physically, emotionally, spiritually, and even financially fit can be a benefit to one, many, or all the relationships we have. It doesn't have to be, though.

Like anything else, change is unavoidable in the many relationships we have with everything, mostly because we change. Our beliefs can change. Relationships can get better or worse from our own perspective. The reactions we have might be different depending on the who, what, where, and why involved. It seems like it's pretty much the same for everyone.

9

Interpretation, Intelligence, Intuition

How we are taught to see or process what we absorb, whether considered good or unfortunate, at any stage in life can be different. The many factors of a particular individual's life can lead to certain motivations or none at all, depending on the questions of who, why, what, where, when, and how.

Many people all over the world encounter the same scenarios in life every single day. They can been seen as good, bad, or indifferent. Some people do things the same way others do. The results might not be exactly the same, but then again, they might be. Others do different things for different reasons.

How one part of the world sees other parts can be the same as it would be with two neighbors. With the world as big as it is, not everyone's beliefs will be the same. Oftentimes, we make our own judgments based on what we feel, believe, or know. Sometimes we might not have the full information to understand what others do or why things happen.

People's interpretations of people, places, and things are heavily based on what they learn, their ability to process it, and their intuitive ability to understand what it meant in the past, what it means in the present, or how it affects the future.

There is no doubt that people from every part of the world throughout time, both male and female, have done things to enhance, teach, and share with humanity. Some of these things have been amazing, beneficial, and enhancing to the world. Others have done the opposite. There can be debates on both sides for any of them.

Today as whole, the world we live in is evolving quickly in almost every facet. Technology has come to new levels and grown by leaps and bounds. Go back fifty years, and look. Then go back another fifty. Then another fifty. Do that ten times. Do it twenty times. Go back in time as far as we know.

With what we are exposed to now and how far we have developed over time, it seems as though the learning curve has progressively gone up. With the gifts of intelligence of many people throughout time in every area, life has become easier in almost every way. Some today live in ways that are primitive by the standards of others. Sadly, that's true in all parts of the world.

The intelligence level of almost everyone is different by either a little or a lot. That isn't exactly a bad thing, though. Depending on the factors, which are many times out of our control, what we experience can create either positive or negative events. How one uses an experience and the direction life goes from it differ from person to person.

There are different kinds of intelligence. These can be learned or natural gifts. Many people excel in different ways in life because of how they use the particular kind they have. Intelligence and intuition, which everyone has some degree of, can be useful for anyone.

The intentions for the use of intelligence can be different. The path one chooses and the reasons for how one thinks, feels, or acts can be influenced by personal experiences and choices or those of others. Because experience, survival, and necessity can be different for all of us, the perception of how people, places, or things are can sometimes be distorted from reality. We also gain intelligence by observing and doing.

Many factors can affect the way people see themselves at certain points in life. Reactions to experiences will differ. How much a person knows or doesn't varies, and the ability to find solutions can be easier for some than others.

Intuition is an inner feeling that everyone has. It might be stronger in some than others. It is a feeling of knowing without knowing. Considering that no one is perfect, anyone's intuition can be wrong too. Anyone can use it at any time for a number of reasons. It might be a feeling about a person, place, or thing. It can lead us toward or away from an experience or encounter.

Combining all of these together allows anyone the ability to both judge and process any encounter or situation, especially ones he or she might not feel comfortable in.

Using these traits is something people do every day; they are essential. People throughout time have shown this. Unfortunately, sometimes people have misused these traits on many levels.

As we grow, develop, mature, learn, and process, our perceptions of people, places, and things can be the same or different. This makes it seem as if we are all kind of the same.

10

Paths, Directions, and Judgment

The continual birthing of new life is constant and greater than ever today. New life enters by the minute. We also see many persons' lives expire. Some pass from natural causes. They might just get old. But how old is the age you're supposed to live to anyway?

Some have their lives taken or, sadly, take their own prematurely. Some have accidents or make mistakes, and lives are lost.

The paths and direction a person's life takes at certain points can change like anything else. The paths and directions of life might not go exactly as planned for many individuals. Life can go in ways we never imagine. Everyone might have a different feeling about that.

Some individuals are born healthier than others. Some are born into wealth or into poverty. Some have greater or lesser physical abilities than others. Some have opportunities or advantages, higher comprehension skills, or stronger influences in factors regarding how they perceive life or want it to be.

A person's life path can be seen or unseen, planned or unplanned. Life doesn't necessarily go how we think it should. How it plays out can create different feelings, and we may view it as fair or unfair. The direction it leads can cause people to pass judgment on themselves and others.

Many things lead us to the path we are meant to be on, including people, places, and things. These can lead to experiences regarding why we are here, what we are here for, and possibly with whom we are to be here with.

Unfortunately, at any time, we can be led astray from the path we're intended to take. Life can take people down a path they never imagined they could be on. Getting off the path or redirecting it can be humbling. The solution to get away from it can be difficult to see. There might be only one way out of it, though. Situations can occur or be in anything from a persons

relationships of all types to career choices to what we do to relax or have fun. These can range from the highest of highs to the lowest of lows. They can also lead to other paths or directions in life that might be seen as good or bad?

In whatever situation we are born into, we are automatically propelled onto a path in life, whether or not we realize it. The direction life takes plays into the many factors written about earlier. No one can expect to have the same results or experiences as anyone else. People can be inspired, though, to have similar, if not greater, ones. If they don't achieve it, though, that doesn't mean they aren't a success.

One might take a path for the lessons learned or benefits for one or many. A path can lead to fame and glory or shame and embarrassment. It all depends on the outcome and how it's received.

The judgments and comparisons people make about themselves, others, and life in general may be spot on just as much they can be harsh and unjust too. Having all the information about a particular topic, whether it's a person, place, or thing, and trying to come from unbiased thinking position can be difficult due to many factors one can be surrounded in.

There are times when people feel less at ease when they are being judged. There are times when judgment is a good thing. There are things that are obvious. Conflicting ideas of judgment can change anyone's path in life in a split second. These can happen over short or long periods for anyone. The path of one person can influence, inspire, or reject depending on how judgment is taken in either direction. In contrast, some aren't affected by others.

With so many people on Earth, the intersecting paths of people we encounter might be for a moment in time or a lifetime. For some, a connection is lifelong, or for as long as one person's life is.

Because we grow more and more intelligent as time goes on, there is much more to feel about the experiences we encounter or would like to, including what we see, how we are taught, and the internal and external responses to the actions we take or don't take.

How we feel about anything and everything is what creates the judgment of the things in our immediate surroundings and everything else in the universe. The paths people take, whether willingly or unwillingly, have the ability to change. There are exceptions due to some permanent mental, emotional, and physical limitations for some.

The path taken isn't always the best or right one for each person, nor do others always understand it. We don't always have to be understood. Sometimes we have to live out the path to explain it. It might also create new strength in different ways.

Inner and outer strength for everyone is different, though. The mind-set to get through tougher moments, go beyond or fall away from them, or even redeem oneself might cause different reactions from different elements at any time. It is the human side in all of us. We are all the same.

11

We've All Been Here Before

This concept might be difficult for some people to understand due to people's different belief systems and the fact that it is hard to physically prove. It might scare some people, and it might make complete sense for others.

There are certain things to consider. Science has been able to predate almost anything it can find today. Archeologists have found bones of human beings all over the world. They've also found pots and other artifacts of many sorts from all different parts of the world. Human life had to exist for those to be created.

Many of those objects date back to well beyond the BC status, to a time that can't be judged or numerically identified today. Many religions base their stories on such times and ages of people involved. So in its own way, religion shows the ancient existence of people.

Researchers have also proven the existence of dinosaurs of all types that go even further back in time. Science has even put a number on how old Earth is, as well as the universe we live in. If you think about it, it's quite amazing. But let's focus back on the human side of things.

We have figured out a lot already, but there's more we don't know that we continue to look for. The idea of religion is a fine place to start. Some religions believe that our soul never dies. The body dies, but the soul goes back to where it came from.

That idea can be difficult for some, I'm sure. Thinking about one life in the thousands of years of human existence just doesn't seem fair. Does it? Especially when some lives never even start, are taken by others, or are lost to sickness or just bad timing. How many people have lived and never achieved a goal, a plan, or experiences for themselves or with others?

How many people have experienced horrific events or done horrible things to another or many more? Pick out points in time and people in time, and see what has happened because of acts of cruelty, misunderstanding, mental illness, and hate. What if a soul had the ability to right a wrong or experience a different view of life? Can that be possible?

Some believe we have all been here many times simply to experience the many different forms of life the universe has to offer: being male or female; being a mother, father, sister, or brother or even being alone; being strong or weak mentally or physically; being led or being a leader; helping, aiding, or assisting; being helped, aided, or assisted; fighting, rebelling, or inciting; being rich or poor; seeing the many facets of life throughout time and the changing of life and maybe even adding to it; and creating history.

Maybe we return to right wrongs made in the past. Considering no one is perfect, according to some religions' beliefs, hardly anyone would qualify for what is considered heaven. But what if over time, we are given the ability and opportunity to experience all that we want, with whom we want, and for how long we want?

The possibility for some might be to redeem themselves. There is also the thought of becoming whole as a spiritual being. Whether emotionally or in the physical form, the entire package of multiple lifetimes allows us to experience whatever we seek next.

What if you suffered from something in one life and then, in the next, having gone through it previously, had the ability to cure it? You could help yourself and others—maybe even millions later on. What if you were a criminal in one life and lived honestly in the next life? You would get to experience both sides, and in doing so, you would become whole. You could be a man in one life and a woman in another. The ability to experience anything and everything would be possible. You could have different experiences of religions, health, wealth, and happiness. You could also learn the lessons of living the opposite way. You'd pass away in the physical form to experience the next.

We would also have the ability to use previous experiences in how we live life today. How? By what we are drawn to in careers and hobbies and with the people we live with today.

We might not understand it because we experience these things in living time, but there is a lesson in every day and every life. Some lessons are repeated over and over. Some we enjoy; others we might not. Some are necessities; others involve things we would like to do or have.

All of them create who we are and how we live life.

They can also have other effects on many things, including how we see ourselves and the world around us, the world we live in directly. What is the difference between being born in one country or another at the same time in life? Depending on the circumstances, a lot. On the other hand, life in different countries could be similar.

Sometimes people meet others and have the feeling they have met before, but they aren't sure where or how. It's like an immediate connection but an unknown one.

Science has found that we only use a small percentage of our brains, roughly around 10 percent. So what do we do with the unused parts? Do those parts store things from our past experiences?

People of all ages who have gone through traumatic episodes in life can emotionally block life experiences out. Some get hypnotized to help clear the path for a way to work out the experience. The experience is stored somewhere in the mind.

In some cases, the storage of past lives might explain why someone is naturally skilled or gifted in some area. It might also show why some people have a fear of the dark, heights, animals, or even people. What if all of our experiences are stored somewhere in our minds?

Some will say this isn't possible. Limited beliefs will stop some from ever even considering it, which is fine. If you look at all the things that have happened so far that science can't explain, what's one more? For some, this knowledge might be evident; it's just internal.

Finding physical proof of this concept might be impossible. However, things are the same for everyone because we all exist in this life today, so we're all probably experiencing another one now.

12

Karma, Destiny, and Miracles

Everyone goes through different experiences in life. Where and for how long are usually the only differences. Good and bad experiences and highs and lows happen for almost everyone. Why does something happen or not happen? The answers can present themselves at times when they're least expected. Maybe things happen for a reason known as karma.

Karma is the concept of doing something good and having something good happen in return somewhere down the life path of an individual. It can also be instant. It's considered good karma. The opposite of this is bad karma.

Some religions believe that how one led past lives determines how this and future lives will go. The concept of paying it forward or having higher morals is an idea in other religions. The spiritual belief in it is strong for many people throughout the world.

If that's the case, then it could be considered a superstition. What if it's true? What if every person in the world today has experienced multiple lives and was nice in some and unkind in others? Then good karma would be like a reward in a way, and bad karma would mean things might not happen how we want.

It has nothing to do with being rich, poor, healthy, or unhealthy. Our life experiences and the value of life aren't about that. A person can have all the money in the world and not be happy or enjoy life itself, and another person who does not have as much or any at all can live a fulfilling and happy life. The latter might learn or experience greater lessons and be able to touch or help another or more with less.

What if a person has the internal instinct in him- or herself or has been be taught to hurt, harm, steal, lie, or cheat? If caught by society while doing any of these things, the person will face repercussions. Society has laws that carry different levels of punishment. If a person never fully pays for the actions of a past life, then a punishment may occur in the next.

The same concept applies to doing something considered good. What if a person does something nice, kind, or compassionate for others but never has the opportunity to be a beneficiary of kindness due to various factors? Could that individual be rewarded in one or multiple ways in the next life? Karma is the great equalizer of spiritual time and history for each individual or soul to ever walk the earth.

Is there also the possibility in every person's life to change karma then? We can change the way we look at people, places, and things and the actions we take. Because time never stops, change is always occurring. We are in a state of constant change. That makes it possible. Karma is based on action and how we react to everything we encounter and experience.

Our reactions to everything; skills, talents, and abilities; belief systems; circumstances upon entering life; available resources at certain points in life; and how long we are here all create our destiny.

How and why we do the things we do, where we go, what we experience, the results of those experiences, and the feelings about and reasons for our actions create our destiny. Like anything else, we can change our destiny. In the same sense, others can change ours, and we can change others' too.

The destiny of one's life can be combined with those of others. Destiny can be considered good or bad, depending on all the factors of life. A person's destiny can change in a second just as it can be built over a lifetime. It also might not be in one's own control. It might be based on the destinies of others or what may be seen as an act of God.

An act of God can be anything. It can been viewed as good or bad.

It can be an act of nature, such as weather. It can be an illness or healing that is not understood by one or many. It can be an idea, invention, or solution that benefits one or many.

The concept of an idea or thought being an act of God might not make sense to some, but when an idea or solution to something seemingly appears out of thin air or comes to mind from nowhere, where does it come from?

Knowledge and thoughts that seemingly come from nowhere have to come from somewhere; we just might not recognize it. In the many thousands of years man has walked the earth, our development and intelligence have had to come from somewhere. The human side of us gives recognition to individuals, lots of people throughout time, but the real credit should be given to whoever or whatever created us.

Miracles are unexplainable events that happen—for example, when things seem to appear, when change occurs in circumstances that are unchangeable, in dire moments, or when a certain need for immediate change is met in any facet of life. Many people pray for miracles for themselves and for the lives of others.

People define miracles differently all over the world. Miracles have been performed throughout time in multiple religions. Miracles still continue to happen today. We sometimes take them for granted when they do.

We can try to explain miraculous events as coincidences. But what if there aren't such things as coincidences? What if certain things happen because they are meant to happen? Not all things just happen, though, simply because of the free will that all human beings have.

However, there are things that happen that can only be defined as miracles. Miracles have happened not only in religions but also in science, medicine, weather, and plenty of other areas of life. They can also be in our thinking, processing, and understanding of the lives we live, the world we live in, and all that is around us.

Many people try to debunk phenomena considered miracles. Why? Because that's what humans do. We are always looking for proof or some understanding of how things happened. Sometimes there isn't a reason or answer for why things occur, though. Sometimes the only answer is that a miracle has occurred. Our existence on this earth in this universe is a prime example. We still question how life started.

A miracle could be saving a life or creating a life, winning the lottery, surviving a crash or accident or not being in one at all, experiencing a change in health to get better, or passing on to relieve more pain and suffering. The definition is different for everyone. Living, seeing, or learning of a miracle can be life changing and inspiring in multiple ways for many people.

Miracles happen. Are they related to karma? Do they have the ability to change a person's destiny? The answer to that is up to each person to decide for him- or herself. Whether or not the intentions of a person can create good or bad karma, how we see life can help us find our true reason for being or experiencing this life.

Sometimes a miracle—or two or more—has to happen in order for us to achieve it, though. When miracles happen, we might not even know it.

Many people who do believe in miracles, however, think they can't happen for them. They think it's their destiny for them not to happen, which is sad. Because we are all the same, miracles can and do happen for everyone. Recognizing them is the hard part—maybe because we are human and take many things for granted.

We are only here because something much greater than all of us allows us to be. It sees us all the time and helps us along the way as we go. There is debate surrounding who or what that is. Beliefs regarding a higher power have existed for as long as time has been, and they still go on today.

Though disagreements about the definition of a miracle continue, miracles do happen. Unexplainable things can happen to or for anyone, which again shows that we are all the same.

* * *

In the next two parts of this book, I hope you will see how the things you've just read about can affect people in different ways. I am one person, yet it took many others to help make my story play out. All the others have their own stories, and I'm as much a part of theirs as they are of mine. Further, the following might illustrate that we all are here for reasons we might not understand. It might also show we all are trying for common goals, just in different forms. We might be here to fix or change certain things that those before us failed to fix or change. We are here to enhance and grow individually and as a whole. We are all the same.

Part 2

13

How It Starts

Five weeks shy of my fifth birthday, my father was suddenly stricken with a stroke and taken off life support. He was forty-two. Taking him off life support must have been the most difficult decision my mom made in her life. Before that, life was pretty good from what I understand. I was so young when it happened. The ramifications of it played out the way they did.

Left behind were my mom, who was forty-one, and my two older sisters from my mom's previous marriage, who were fourteen and fifteen years older than I was. My mom's first husband, their father, had been killed by a drunk driver. My mom had three children with my dad: my older brother by three years; me; and my younger sister, who was eleven days shy of being a year younger than I was.

As I was at such a young age when the dramatic occurrence happened, only now can I see all the things lost from it at every point in life and with everyone in my family and how the loss played a part in everything. No one could understand how his stroke and death could have happened.

My dad liked to drink, and he also smoked. But so did everyone else. He wasn't out of shape or sick or anything like that. He wasn't a bad guy; everyone liked him. How could this have happened? Who would take someone like that from his family?

There were no answers good enough for my mom to hear, nor for my grandparents, my sisters and brother, or me.

An event like that causes rippling effects on everyone. The removal of the person he was to everyone and everything was a pain and strain on multiple levels. Sudden death is something no one is ever prepared for. Moving on and going forward with the emotions surrounding the death can be a roller coaster over the short and long term. The experiences are different for each person.

I asked questions about it at that age, and as I've gotten older, the answers given still aren't good enough. Where did he go? Why did he have to die? Does God not love us? The answers, as genuine and nice as they could be, never made sense to me.

All I knew was that he wasn't coming back. The whole thing was unfair. His death created a hole, an emptiness, a void. As I grew up, it made me think about things I never would have if it hadn't happened. Why didn't this happen to other people? The feelings created from the experience led to more questions that had no answers.

Life never stops, though. It keeps going on. It leads to more experiences that you might not necessarily be prepared for. Looking at how his death took a toll on my mom while growing up with my siblings and what she went through was nothing short of amazing. She wasn't perfect, but considering her ability to go through it and do what she could for her children after the emotional trauma she'd endured, she is by far the strongest person I know.

Wondering how we were going to get through situations that had seemed normal one day suddenly brought a completely different perspective of life. Raising a family and doing it as a single parent was never easy for my mom. My mom tried to be both a mom and a dad. For one person, that's hard, as you might expect. While going through her own emotions of what she'd been through, it wasn't easy. Being comfortable in trying to raise five kids, getting the oldest two through college, and keeping the other three happy after what had happened wasn't easy.

The loss of her husband took a toll in many ways. Emotions, finances, time management, and spiritual beliefs, to name a few, all changed when the dynamics of life changed.

My older sisters were not there to help my mom for periods of time when they were busy with school. It was tough to think about what they were feeling. They had now had two fathers taken from them. My dad had taken them in as his own daughters; he'd loved them, and they'd loved him.

My brother, my younger sister, and I couldn't understand it. As with everyone else who has something like this happen in his or her life, moving forward was all about going on and dealing with it. Because of my siblings' and my ages when it happened, it seemed to change the way life went for everyone involved.

While growing up as kids, we were all different. My brother wasn't into sports much. He had no desire to play in Little League or stuff like that. He enjoyed reading, music, and things like that. He was creative. The last thing he wanted was to be bothered by his younger brother most of the time and, for the most part, his younger sister too. He had his group of friends growing up, and he made more, it seemed, wherever he was led in life. He went on to college after high school and transferred to another to complete his degree in marketing. He made my mom proud. He was true and genuine. He loved everyone and everything, especially his family. He made people feel good; he made them laugh. At one point, his and my relationship fell into place that it probably shouldn't have. I take full responsibility for that. I'll explain later.

My younger sister was athletic, competitive, and fun. She is still that same person today, except as I look at her now, I think she is even better. She is smart, caring, and genuine. She isn't perfect either. No one is. While growing up, we tortured each other in every way we could. We were always trying to get ahead of each other, no matter what we did.

I have had some of the greatest experiences of my life with my siblings. I've been blessed with these people. I have let these people down too. I've hurt them all by hurting just one.

Two of my sisters are married, and each has two daughters of her own. They all are blessings for the entire family. Seeing them, especially with my mom, is enjoyable. To see them all together is rare, though, now. It's just the way life is. The last time I saw them all together, it was not under the most comfortable of circumstance. I'll get to that too but not yet.

I'll talk about me now. I have found my life from the day it changed with my dad's passing. There have been many highs and lows. Some things that happened were a direct result of my being unable to learn from an experience or influence and, most of all, not being honest with myself. That last one is the one I have to live with and be aware of for myself. I have also learned I cannot blame anything on anything today. It's just the way it is.

I'm not saying life has been one tragedy after another, because it hasn't been. Some experiences, though, have taken me to hell in my life. I've had experiences I've enjoyed very much in different ways. There have been many things I can't explain. Some things I either allowed to happen, or I grew from how they were handled, including from a young age through adolescence and throughout my adult life. I don't see myself as more special than anyone else, though. I used to. That was my ego. Many times, I felt that way because of fear, perception, and self-pity.

My experiences have also affected others in both good and bad ways. I've come to the conclusion that life is supposed to be a certain way for a reason.

Growing up under the circumstances we did, having all the things a kid would want wasn't gonna happen that often. Money was tight; my mom had no income after my father died. She went to work. It was difficult, but she found a home in a good neighborhood and school district. She was still not two people, though. Raising five kids at different ages while going through what she had and with the limited resources she had was hard. No one would ever envy being in her shoes.

We were blessed to have the influences of going to our grandparents' homes on both sides of the family often. We all looked forward to those times, even my mom. The visits gave her a break. We would often stay overnight at least one night on the weekends. I now see it as my mom sharing us with all of them. They spoiled the hell out of us. It was great to be at either of their homes.

Both sets of grandparents lived in older homes in fading parts of town. My paternal grandparents lived close to the city, which was about twenty minutes away. The house had the feel and smell of the city close to it. It wasn't big, but it was enough for what they needed with just the two of them. It must have been built in the 1930s or '40s. It had two bedrooms, a kitchen, a dining room, a living room, a storage room, and a small enclosed wooden deck addition that led down to grass and a pea-gravel driveway with an old wooden garage door that was heavy, at least to me. The basement was tight; it held many things from their past, including furniture, clothing, and tools.

My mom's parents lived about twenty minutes away in the other direction. They were actually her aunt and uncle. Her mother was killed in a fire at their home when my mother was young. Only one of her other siblings survived. Her father opted to keep her brother and not her.

As you can imagine, it left her feeling hurt in many ways. Her father never told her why he rejected her either. I often wondered how she felt, but I think I knew. It wasn't something I wanted her to relive.

My other grandparents' house was huge, with a big living room, a dining room and kitchen, four bedrooms upstairs, and a giant attic above. It had a lot of room to hide and play; for a kid, it was amazing. The basement was as big as the ground floor above it. A two-car garage was at the back of the property, past a small backyard surrounded by private hedges.

My grandfather had worked in the mills, and they lived at the top of a hill in the town. At the bottom was the river, on which everything moved in and out of the city. The house was built in the early 1900s. It too had the warm feeling of our grandparents. My older sisters had grown up there after their father was killed. They had many good memories of it.

My mom was blessed in many ways by both sets grandparents. All of us were. What's amazing is how the dynamics of life changed simply because they had to. One by one, over the next ten or so years, as we got older, they all passed away. First was my mom's mom, Gram. She was my mom's best friend and the most influential person in her life. As I would learn over time, she was the person my mom missed most for multiple reasons. Her mother's death hit her hard, as you might expect.

Next was our other grandmother, Granny. She was great. I always will remember the feelings I had when seeing her. She was funny and a lively soul. She drank whiskey and water—a highball, as it was called.

Her husband was the next to go a few years later. He wasn't the same after Granny passed. He was in a way, but he was quieter than he'd been before Granny's passing. He was great; he was the one who really spoiled us when we were there. He always had a joke, and he always said to be polite and respect my mom. I can still hear his laugh in my head.

He would ask me if I wanted something to eat or drink. I'd always say yes. He would reply jokingly, "Well, you'd better ask Big Red. I don't want to get in trouble with her," and then he would laugh. He was referring to my mom. My mom had very red hair. Most of the time, she said it was okay for me to have a snack.

He called her Big Red because at five foot two, she was taller than he was at his age. He made sure he had her permission because he was a respectful person. He made a mean root beer float. He did a heck of a job with ice cream and wasn't shy on cutting a nice-sized piece of cake either.

My mom's nickname of Big Red has stuck to this day. I kept joking with her even when he wasn't there. The first few times, I thought she was gonna smack my lips off, so I called her that from a distance. Over time, she became okay with it; she knew it was done as a joke. As I grew up and became taller than she was, I started to just call her Red, the joke being that she wasn't big anymore.

Today she is eighty-plus years old—she quit counting after that; she says that's a number she's okay with—and has a head of hair that is now gray, but I still call her Red. My siblings still only call her Mom most of the time, but every once in a while, they'll call her Red too. She is now just under five feet tall.

The last grandparent who passed was her father. They had a tumultuous life together. At many times, I learned she really didn't like him. Trying to understand why was hard sometimes because she would get so upset with him that she would get sidetracked by emotions and not make sense. She had her reasons, though. He lived ten or so years past Gram, and we went to visit him every Saturday. He was stubborn; he didn't want to leave his house for a nursing home.

My mom finally convinced him to move to a home. It was a blessing for her, but he was miserable after his wife died. Just like my other grandfather, he felt a huge part of him was gone when his wife passed over.

After they had all passed on, at the time, it never really dawned on me how much their loss took a toll on her. She hadn't gotten a break for a long time. Everything she did always seemed to be for someone else. She was trying to fill so many different shoes. It seemed unfair. But what is fair?

14

And Away We Go!

As I grew up, I was a shy, quiet person. I never enjoyed school much. Physically, I wasn't big size-wise to start with. I enjoyed sports, though—all sports. They were a big part of summer when I was growing up with the kids in the neighborhood. I played Little League baseball and swam at the neighbors' up until the age of around eleven or twelve. Things were harmless.

I found myself in serious trouble only once. I was nine. One of two brothers who lived in the neighborhood decided to jump into an open window of the neighbors' house. His younger brother and my brother jumped in after. I was a lookout. I couldn't believe what was going on. I was shocked my brother had gone inside. I was shocked any of them had. They weren't supposed to be doing that.

They were in and out in two minutes. I could see the terror on my brother's face as they exited. The younger of the brothers asked, "Why did we go in there?" as he peered around after he'd jumped out. The older one had magazines in his pants, covered by his shirt. He ran into the woods behind the houses to stash the magazines.

The people who lived in the house were nice people. They had a son my age, whom I played with all the time. I couldn't understand why they'd done that. The dead giveaway was that the kid hadn't closed the window the way it had been when we found it.

A few hours later, the neighbors can home and came to my mom's house to inquire if anyone knew anything about the missing magazines. He knew neighborhood kids were always running through the backyards to go from house to house. He was mad and rightfully so.

As I was all of nine years old at the time, he scared the hell out of me. My mom had no knowledge of the incident and was surprised by the overwhelming tears and emotions that came from me. Then she got mad quickly. She was beside herself upon hearing me tell what had happened.

I thought I was going to jail. A few phone calls later, it hit the fan. My mom's normal reaction was that a good beating would solve the problem. A smack or ten was perceived as okay for a child growing up in the world then. At that time, it was considered justifiable.

Our punishment came with more than that, though. She called my uncle to come over to speak to us the next night. After the phone call to him, she said he would handle it tomorrow. We could hear him through the phone while he talked to her. Her initial response was to immediately ground us for multiple weeks. The idea of my uncle coming was terrifying. Thoughts of what he would do played havoc on my brother and me all night and the next day.

No one could believe such an incident had happened in my family or in the neighborhood. The word quickly made its way around. My mom was crushed. She kept saying she hadn't raised us to do that. The thing was, she hadn't. She was disgusted at the sight of us. She kept reminding us that at six o'clock, our uncle was supposed to be there.

As the clock moved closer to that time all day, the idea of seeing our uncle was less appealing. I didn't see him often, but when I did, he was always a nice guy. He had a loud, booming voice, though; you knew he was there. He and my dad were really tight. My dad's passing years before had been tough on him as much as on anyone. They'd had a special bond while growing up.

My brother didn't say much that day. I could see he had the same fear I did and was wondering what might happen. I think he was more ashamed of what he'd done than what I'd done. He felt more guilt than I did. I didn't really do anything, if you think about it. But no one saw that. My brother and the two other boys weren't going to listen to me anyway, so how was I supposed to stop them? I wasn't going to run and tell my mom what they'd done. They would've killed me. That was probably the thing she was most mad at me about.

My uncle rolled in a few minutes after six o'clock. He had a small bag under his left arm. I had no idea what it was as I looked out the front window into the driveway and saw him walking up the steps and walkway. He casually walked into the house when my mom opened the door for him. He said hello to my mom with a smile on his face as he entered. He then looked at my brother and me as we sat on the couch, and his tone changed in a split second.

"To the back porch—now" was the first thing out of his mouth. We both got up without saying a word and made our way through the kitchen and onto the screened-in back porch. My brother and I sat on opposite sides of the picnic table. He and I knew we were a few moments away from something we didn't want. We had no idea what, though. We could hear our mom and uncle talking inside.

He came out a couple minutes later, holding the bag under his arm, along with three glasses I hadn't seen before. He sat down next to me and placed a glass in front of each of us. He then pulled out two six-packs of beer. He was close enough to me that I could smell his scent. It was obvious he had been drinking before he got there. I could barely look into his face.

He started by pouring a beer into each glass. He then proceeded to yell loudly about how ashamed he was of us. He said we must have thought we were now men. He started encouraging us to drink the beer: "Go ahead! Drink up." He picked each one of us apart for what seemed like forever. Slowly, I sipped the beer. My brother sat across from him. My uncle continued to badger him to drink. My brother kept saying no.

I had sipped beer when joking with my grandparents years before; they'd thought it was funny. Now I, at age nine, was drinking alcohol because my uncle wouldn't stop yelling at me if I didn't. My brother never touched his, which seemed to make my uncle madder by the minute. He drank his beer and filled up another glass. Then he looked at mine and topped it off full.

My mom watched the first few minutes of the ordeal and then walked away in frustration all over again. She told my younger sister not to listen, as we were in trouble, not her, but it would have been impossible for her not to hear. I looked behind me to see her standing there in the doorway, looking at me and my brother with a blank look on her face. She had never seen that side of my uncle either.

I noticed I didn't mind the taste of the beer. The flavor wasn't all that bad. It was different. I did start to feel the effects of it, though. After a couple more top-offs of mine, I felt different for sure. Still, my brother never touched a drop of his. He just stared at my uncle and said, "I'm not drinking it."

My uncle finally succumbed after that stand from my brother. He backed down for the first time in what must have been about an hour or so of yelling. He went inside and talked to my mom after that. We were instructed to go to our room for the rest of the night.

They went over to talk to the neighbor and apologized again. My uncle never came back into the house before he left. I slipped out of my and my brother's room to see if he had left. I ran into my mom's room, which looked down onto the driveway. The window was open, and I could hear him and my mom talking about the whole evening. Standing on her bed and ducking down, I could see them talking.

I stayed low so I would not be seen. I noticed I was kind of dizzy. I realized I felt pretty good, to be honest. I listened to them until he left ten minutes later. Before my mom could get back into the house, I slipped back into our room and jumped into bed. My brother was already in his.

We both pretended we were already asleep, so my mom hopefully wouldn't subject us to another round of yelling, but she did. She said the neighbors weren't pressing charges. We were nine and twelve—what jail were we going to anyway?

Before she finished her rant, she grounded us for two weeks. She closed the door. It was eight o'clock at night—still light out—and we were already in bed for the night.

After a few minutes of lying there, I said to my brother, "Why didn't you drink the beer? He would've quit yelling at you at least." I waited, but my brother didn't reply. "I can tell you this: I'm a little dizzy, but I feel pretty good, like warm all over."

My brother finally replied, "I'm not doing that. What would it prove?"

In only a few minutes, I was asleep—out cold. I woke up the next morning. I didn't feel good at all.

The next time I saw my uncle was at his funeral a few years later. The drinking and smoking he'd done all his life had caught up to him. He wasn't even fifty. I didn't feel bad about that either. I didn't really like him after the last time I'd seen him. He scared me, and I didn't care that he was gone. I don't think my brother did either. I never asked, though.

Drunk at the age of nine—I'm not sure my dad or his parents would've approved. But it happened. I think after it happened, my mom realized that calling my uncle had been a mistake. The incident showed that harshness was the only thing he knew and showed how he handled situations. I blamed that moment on him for a long time.

Between grade school and middle school, I had a couple friends I hung out with more than others. There were different groups of kids of all different ages. Some kids had older brothers and sisters, and one of my friends had an older brother from whom I learned some things.

My friend and I had been friends from early on in grade school. We played baseball together. I was at his house all the time. He lived about a ten-minute walk from my house. His parents were generous to him and kind to me. His older brother never said a word to me. He was a few years older than we were. He was pretty much an asshole to my friend.

His brother might have said twenty words to me in the ten years I'd been at his house. One word he used often was *no*, usually when I called to see if my friend was home. Whether my friend was there or not, he rarely picked up the phone unless he was expecting a call.

The brother was skinny, with fairly long, greasy hair. He was taller than my friend was until my friend turned about fourteen or fifteen. They were the same height by then. By that time, he was seventeen or eighteen. His brother had a motorcycle, and he dressed the part. He worked on his bike and smoked cigarettes constantly. He specifically warned us to stay away from his motorcycle.

My friend said his parents had helped him buy it. His brother had a job too. His friends all had motorcycles, and we stayed out of their way when we all were there. One day, though, my friend's brother started to mess with him to impress his friends. He picked a fight with him.

The dumbass, who was barely taller than my friend by then, didn't realize his younger brother had been playing football and working out regularly. My buddy easily got the best of him after about a three- or four-minute battle. My friend did everything he could to avoid it, but his brother crossed the line. The moment my friend thought the fight was over, his brother got in a cheap shot to impress his friends and save face. His brother's friends harassed my friend as they got on their motorcycles and drove away.

A few days later, we were hanging out in his room, watching TV. My buddy reached into his drawer and pulled something out: a small baggie of marijuana. Surprised, I asked him where he'd gotten it. He said he'd been pissed off at his brother after the fight, so he'd gone into his room to either take something or break something. He'd searched around and found a safe he had given to his brother a couple Christmases back. He'd figured there was something of value to his brother in it. He'd slid the pins from the hinges on the back. He said it had been easy to put back. He said he'd found about eight small baggies completely full, bulging, inside, so he'd taken a little bit from each. He was confident his brother wouldn't notice. As it turned, he never did.

His parents both worked and weren't home during the day, and his brother wasn't there either. A couple other friends came over, and we sat on his back porch that afternoon and smoked all he'd taken. It didn't take much to feel the effects of it. No one knew what to expect. One guy didn't participate; he said it wasn't for him. He never came back after that either.

We sat on the back porch, laughing for a while over stupid things, and then became paranoid about every sound we heard or thought we heard. Eventually, we raided his kitchen for food. We repeated that routine all afternoon. I was eventually ready for a nap by late afternoon. That day, when I got home for dinner, my mom looked at me and asked what I'd done all day.

I barely noticed that my eyes had become pretty red. They weren't fully open either. My quick response before she could ask was "We were in the woods. My eyes have bothered me the whole time."

She looked at me, not suspecting what had really happened, and said, "Maybe you should watch where you're at then. Looks like you're allergic to something."

She had no reason to think anything else. I'd never given a reason before. She also knew that as young boys, we could end up anywhere, doing anything. I was always honest with her about where I'd been and what we'd been doing. But we'd never crossed the lines we'd crossed earlier that day. My sisters and brother never gave her a reason to be suspicious of anything like that.

From that moment on, subtly, things changed in ways I didn't even realize. Smoking was something I probably shouldn't have been doing to start with. It seemed cool, though. Everyone else had a good time. I did enjoy the feeling; there's no denying that. It seemed there was no harm to anyone. I knew it was illegal, though—we all did.

That was the day I perfected lying to my mom's face. I felt good about it too. It was easy. It was something I'd be able to perfect to greater levels as I got older. I did it everywhere to almost everyone. It would serve me well—or so I thought.

The marijuana supply became a regular thing that I and other friends could rely on. Smoking it led us to meeting other people and new circles. I learned to keep eye drops with me at all times to combat the red eye, and I always tried to have gum.

Hanging out with my other friends' older siblings and friends led to some parties and stuff like that, which led to drinking alcohol on a more regular basis. No one really knew us, so smoking weed with them was an easy way to meet people.

Seeing how and what others did was a lesson in itself. Some were loud; some were quiet. Some were mean; some were nice. As girls became more prevalent in social situations as I matured, my shyness and quiet side were more obvious. Alcohol and weed were an outlet to come forward some. They allowed me, or what was inside me, to come out of my shell. I would best describe it as a Dr. Jekyll and Mr. Hyde situation. It made the uncomfortable a little more adjustable.

After a while, my friends and the different groups of people I knew expanded. Attaining alcohol seemed to be no problem from age fifteen on. By the end of high school, my friend who'd introduced me to weed originally had slowly slid into another group. There were no hard feelings on either side about it. He went his own way.

He also got in trouble for drinking and driving. It was better for me, from one perspective, to get away from him, at least as far as my mom and family knew. They'd heard stuff. That was just the way it was. No one put together that I was with him a lot and was doing the same things. He was the only one who got caught.

Another friend I hung out with was a true businessman at an early age. Learning from our friend's older brother, the effective use of selling marijuana to supplement his income had him getting weed in bulk, a quarter pound at a clip. His profit was great. I would help him find prospective purchasers. He'd control who got what and the price. I'd get a much better deal on mine. It was a win-win. I always had weed; I was high all the time.

I got hired at a supermarket when I was around sixteen. It was a nice introduction to cash. My friend was working at a fast-food restaurant. We and a small group of friends would meet almost every night in the summer evenings to split cases of beer and get stoned. It was a perfect deal. We played sports and had a lot of fun doing things and just hanging out.

After high school, my friend met a girl he worked with, and they moved in together. She liked the money he was making from the weed, as they could afford whatever they wanted. They weren't living big or anything, but they had a good time.

He was going to a trade school. His dad had some influence and knew people, and he pulled some strings to help that along. He had to go to night school as part of the deal.

I went to college for a marketing degree. I hated being there every day. Being indoors was tough for me. I felt I was being forced to take classes I'd never use. I looked at it as a waste of time, both mine and theirs. It was just about money—mine becoming theirs. Or, rather, my mom's becoming theirs. I knew college was wrong for me. I even told my mom that. I knew it could only end badly.

In between the painful time in class and what had become a miserable part-time job, I started dating a girl who worked with my buddy and his girlfriend. She was a couple years younger than I was. She was beautiful. We had a great time together, getting to know each other.

Over the next few months, I started to get out of control and drink more. The first month or two, I was on my best behavior when I was with her. I never told her I was getting stoned or about the situation with my friend. If she would have known, she would have been gone quick.

We had a talk that would soon take my life in a direction that ultimately changed my life and the path it would take. I'm not saying I made a mistake, but I made a choice. It was free will, I guess you could say.

The beautiful young woman asked me to quit drinking so much. She didn't drink. She hoped I could change some for her. She even volunteered to help me with the college courses she knew I was failing. She was willing to help me at any cost. She wanted to be with me and see me succeed in every way.

If she had known I was smoking weed too at the time, she would not have ever stayed. Not only had I been letting myself slip, but I was lying to her the entire time. Lying had become easy. I never considered her feelings. I was hurting her emotionally and never saw it. How could I have, though? I was consumed solely with seeing only myself. I didn't care about anyone but me.

With the simplest of ease, I stared into her beautiful hazel eyes and said, "Well, I don't think I'm quitting drinking anytime soon." I started to laugh, catching myself, as my words came out. "This is who I am. I'm sorry." I was emotionless when I finished speaking.

Tears appeared in her eyes as she dropped her head. The only understandable word that came out of her mouth afterward was "Goodbye!" Crying, she smacked me on my chest and arm as she walked out of my life.

It's with a heavy heart that I think of her and how things would have been different had I agreed to her request. I would have taken a different path. Better, worse, easier, or harder? I don't know. I would've had different experiences no doubt. But I didn't.

15

New Career Time

It didn't take much time for things to go in another direction after the breakup happened. I'd been commuting to school via the bus. It wasn't hard to catch a ride or walk the ten to fifteen minutes to the bus stop. A girl I knew from another school district took the bus too. She and I had smoked weed together for a summer back in high school with some mutual friends, so when we met again on the bus, there was an immediate connection.

This girl was smart, and school was easy for her. She was also street smart. Her goal was to be an attorney, but she wanted to have a background in business to go along with that. She was good looking on top of that. She didn't try to flaunt that she was. She was pretty open about everything she saw, and she would say whatever she felt. She was confident. It carried well for her, and she knew it.

She was still dating a guy I'd met with her a couple years back. He always had good pot. After a couple weeks on the bus, she and I made plans to hang out and get stoned after classes. I ended up meeting her boyfriend there and a few more of their friends soon after that.

I was opening myself up to a whole new group of people. A few of them were just like me, a little different, though, in how they perceived things. Soon after that, I found I was doing more things with these other people and not her. I hit it off well with some of them.

The girl who'd introduced us was not happy about that. She let it be known by some of the comments she'd make. She was a little offended. I also got the lowdown from them about her. They didn't tell her half of the things they did. They did enjoy getting stoned with her and her boyfriend, though. They liked them both a lot.

I started to work on the side with one guy whose brother owned a business. At first, I worked one night a week if I didn't have class the next day. He was a little older than I was, and he was short in stature but was funny and loud in everything he did. Everyone liked him. My first impression was that he was a little shady but harmless. It didn't take long for us to hit it off after a while together. We saw things in the same way. Our work was more about just having a good time a lot of the time.

Working together was something we could only do when the stores weren't open. We were either locked in alone or there with managers on overnight, doing cleaning. We mostly cleaned supermarkets. There were stores contracted to clean regularly, and they had multiple crews working nightly.

My new friend and I usually handled stores that needed some specialty stuff done or larger projects that had to be done correctly. He'd been doing that work since he was thirteen. By then, at twenty-one, he knew everything like the back of his hand. He was fast, efficient, and, most of all, good. He knew how long and what it would take to do everything and had fun at the same time.

On a normal evening when we worked, we would usually start the evening by having a couple drinks somewhere first. I was nineteen, looked that age, and had no identification, but he could get me into places and get us served. To me, it was awesome. We'd also get pretty stoned before we went in to work.

Normally, we would work alone. There were times when we met up with others to help them out, depending on where we were scheduled to be. We would do maybe two to four stores a night, working from about eleven o'clock at night until six or seven in the morning.

With the evening starting off so late and lasting till the early morning, the work was at times exhausting. Finishing the job and doing it well were the priorities every day. Anything else was unacceptable. The demand of the job was point-blank: just finish on time—no excuses.

Soon after, the introduction of certain things prevented the tired moments from happening. The way I looked at it was that I wasn't hurting anyone and was doing what was required. The fact that I was having a good time while doing it was a bonus.

Unfortunately, over the next couple months, those certain things became a little more addictive. I found myself having a greater desire to have those certain things when I wasn't working on regular nights.

While I tried to maintain my other friendships and those connections, my college experience was getting worse. Explaining that to my mom in the most delicate way to make it sound like it wasn't my fault wasn't easy. I'd become proficient at blaming things on anyone other than myself. I had excuses for almost everything.

I was also trying to keep my job at the supermarket. Life was starting to blur for me. Being in it, though, I couldn't see that. None of it was my fault.

I had been at the supermarket for a couple years and had moved from department to department. I'd somehow pissed someone off in each department with my smart mouth. I think I had done everything there. I did enjoy the meat room, though. There were two drawbacks to it: the cold and the department manager. He was not someone I admired. We never got along well. He knew it, and I knew it.

Every chance I had, I made fun of him. A few times, he was ready to hit me, but he couldn't. Some people enjoyed my verbal shots at him. I know because they told me so. One guy even coached me on how to hit some sore spots with him, as I had the ability to get the guy worked up when others couldn't. We always worked Sunday mornings at seven o'clock. It sucked. He had an ax to grind with the manager, and I was more than happy to take his help to get the most out of the manager.

Working there had become an aggravation more than anything. When there, I was robotic, almost contained. I liked it less and less, but it was a simple source of income.

I'd also met another guy who knew the girl from college and the guy from the floor-cleaning business. They had known each other for a few years. He offered me a job helping out a couple days a week with a landscaping company he was part of. He liked the work and thought I might too.

I liked money, so I agreed to meet his boss and do a day with them. We agreed that if he liked me and I liked the work, we would talk about my doing it again the following week. More or less, it was a live working interview. I had no idea what I was doing, but it was just grunt work, I assumed. I wasn't wrong. Being about six feet tall and 160 pounds, I could handle it.

The guy, who was named Dave, picked me up at seven forty-five, and we started at eight. It was a five- to ten-minute drive, depending on the lights. I met his boss immediately as I got out of his car. He was loading tools and plants into his pickup truck and into the dump truck he owned. He'd been renting the place to work out of.

The day went smoothly. It was some hard, heavy work, but I enjoyed being outside in the warm air. The conversation was good for the most part. It was mainly about the next week's projects or stuff they did. We also talked about sports and hobbies and checked out women we saw during the day.

When the two of them spoke about plants and plans, though, I felt as if they were speaking in a foreign tongue. At the end of the day, the owner told me that if I wanted to help them the next week, I was more than welcome to join them again. I agreed and said I would be glad to.

I ran into Dave over the weekend, and whether it was true or not, he said his boss had spoken well of me, including how quickly I finished the work and how polite I was. He was looking forward to next week.

The following week, when he picked me up in the morning, we got stoned before we got to work. After that, we got high almost every chance we could. When the boss left, we would find a place on the property or get in the truck and drive around.

Working one day a week with them wasn't tough. I actually looked forward to it over the next few weeks. It was better than what I was experiencing at college. My dislike for that place grew by the day, mainly because I didn't do the assignments. My job in the meat room wasn't all that bad other than the manager, and I seriously was considering learning how to become a butcher. The idea of being in a cold environment was the only deterrent.

I had to start thinking about my future, as I wouldn't be in college much longer. There would be a reaction from my mom that wouldn't end well. I was positive of that. I had wasted her money and my time. From the beginning, though, I'd said I didn't want to go.

My argument wouldn't stand well with her, I knew. I'd be a disappointment to her. I knew that. My brother was close to finishing his degree, which made my mom proud. She had the same expectations for me. There were no other alternatives, at least not in her thinking.

She had a cookie-cutter view of how things should go. Anything less meant I was not applying myself. That was where things started to go terribly wrong. The introduction of drugs and alcohol along the way and the feelings and emotions prior tipped the scales that helped define the path I ultimately took.

With no desire to be there, I knew that sitting in a classroom and trying to learn things I had no interest in that would have no bearing on my life was a waste of time. As the school sent home letters about academic probation, things progressively became worse on all fronts.

I didn't have suitable answers readily available, and things seemingly were falling down for me on the school front. The last couple weeks before the semester ended, I decided there was no need to attend many classes anymore. I maintained the appearance that I went to school, but I didn't. There were still places to go and see and things to do. I could get lost anywhere to kill the day.

Though I didn't see the girl from the bus much anymore, we still were on good terms. We didn't take the bus together much anymore, but we still would hang out in between classes or go to lunch when we could. Talking with her was always a fun time.

I thought her brutal honesty about things was great. She was a little too critical about some people at times, but she wasn't far off all the time, in my opinion. She was unable to see or didn't realize she had some flaws, though. She thought she was perfect. I learned early on from her friends that she was that way. I learned that when she was provoked, she would become defensive. She would quickly go on the verbal offensive toward her attacker. Rarely did she ever take a joke well when it was made in her direction. She took the smallest thing toward her as an attack in some way.

Sometimes people can take a joke, and sometimes they can't, depending on the factors of where, when, why, who, and, the biggest one, how. None of those mattered with her. Her responses were as quick, sharp, and personally cutting as possible. She would usually say something derogative after the person left. Many times, her comments were racial, cultural, or personal slurs. I wondered where those feelings came from. Her parents? Her friends? Past experiences? I didn't understand what got her to those places emotionally so quickly. It was messed up.

Her need to feel in control and superior to or dominant over others was her downfall. Her buttons were easy to push. Her ignorance showed. Her comfortable place was in feeling she was in charge or smarter than everyone else. Her bark was worse than her bite.

She could be a nice person I enjoyed being around, but it was as if she flipped a switch or something. In many ways, it was scary. The energy she gave off showed something about her. I wondered what she said about me. But I didn't really care that much; I just got stoned with her. I didn't really care much about anything at all. She was a way to get high; that was how I looked at her.

On one of my last days of school, on my way in, we rode together on the bus. It was an unexpected meeting. Her early class was canceled, and she caught the bus I was on. We caught up on some things and how things were going. I told her things looked bad for me regarding school for next semester. She had straight As all the way across the board, as usual.

She mentioned that she and some of the friends she had introduced me to were meeting for a Grateful Dead concert later that evening. I agreed to meet her and walk to the concert venue. I had no problem finding a reason to miss my last class to go with her. It was a five-minute walk at best. We did not plan on going into the concert. The idea was to take in the atmosphere of the event.

There's no need to sugarcoat it: if we could score some type of weed or something else synonymous with what went on at a Grateful Dead concert, well, that was the plan. We were sure we'd find something.

It was a beautiful, warm, sunny day. The temperature was in the seventies. Many people had the same idea we did. We saw people of all ages, from teenagers to some seriously old people. The parking lots filled up hours before the show was to start. People were selling

T-shirts out of cars or just walking around. I could smell marijuana in the air. It was a festive feeling—except to the police. Their presence was everywhere, but no one did anything to get them going.

We met everyone in a parking lot. We decided to hang out at one guy's car to watch everything play out. People were friendly, walking and dancing around everywhere. Some had followed the band from city to city. Many financed the trip by selling drugs along the way. We were looking for those people.

Many people around us had started the party kind of early. Some of them appeared buzzed when we got there. Some people with us had coolers full of beer with them. I knew I was scheduled to work later that day, so my plan was to stay a couple hours and then catch the latest bus possible not to be late. I was going to have a couple beers anyway. I told myself I'd be okay. I could cover my breath with gum or candy or eat something. I'd call off if it was that good of a time.

After I'd been there for about thirty minutes, the plan quickly became to call off work. It was starting to get fun. A couple beers and a few joints later, there was no way I was leaving. I planned to call off about an hour before I had to be there. A friend had agreed to let me use his phone when I needed to. He was the only one who had one.

As people filtered in, a couple of my friends made new friends themselves. They found a guy who was selling everything from weed to pills to mushrooms and LSD. He said he had to go get what they'd asked for, and he pointed to the top floor of a hotel, where he said they were making the drugs. I assumed he was talking about the LSD.

How the people trusted each other so quickly amazed me. Neither knew the other wasn't a police officer, yet the deal went down fast. The man was back twenty minutes later. He concealed everything in his jacket pockets, which were bulging on his sides. It was seventy degrees outside, and he was wearing a jacket—that should have been a red flag.

He and my buddy made eye contact. They had a plan already that no one knew. He walked over to the cooler in the trunk of the car, grabbed a beer, and emptied his stash. The cash was already there. The transaction was so smooth that hardly anyone even noticed.

There were more people in the parking lot, so few, if any, expected that transaction to go down. I didn't believe what I'd just seen. I asked my friend about ten minutes later if the order was all there. He said it was.

He then grabbed my hand and put some dried mushrooms in my palm. "Try 'em!" he said. "Tell me what you think. I had some a few minutes ago." I didn't bat an eyelash: I ate them. They tasted horrible, but I chased them down with my beer.

I laughed off what I had just done. No one but he and I knew. I looked and walked around my environment for what I thought was twenty minutes, taking in the people, the warmth of the sun, and the music.

My friend from school came up to me, smiling. She knew something was up. She said, "Did you call off work? You haven't said a word in almost three hours. What the hell did you take? You've been smiling and laughing the whole time."

I was shocked. I'd forgotten to call off. "Oh my God!" I said, disregarding her questions. I grabbed my buddy with the phone and told him I needed to use it. He handed it to me, laughing hysterically. It was about fifteen minutes before I was supposed to be there. I went into panic mode for a moment.

My call was patched through to my department, and my manager picked it up. He asked why I wasn't going to make it. My reply was "I fell. I think I broke my leg. I have to go." As I pulled the phone away from my ear to look for the end-call button, I heard him yell out, "What!" I hit the button before I could hear any more.

My friend next to me was losing her mind laughing. When she regained her composure, she asked, "What did you just do? What did you guys take?"

Realizing my words on the phone, I laughed too. "I'm not sure about anything right now."

I'm not sure how I got home—or anything about the rest of that day. I woke up in my bed somehow. I wondered to myself what all had happened. My mom's first words to me shocked me: "How do feel? You must have been really tired. You slept for the entire day. I know you've been doing a lot lately; maybe your body is telling you to slow down some."

It dawned on me that she'd said I slept for an entire day. I'd been scheduled to work the day before. I knew that couldn't be good after I'd called off the day before in the manner I had. I'd missed an entire day, and I hadn't called off at all that time.

I remembered telling the manager I might have broken my leg. Obviously, I hadn't. There was nothing wrong with me at all. I was scheduled to be there that afternoon. Something was going to happen. They would either let it go or fire me—it was as simple as that. They never called me, so I figured they might let it go.

I knew the department manager was off that day. That was good for me too, I thought. However, when I went in that afternoon, I saw his car in the parking lot. I had a bad feeling right away. I made a beeline to the back to punch in, talking to no one. I could feel people staring at me.

I punched in and grabbed a white coat before I entered the meat room. The only woman who worked in the department said as I entered, "What are you doing? You're done. No-call no-show. You're out." She had a deadpan look on her face.

One second later, the department manager burst through the door, yelling, "Get out of here! You're out of here!" He was flipping out. He'd been both waiting for and hoping for that day. He was going to take full advantage of it.

He unleashed a barrage of insults at me in front of everyone. No one said a word. I was embarrassed. I'd screwed up, and it was reality now. I took off the jacket, looked at him, and said, "Fine."

I turned around and walked out without saying a word. He followed me out to finish his rant one on one. I had it coming. One insult he used stuck out: "Your best day in life will not be comparable to my worst. You are nothing. You're beneath me in every way." He then berated me as a drunk and a waste.

When he said that, I stopped and turned to him. I was about fifteen or twenty feet away from him. My embarrassment over my actions turned to anger. He was right about my drinking and drug use; my actions must have been fairly obvious for him to say it. I wanted to punch him, and he wanted that too.

My voice rose as I spoke. "Oh yeah? You keep in mind one thing about yourself. You're not all you think you are, little guy. You're not liked as much as you think you are. If fact, you'd be surprised how much you aren't. People only listen to you because you're in a position of power." He was about four or five inches shorter than I was. "You're little, you're loud, and you think you know everything. Everyone sees through your act. You aren't as perfect as you think."

That hit the button I'd been trying to hit. He came toward me and confronted me in only three or four steps. Face-to-face, inches apart, he wanted me to touch or hit him. His barrage of insults started over. As we pointed out each other's flaws and issues, the best thing I had going for me was the presence of cameras all over the back stockroom. He was madder than I'd ever seen anyone before. I felt good about getting him there. A couple people heard us yelling and came to see what was going on.

In the end, nothing was solved. I was no longer employed there. I still had to deal with getting fired and failing out of college and explaining how it was the fault of everyone else to my mom, family, and friends. The landscaping and floor-cleaning businesses were what I had left to work with.

As you would expect, my family had some obvious questions about how I was living my life and what I wanted to do with it. They had every right to be upset by what I was doing to myself. They could see a change in me. Pinpointing it wasn't on them, though. They were all doing well for themselves from what I'd seen and heard.

My mom was working hard and had taken on a job at another supermarket in the area. She had been working the morning shift, starting at four or five o'clock. By nine or ten every night, she was in bed. Some weeks, she worked six or seven days because of how busy they were. My being fired for not showing up was inexcusable. I would have fired me too.

16

Landscaping It Is

I'd been juggling doing both the landscaping and floor cleaning kind of on and off for a while. I tried to keep some entertainment in my life by playing hockey with my friends. It was basically ball hockey on a sport court, an enclosed rink about half the size of a normal ice hockey rink in length and two-thirds of the width. I'd been a huge hockey fan since I was little. My mom had taken me to my first game when I was eleven years old. It was a Saturday afternoon game. I'd been hooked ever since.

As kids, we always played different sports as the seasons changed. Some older kids had some ice hockey nets we would carry around to wherever the game was. As we got older, we put them into car trunks or truck beds and moved them much more easily.

Years later, a player got drafted to my team who changed the dynamic of the team and the city itself. The number of people playing ice hockey grew quickly. Ice time was limited because there weren't many rinks, so we played places where we could run around instead of skating and use a ball instead of a puck. We needed fewer pads and other pieces of equipment, which kept the cost down too.

Rinks emerged at certain points around the city. People of all ages and skill sets could play in different divisions of talent and skill level. I was around nineteen when I first started to play in that format. It was fun from the beginning. An older friend of mine asked me to play in what was considered a higher division. He'd convinced a bar to sponsor his team. He was twenty-one.

I also played with some friends of mine who were my age or younger in a lower division. Games lasted less than an hour. Some became intense. The skill levels of some made them think they were pros or something. Some people played for the fun of it. Nobody played to lose, though. There were often disagreements, and occasionally fights broke out.

Seasons were twelve games long, plus playoffs. Some playoff series were three games. There could be as many as three series in the playoffs, depending how many teams were in the league.

Depending on schedules and who showed up, the playing time varied. Everyone always wanted to play a lot, but having a couple subs would give players a breather, which helped out depending on the competition. It helped how one felt the next day. Guys were usually pretty sore after the games due to the intensity of them. Bruises and welts were commonplace.

My friend from the floor-cleaning business was not into hockey at all. It wasn't for him. He never got why I enjoyed it so much. I asked Dave, my landscaping friend, to play. He jumped at the opportunity. He was competitive. His skills were not so great, but he could run.

During the first season, he played in the lower division I played in. While he was playing, something happened. My friend from the floor place was seeing Dave's girlfriend behind his back on nights when we played. She and Dave lived together.

I found out when I saw them kissing in front of his house before we left for work one night. My game had been canceled, so I drove by to see what he was up to, hoping to work with him that night if they needed me. It was a letdown to see that happening. What do you say when you see something like that?

His jaw dropped, and the girl was embarrassed about my seeing them. She didn't know what I was gonna do or say. She saw me before he did, and she abruptly pushed him away and headed to her car. He then saw me and understood her reaction. He said to her, "I'll call you later."

I was out of my car by then, looking at him. "How long has that been going on?" I asked as I walked toward him.

He replied, "A while."

It wasn't my place to say anything. Those situations happen all the time. Seeing it, though, I knew that disappointment, anger, bitterness, and all the other feelings and emotions that came from it were about to begin. I was disappointed in them.

He started talking about all the reasons they had for going behind Dave's back. After he was done trying to explain everything, I was frustrated with him. "It kinda looks like you just stabbed you friend in the back. There was probably a better way this could've happened. There's obviously gonna be stuff that goes down because of it. You actually did Dave a favor. You saved him a bunch of time going forward with her. He's still gonna be pissed at you both."

I felt bad because I didn't tell Dave about it. I could have told him, but I never did. I had opportunities, but I never got the courage to do it. Telling someone bad news is hard, and I didn't know what kind of reaction he would have or what he'd do. I also thought it wasn't my problem. I didn't know what to do, so I did nothing.

Over the next couple weeks, it all played out, and the inevitable happened. Dave caught them together himself. As expected, because of what transpired, there were some difficult moments, and things almost got out of hand. Other things I expected to happen didn't.

Dave was upset and had every right to be. He was crushed. He took the high road and didn't beat the hell out of the guy. My friend who did the floors talked a big game, but my money would have been on Dave in a physical confrontation ten out of ten times.

I helped Dave move to another apartment with some other friends. One of the guys helping was the older brother of the guy who'd cheated with Dave's now former girlfriend. It showed a lot about their friendship. He was upset with his brother too.

A week after that all went down, the landscaping business offered me a full-time job. It was the perfect time. I then had a direction at least. I liked the idea of working in the day much more than being out at night. The energy of the company was good. Dave and his boss seemed like good people to be around. I felt comfortable being there too.

17

The Lesson Learned

How we get to where we are in life and the circumstances that develop because of it involve a time, a place, and things that make up the moment. These may be seen or unseen, known or unknown, understood or not. The smallest thing can change the destiny or path of one or many lives touched by it. The trickle down of elements can affect individuals' reactions to what they are taught, see, or learn or their intention and can define people, concepts, and goals set. They can develop and grow or dissipate goals.

Certain circumstances can allow us to notice the natural God-given skill, talent, or ability one or another has or doesn't. When something feels comfortable, safe, or enjoyable or there is some type of reward financially, emotionally, or spiritually in a career, hobby, or belief system, that entity can affect the direction we are pulled to experience what we are here to experience. Things might not go exactly how we anticipated.

At the age of twenty, I never would have thought I would experience what I did in the next fifteen years. My "office" in the landscape world seemed to change every day. I liked that a lot. Being outside was great. I found I could always dress for the weather. If it was hot or cold, it didn't matter. I could still work in the rain; it just wasn't all that much fun, and sometimes it was counterproductive. It wasn't great for morale.

The first couple years were by far the most fun. The money wasn't great, but it was constant. There were always plenty of ways to make money legally. My mom instilled that truth in me at an early age. I had a paper route as a kid. I wasn't afraid of work by any means.

I played hockey more and more and loved it. I also drank more with my friends who were younger than I was, basically priming myself until I could go to bars legally. With some of the guys I played with, I would try to filter into the bar that sponsored the hockey team. I'd try to make my way into the back room with the illegal poker machines and drink with people I didn't know. I certainly didn't look twenty-one.

The bar manager politely asked me many times not to come back until I was twenty-one. The bar would be glad to accommodate me when I was legal, he said. Dave worked there over the winter as a dishwasher to earn some extra cash. Many nights, he was playing cards well into the wee hours having a great time. Hearing that made it all the more inviting for me to be there.

When I did turn twenty-one, let's just say things were a blur for about a month after. Work-wise, with the experience Dave and I had, we started meeting people who wanted side work done—cash only. We would borrow the tools from our boss, which he was good with, and knock out jobs with ease. If we needed a truck, it was at our disposal. Dave was good about knowing what it would take to finish a job.

Another hockey rink opened up, and I started to referee there. It was indoors. I coached kids as a promise to the owner there. He gave me a fair amount of games during the winter when we weren't working. There were two refs, but sometimes I did the games on my own. The young kids' games especially were easy.

As I became more involved different places, I hung out with more people whom I saw as excellent manipulators. I was learning firsthand, adding to what I already knew. These weren't people I considered bad in any way. It was just what I was exposed to. No one ever admitted to doing anything illegal either. It was just who they were, and who was doing what was sometimes questionable.

When involved with things, you can't help but absorb and be influenced by your surroundings. My own intentions for using the techniques I was acquiring were different from the purposes and reasons of others who were using them for. Sometimes you don't recognize the subtleties you're developing; they just develop.

I knew I was drifting away from my family slowly but surely, mostly by choice. I didn't tell any of them what I was up to because inside, I knew it was wrong to me based on my idea of what was right and what was wrong.

I didn't seem to care much about the events going on in their lives. I cared only about what felt good for me. Things were all about me. How I felt was all I worried about in the moment. I didn't care about others or much else. The only person I didn't try to piss off was my mom.

Although technically living at her house, I was never there. I talked to her all the time, but I'd always tell her I had something to do. I didn't tell her what I was doing. I always made it sound as if the world were against me. I had convinced myself that it was.

Things went smoothly for a while. A year or so later, at work, my boss decided to expand the business and hire some more people. Dave and I told him about a friend of ours who had experience in landscaping both in working for a nursery and working for another company. He would be a perfect fit, we said. He was hired, and a friend of my boss came on with him.

Both new editions fit right in. The older man brought on board was similar to us in that he liked smoking weed too. We knocked out all the work the boss could give us. Sometimes the weather played a factor in things, or something else was added on, but it seemed things always worked out. For me, landscaping was something I enjoyed every day.

My boss had been living at his parents' home since I'd known him. We met in the mornings at a few different places. A couple months before hiring the new workers, he had purchased a house. It was a sign to us he was committed to being there and expanding.

The house was a little rough looking. It was located off the main road, and one could barely see it. He liked that a lot. It had a long driveway that opened up into a parking area, plus a place for all our cars and the multiple trucks he now had. The house sat behind it.

My boss was aware he wasn't hiring a bunch of angels to work with him. He knew we all liked to go out and have a good time. He had a pretty good idea we ventured into things other than alcohol. He wasn't dumb. Just in looking at us and listening, he knew.

His own life experiences had taught him many lessons. On occasion, he would bring up horror stories from his past. It was as if he were reliving each incident as he spoke. To us, the way he delivered the stories was funny. He would laugh about them too, though he was actually warning us not to do what he'd done. The stories made us feel he'd been just like us.

No matter what we did on our own time, we were expected to be on time and ready to work, fully capable of delivering a day's worth of work. That is what every employer would expect of any employee.

He was more aware of things than we gave him credit for. He always thought one step ahead, if not five steps ahead, in all he did. His refinement of his skills, education, and experiences made him a good boss. The one thing he had going against him all the time was time.

He usually ran a little late in trying to juggle all he had to do. He would try his best to be on time, but more often than not, he wasn't. There was always something that prevented it. He was the boss, so it was okay. It was not okay for us, though. His excuses were fine; ours weren't. We often felt he was pulling a double standard.

He would get upset if we were late or weren't done on time. Oftentimes, he seemed to forget that the same things that held him up and made him late were the same things that affected us most of the time. We couldn't stop people, traffic, the weather, or time itself. That being said, he was teaching us to be responsible and prepared. We didn't always see it that way.

We would hear about his being lateness from clients and other people at companies we worked with. We would hear it from his mom and dad. His parents were a big part of his life. They were proud of him and supported him fully. They were kind to all of us who worked for him.

He had his dad work on the business side of things with the books. He did the payroll and other things to help save time. His mom didn't have anything to do with it, but she was as important as anyone. We all enjoyed seeing her and talking with her.

A couple months into the new season, my two coworkers and I decided to go on a weekend excursion to a sporting event. My boss's last words were "I'll see you Monday at eight o'clock, ready to go." He knew there was the potential of one or all three of us not making it in.

We went pretty strong all weekend. It was what we did: we worked hard and played hard. We felt entitled to be that way. We didn't always make the best decisions.

When we arrived at our destination on Friday night after work, we had twice as much alcohol and other stuff as we needed for the entire weekend. Our ignorance showed when we agreed we would finish everything before we left. I took it too seriously. I pushed myself to where I shouldn't have. By the time it was all said and done, I wasn't in much of a condition to drive. Nobody was.

We got in line to leave the event, about to engage in a six-hour drive home on the highway. Frustrated by going nowhere quickly, we'd moved only inches an hour after the event ended. A car cut in front of me while leaving the parking lot. Dave, who was riding shotgun, tossed a small pebble at the back window of the car in front of us.

The people in the car ahead of us told the troopers directing traffic at the exit about the incident. A trooper approached my car. He saw a beer in the drink holder. He reached into the car and pulled me through the window, and then he opened the door. I stumbled, having no footing. I was charged with DUI. I was released about six hours later.

I now see the arrest as a blessing, as it gave my friends time to sober up to drive. The DUI probably saved our lives and perhaps the lives of innocent people on the highway. A terrible moment for me was a blessing in disguise for others. I was still plenty pissed off about what had happened. It was easy to put the blame on everyone else.

As much as it was an inconvenience to lose my license for thirty days and pay an attorney, which actually cost more than the fine for the DUI charge, I knew I was lucky. Unfortunately, I didn't learn from the experience. A false sense of invincibility came over me. My drinking and drug use increased. I was smoking a pack of cigarettes a day, if not more. Of course, I felt that nothing was wrong with anything in life at all.

I was able to keep the news of my trouble away from some of the people in my family. The ones who did find out were disappointed. I begged them to keep it to themselves. I think my boss knew there'd been a possibility of something like that happening.

Over the next few years, I never felt anything getting worse, but it did. I had a girlfriend for a couple years, and our relationship was all over the place. Our common bond was drinking and having fun. The relationship ended because I never had the intention of being with her in the way she wanted.

I manipulated most of the relationship to my advantage in every way. I managed to ring up another DUI with her in my life. I blamed that on her. My first DUI never showed up because it was from another state. It was as if it had never happened. The penalty that time was again losing my license for thirty days, plus a fine that took away from my drinking funds.

I introduced her to my family once, after about a year. Let's just say it didn't go well. The thing she and I had most in common was drinking. We did that well. We did have a great time together. We also had moments when we didn't.

I had built up an extreme tolerance for how much I could drink. I looked at her as the one who had a problem with drinking, though. I'd gone from being with a girl who didn't want to drink to one who drank too much. With both, I failed to look at me. Eventually, when she realized I had no plans other than having a good time with her, she said that was enough after a little more than two years.

During my time with her, the bar I went to changed owners. I didn't care for the new owners much. The father worked for a professional sports team. He had pictures on the wall of him with athletes he knew. There were always about five or six of them hanging on the walls in the bar.

I had known his son back in the day. It had been a few years since we'd seen each other. It would have been all right if it had been a few more years before I saw him again, in my mind. I'd never really liked him.

I knew who he was when I saw him. He remembered me too when they introduced themselves to everyone who walked in for happy hour that afternoon. From that day on, every time I saw him, I liked him less. I resented that they owned that bar. I found out I wasn't big on change. I was kind of a creature of habit—even bad ones.

The guy I didn't like did have value in mine and my friends' lives. Let's just say he was another entrepreneur. He had favorites as far as some of the people I hung out with. He and Dave got along well.

I already had multiple outlets to get whatever I wanted, but he was another, and it was convenient.

A few months later, Dave left the bar late one night and was pulled over by the police. They found him to be in possession of a certain item. The police were pretty sure they knew where he'd gotten it from. They'd been watching the place for a while. The police said he could testify against the dealer, and there would be no trouble for him. There would be other consequences if he didn't.

Word was they had been after that dealer for a while. Different levels of law enforcement were aware of who he was and what he was doing. They wanted him and his source. They believed Dave could make that happen. Dave didn't budge on that offer, though. Dave's legal bills were taken care of, and he received a minimal penalty.

The way I learned about the situation was odd in its own way. Dave missed or forgot about his court appearance for whatever reason and was taken into custody. He missed a day of work and had to come clean with our boss. Our boss saw the writing on the wall. We were all getting caught up in things that could've been avoided.

Our boss had always warned us about spending time where we and doing what we were doing there. He was frustrated because he'd been aware of what could happen.

Dave's silence created a bond among my group of friends, which got us access to the bar owner's line of entrepreneurship more easily. I still didn't like the guy, but who cared? I was getting what I wanted when I wanted it—and easily. Dealing with him was the cross I had to bear.

Dave also landed some easy side jobs fixing up and adding to the landscape of the bar, their homes, and some of their friends' homes too. I benefited greatly from all of it.

As time went on, we agreed not to mention anything pertaining to stuff outside of work in front of our boss. Things actually had calmed down by then, but it wasn't the same at work. The friendly, relaxed environment wasn't the same.

The lack of conversation about many of the things we normally would have felt free to speak about was obvious to our boss. He was shut out. He was just the boss. We blocked him similar to the way I had blocked out my family. I still liked him and was on board with working for him, just not with talking to him the same way as before.

The following year, in the off-season, my boss met a woman. It wasn't all that long before they were engaged. He hired his fiancée's younger brother, who was going to college, and he brought in multiple people.

They all were smart, did whatever was asked, and were funny as hell, and they wanted to go out after work to have a good time. Plus, everyone was of legal age. It seemed things were going back in the direction they had been years before. It was good again.

Suddenly, it seemed the boss actually encouraged the new people to go out with us to build some bonds outside the workplace.

With the expansion, my boss wanted us to run about three or four groups of four or five people. By spending time together, we could learn who fit better with whom and about personalities and whom we preferred to work with. The arrangement was perfect, it seemed. I was happy, comfortable with almost everything, and enjoying things. The same was true for the other guys.

For me, making money was easy between regular work, refereeing, and side work. Most of all, my family never saw me doing what I really was doing. I didn't let them think I was doing too well or too bad. I felt, and hoped, I gave my family the impression I had it all together.

One evening, I called a friend of mine and told him I'd come into some cash. I was going to surprise him and some of the other people I hung out with. He didn't hesitate one second and picked me up on his way.

We stopped at our normal connection. The guy liked my buddy more than any of us. No one understood why. No one could explain why. He just did. It was great. He hooked him up better than all the rest of us.

We stopped and had a couple beers, played the poker machine, and picked up what we wanted all in about twenty minutes. We said we'd be back later on that evening. Everything fell together. It was perfect. I thought I'd be nice and surprise everyone.

As we pulled up to the home where we were to meet everyone, no one was aware I'd bought what I had. We usually pooled cash together and usually on a weekend. It was a week night, which wasn't normal but wasn't out of the ordinary either.

I had a beer with me that I'd taken from the bar. As we entered the house and said hello to everyone, the verbal jabs and insults that were normal to everyone flew. I pulled out what I thought would be a nice surprise. My friends asked what the occasion was. I answered, "I just wanted to."

Not one person said he or she didn't want any as I took it out of my pocket. One particular person was pretty loud and straightforward about just about everything. In fact, the person could be mean. This person was critical of everyone else yet sensitive to his own issues. This person judged everyone as if he were better than everyone, which made him an easy target in return.

Still, none of my friends were bad or overly mean people. I liked to think they all were good people who, like me, partied a little bit more than others. Sometimes it got to be a little more than that. Sometimes funny or crazy things happened. There was never any bad intention. I hung out with like-minded people.

That time, though, the one person in particular made a comment about my having a beer. I wasn't sure if the person had had a bad day and I'd just walked into it or if I'd offended this person prior and didn't know it, but the comment was harsher than the insults we tossed around carelessly and considered normal.

The person also didn't know what I had or that I was about to share it. If this person had, I'm not sure the comment would've been said so bluntly. The words hit me with the truth of what I had failed to see about how other people saw me, both people I liked and those I wasn't all that crazy about.

"You know, all you are is a functioning alcoholic! You drink every day no matter what. You drink a lot—you drink to excess. You drink and drive everywhere; plus, you're stoned. Everyone knows it. You should hear what people say!" The insult rolled out of the person's mouth with venom. There wasn't any gray area about what the person had meant by it.

I paused for a second, stunned, embarrassed, and angry about what had just been said and the way it had been delivered. I went after what I knew was a sensitive area for the person. Before, I'd always stayed away from the topic. Everyone had—until then.

Everyone stared at both of us as if watching a tennis match and waiting for the return. My reply was like a missile with strategic placement. I calmly looked this person in the eye and said, "Well, thank you for your concern. How about you worry about your weight then? I'll worry about how much I'm drinking, and then things will be fine between us."

There was another moment of dead silence as everyone processed my words. I had hit the person's weakest point. That was the way I was, and I went directly after it. The sore spot, the nerve I knew which was available.

Everyone burst into laughter and watched as the other person exploded with explicit words about me. I then pulled out the surprise I was ready to share with everyone. I glanced over to see two guys crying from laughter, smiling from ear to ear. "Do you guys want any?" I asked.

The person I'd had the words with remained mad about what I had said. The rest of the night, there were no words between us unless they involved drugs. The person's anger didn't stop or even slow the person from participating in what we were doing.

As planned, we ended up at the bar again that night. The people I was with let a few other people there know what I'd said and the effect it had had. A couple people came by afterward and thanked me for doing it, saying they wished they would have seen it go down.

Even though it felt good to defend myself from that person, what the person had said about me made me think more and more about how things really were. What did others think of me? Was I really that bad?

The person's insult wasn't all that far off from the truth. In fact, it was the truth. I finally realized it. I admitted it to myself. My defense had been to attack the attacker with words I knew would be more harsh. It was like dropping a bigger bomb or throwing a counterpunch that was a knockout blow.

My approach had worked perfectly. I'd achieved what I wanted to do: hurt the other person worse. However, the comments about how others saw me made me think. Those thoughts took over my head for the rest of the night—and the next day and so on.

18

Sometimes You Don't See Where It's Going

Over the next few years, changes occurred in all phases of my life. Some were obvious, while others were subtle. Work had really expanded. My boss had moved our headquarters and meeting place from his house to a warehouse facility a few minutes from his home. He'd been married for a year or so, and it seemed logical not to have the entire crew saying good morning to his wife every day in their kitchen. Expansion was the reason he used, but privacy was what we all knew his wife wanted.

They appeared to be different people, and their being together was an example of opposites attracting in many ways. He liked to go camping on the weekends and would go hiking to places where none of us ever would have considered spending a weekend. It didn't appear that camping was as appealing to her.

In the beginning, after they met, she would go with him on his excursions. She'd say things to us about the trips when they got back and when he wasn't around. She seemed more refined and preferred to be at home or go away to more civilized places for the weekend than the places they were going. Living in a tent and taking long hikes in all types of weather didn't seem to suit her.

The more we got to know her, in some ways, it made sense that they were together. They had some things in common, but for the most part, they were completely different. They had met after being set up on a blind date.

A change of venue was needed. Everything else was changing too, but why wouldn't it have? Time doesn't stop for anyone. Things became more complicated.

My friendships were still good. At times, there were some strained moments due to the pressures of the job and some of the stuff that went on outside of it. Considering how much time we spent with each other, those people had become like brothers to me.

My relationship with my family was fading, at least to me. I was drifting away further. They, on the other hand, were all doing great. I began to think they were better off without me. I kept my drinking and drug use away from them, so I didn't go around them. If I stayed at my mom's house, I made sure I didn't come home until she was asleep, or I stayed at different friends' places. I had multiple places I could fall into.

If anyone ever asked where I was, if need be, I'd lie about it, saying whatever came to mind to fit the circumstance of why I was not available. Since I wasn't in legal trouble, there wasn't any reason to be concerned with what I was feeding them.

I managed to wreck my car because of drinking but didn't get in any trouble for it. After that, I decided to get a small truck. It was manual drive. I'd learned to drive a manual by driving the dump trucks at work. One particular Saturday, two friends and I were finishing up a project. They asked me to go check the backyard to see if we had left any tools there. It was normal to perform such a check.

As I was opening the gate to the back, I heard one of the trucks start. I figured someone was pulling out. There was no need for both of them to wait for me. When I came back out a minute later, I saw that they were both gone. The only thing there was an empty truck. The owner of the house stood smiling at the door, looking at me.

"Your friends left. They told me they were going to do this when you got here this morning. I guess you have to drive it home," she said. "Do you think you can do it?"

There was little confidence in my voice as I told her, "I guess we'll find out." The feelings that came over me ranged from fear, anger, and uncertainty to disbelief at what the two SOBs had done. It wasn't a funny joke in my opinion.

I'd been practicing over the past months, tooling around the parking lot of the nursery where we got our plants. It was a flat, wide-open place. It was a perfect place to learn. The problem was, I wasn't there that day. It seemed I'd forgotten all I'd learned.

I got in the truck after I checked to see if it was safe and made sure nothing was hanging out of the one-ton dump truck. I hoped that one of the two clowns was hiding from me on the other side of the truck and that it was all a joke. My mind went all over the place for a second. I sat there in the truck for a moment to collect myself and assess the situation.

I thought of the positives: That was truck I'd practiced on the most. I was maybe three minutes from the shop. I'd watched many people drive the truck thousands of times, so I knew when I should shift to higher or lower gears, depending on the traffic and other scenarios I'd seen before.

The fear of stalling it or screwing up in front of the homeowner was my concern. They'd left me on a sizable hill, going upward. Ideally, I'd have been starting on the flat driveway, but such was life. Hitting or wrecking into something wasn't out of the question.

It was a beautiful, warm, sunny morning that was turning into a magnificent-looking day. I felt better when I started the truck, eased up the street, and shifted from neutral to first and then into second gear. I was soon at the top of the multitiered hill that led to the main road I needed to be on. I was relieved I'd made it up the hill. Once I felt comfortable and confident, my mind slipped. I stalled the truck at the stop sign at the top. Panic again set in instantly.

Feeling uncomfortable all over again, I had to focus on paying full attention to the road. I turned off the radio, needing to concentrate. I was happy it was one of the few days I wasn't hungover, and we hadn't gotten stoned before or during the job. Otherwise, the situation would have freaked me out. Luckily, I didn't stall the truck the rest of the way.

When I returned to the shop and pulled into the parking lot, I started to laugh. I immediately saw not only the two guys who'd left me there but also my boss. They all had known about the plan. It was my first driving test.

The homeowner called my boss after I left to make sure they would come look for me if I didn't return to the shop soon. Smiles and pats on the back greeted me when I pulled up. My boss even said I looked like a natural.

I didn't tell them I'd stalled the truck at the top of the hill. I played it off as if I were a natural. I found myself bragging about something I shouldn't have been. I never at any point had been comfortable with what I was doing. I was lying to them and myself.

I continued to practice driving the trucks more and more with fuller, heavier loads. After I improved my skills enough and took a long driving test with my boss and each of the other guys, my boss purchased another even bigger truck. The plan again was to hire more people for year-round work for all of us. That meant more people, not just summer help. Hiring more people meant training them. That would be more responsibility for me.

Over the next few years, the people my boss hired varied on all levels, from smart to not so much to different sorts of personalities and from physically weak to ridiculously strong. We had a couple women work with us. He hired all races. He hired people of all ages.

The expansion increased the business from four to five regular people to around ten to twelve, plus summer help. The boss was trying to create the vision he'd had from the beginning, when he'd first gotten into the business. He wanted to fade himself out of the physical work. His desire was to focus solely on design and creating new work with the clients.

He expected us always to be professional on the job. He had an idea of whom he was hiring and what he was adding to his company. He was desperate to fill the correct spots needed for what we did. Some people weren't cut out for it. Others didn't want to work. Others were really good.

For many, the job was just a paycheck or a stepping-stone between jobs or careers. Many factors, such as weather and time of year, played into what went on and how things were carried out.

We suggested the new people come to happy hour with us. They enjoyed being included. There were only a couple we never said anything to.

The bar had a volleyball court in the back, which was a great way to take out the frustrations of a day or even a work week with the people we worked with. Usually, we would play old versus new or crew versus crew. Many times, happy hour turned into much more.

Having access to certain other things kept the party going further into many nights. Other friends and acquaintances would meet us there. The volleyball court had lights that took things well into the evening.

We left work behind when we left the company building. We went to happy hour every day in the summer months. My boss didn't like us drinking as much as we did, but he did like the bonds the group formed as far as communicating and completing projects. The others and I felt that when we left work, we were on our own time. It didn't really matter what he thought.

He was aware of what was going on. Work-wise, he asked for even more production. He expected us to perform, and he had every right to feel that way. Unfortunately, he didn't see that the crews he sent out weren't always giving him that.

Because it was tough to fill positions sometimes, we held on to people who became harmful instead of helpful, which led to some uneasy situations. Blame was placed on the leaders for not getting the most out of people. It became a catch-22 sometimes.

Having people on board who didn't always give 100 percent and asking others to do more didn't go over well. Not having a person was even worse, though. Trading someone off wasn't easy because everyone knew who did or didn't work. People talked. Some people didn't work well together with others.

The situation slowly had an effect on the atmosphere of the entire place. The energy of the group changed. Over time, it was clear that different people were better at certain things than others. The skill sets of people were different. The assignment of jobs depended greatly on what was required for each. It seemed everyone was questioning everything. Who was best at what, who was fun to work with, and who worked overall? Those were some of the questions of everyone involved.

There were conflicting ideas regarding who should work with whom and how much would be expected to finish the projects in the projected timeframe. Some were one-day projects, and others would last as long as two weeks. A few were even longer at times.

Our boss reminded us not to do stupid things on our own time that would have effects on the group. The advice usually came from a friendly point of view—even more so in one-on-one conversations specifically about the decision making and what could happen.

Even if I didn't tell the boss everything about me, he had a good idea of what was going on outside of work. He saw the results of my prior night every day. He saw the potential train wreck coming for me if I didn't make changes. He saw what I was trying to hide from my family. The warning signs were there. However, I was in denial that anything could ever happen to me.

One Saturday, after a long day of work, I should have listened. I went over to a friend's house. I ended up drinking entirely too much, and I did some drugs too. I met my friend around four o'clock in the afternoon, and we went from bar to bar, having a good time. We were out until almost two o'clock in the morning. I remember being cut off just before last call.

I ended up passing out at his place, along with some other people who had made the trip with us. I was a wreck, but I woke up not long after and decided I was going to go to my mom's house to sleep there. I don't know why.

I made it about a mile before I saw lights flashing behind me. I was arrested. I blew almost 0.2, way above the legal blood-alcohol limit. Plus, there were drugs in my system. Another problem aside from being in trouble again was that I'd been caught in another county. The ride to the police department wasn't far from there, but the courthouse where I had to go to be sentenced later on was forty-five minutes to an hour away with traffic. If I had been caught a minute or so up the road, the situation would have played out much differently.

With all the legal procedures that had to happen, everyone I knew found out I'd screwed up again: my family, my boss and coworkers, my friends, and even people I'd pissed off along the way. Everyone was aware I had a problem, but I refused to believe it. It was my third drunk-driving incident, counting the one that hadn't been discovered.

My troubles took a toll on my mom. She wanted me to change, but

I didn't. I lost my license for a year and got hit with a sentence of house arrest for thirty days instead of jail time. I got a $1,500 fine to go with it. I found myself at my mom's house full-time for that month. She was again there to bail me out.

I got lectures from family and friends who didn't want me to go through things like that. I said everything they wanted to hear to get them to leave me alone. Their words went in one ear and out the other. It wasn't supposed to happen to me. I was jinxed. No one understood that.

There were several legal stipulations: house arrest for a month, a one-year suspension of my license, and meetings with a probation officer once a month. I had to pay the fine in full to get my license back. I also had to have documentation showing I'd attended twelve twelve-step meetings. It didn't matter if the meetings pertained to alcohol or drugs. I had to attend the meetings in the first two months after my house-arrest release.

There was one last thing I had to sign off on and agree to: not drinking any alcohol or taking any drugs. I signed and agreed. Unfortunately, that wasn't the case. After the house-arrest portion was over, I quickly fell back into my old ways. In fact, I turned it up even more.

My boss was upset at me for messing up yet again, but he actually paid me for the time I was under house arrest. I was grateful for that. It was a huge relief financially.

My coworkers were not happy about that when word of it spread. One of the guys saw a check made out to me before he handed out the checks to everyone else each week. They were all working to pay me now, some felt. I didn't care, though.

My continual lies and manipulation skills were becoming more proficient and effective in ways I'd never imagined. I got so good at it that I actually believed what I was doing was brilliant. In reality, I had become so reliant on drugs and alcohol that I failed to see my life slipping away.

After I got my license back, I felt as if things were finally looking up. I didn't care much about what was happening with others, even those close to me. I failed to see life going forward with others. I forgot that other people had tough things going on in their lives too. My responses to those things were not always the best.

Work had become a different place. It had been a fun place years ago, but it was not the same. It seemed that for a short period, things went badly for everyone, whether my boss or people on the crew. It seemed no one was spared. There was a run of break-ups in relationships, and many people who were normally happy were confused about where they'd gone wrong. Two particularly difficult ones involved an engagement and a marriage. Both ended.

The marriage was my boss's. His mother also passed away during that stretch. She had been diagnosed with an illness before, but her passing was so sudden that it took everyone by shock. It was like a one-two punch to him.

His outlet was his business. He devoted himself to it. Unfortunately, my coworkers and I didn't do as much as he wanted us to. His expectation of us working harder wasn't solving the things others were experiencing at the same point in time.

Those two different events of loss took their toll. Other people there had their own things going on too. The combination of all the events and the reactions to them changed the energy of the place. None of it was intentional; it was just life.

The people, places, and things we had all known, done, or been part of in the past had become completely different. We had all changed in many ways, and the perspective of how things were or were supposed to be had changed also. There wasn't any hate or anything like that; it was more so frustration.

There was some blame going on because of how things were, including finger-pointing and complaining about who was responsible for what. How we saw each other changed. People were airing out issues with each other but could barely see or understand the criticism that was being directed at themselves. The bottom line was everyone wasn't preforming at their best and it had a lot to do with what was going on outside of work.

I just wanted to be left alone to do what was required. I also didn't want to have to do everything. Feeling the way I did—that I was doing more than anyone—I took my frustrations out by drinking at the end of each day. I deserved it, I thought.

Getting people who were able to handle the physical demands a job required for a day wasn't all that hard. Doing it every day was. Being in charge of a group of people and knowing that what you were going to encounter wasn't going to be fun was tough. Trying to keep everyone happy was difficult. You were up against time; the people you had to work with, including if the crew got along and what mood everyone was in; the weather; the boss; the homeowner; and unexpected mishaps that could happen, which usually did. One person on the crew could ruin the energy of others on it. Lack of effort, lack of ability, or someone having a bad day could swing the job in a direction that everyone paid for. Some people simply didn't like working with other people, and a day could be off to a bad start before it even started.

We often recommended people to be hired. Two people hired were skilled entrepreneurs like my high school friend. My boss never knew. He hired one himself. The other was a friend of a person we worked with.

No one wanted to work with the first one at all. It was a blessing to know he was on another crew. If my boss had known they were such entrepreneurs, he would've dismissed them. He just wanted to run his business and get a solid day's work from those who worked for him.

I understood where my boss was coming from. Working with either person was frustrating. I became judgmental of each. Being around either one of them, I found it easier to point out things with them than to take ownership of my own issues. I was doing many of the same things they were doing but felt they had problems, and I didn't.

I also took advantage of their entrepreneurship. Saying something could have come back on me. I didn't want to be known as a snitch. Word spread quickly about people. Repercussions could happen in many forms.

All the things that were happening seemed to add fuel to the fire inside me about how I saw life. I hardly cared about any of it. I started to dislike where I was, but I was afraid to go somewhere else. It was as if I were trapped. I was just happy we were never drug-tested.

My personal life with my family deteriorated quickly after that. They loved me and wanted me to be a part of things, but I was engulfed in myself. I made great excuses. One of my sisters told me it was time to change. They all felt something worse would happen. I assumed she'd been nominated to tell me that. Sadly, her words had no effect on me.

I made it a point in 2003 to ruin Christmas. We all went to my brother's the night before Christmas for half of our gift exchange. We'd do the rest on Christmas Day.

I stopped at a friend's house prior to going to my brother's home. We almost finished a half gallon of rum before I left. I played it off as if nothing were wrong, but it was obvious I was lit. With the tolerance I had, though, I could hide it pretty well. I covered it pretty well, but I knew they knew I had been drinking. After the gifts and dinner, I drifted off without taking my jacket with me, so no one would think I was leaving or try to stop me.

We were celebrating a holiday with everyone there for the first time in a long time, and I left. I topped it off by not only driving away but also going back to my friend's place to keep the party going. The only reason I left his place was because his girlfriend was upset we had drunk so much.

I have no idea how or when I made it back to my mom's house. I was the last one up on Christmas morning. My family had already started opening their presents. I didn't care.

I went out back, smoked a cigarette, and took a couple hits off a joint to level off. Eye drops barely helped that day. I could feel my family's disappointment in me. My mom never said a word to me. If she had, she would have killed me. She didn't want to ruin the holiday for everyone else. That was just the way she was.

After everyone left a couple days later, she pulled me aside and calmly reminded me of what would happen if I didn't change. "If you don't stop doing all you're doing, something will happen, and you will pay dearly. There is a hard lesson to learn in this, and you will experience it. Unfortunately, everyone in this family will too."

I looked into her eyes welling with tears and said, "I'm fine. Nothing is wrong. I could quit drinking tomorrow if I wanted to. I don't have a problem."

She knew there was no getting through to me. Instead of yelling at me, as she had many times in the past, she just said, "Watch what happens. You'll lose."

Seeing her pain didn't bother me at all.

19

Change Is Inevitable Sometimes

The year 2004 started the same as many years past had: lots of big plans on the work front, chasing the same demons and thinking the world was perfectly fine, and using the skills I'd acquired to get as much as I could from anyone I could while trying to make it look like I wasn't trying to take advantage of them.

I was still playing hockey. I found it to be the one thing I really enjoyed. I'd been playing for a long time and still had the same fire and passion I'd had the first time I played. The rink or the court was my place to just be free. I could still run, even though I smoked cigarettes and plenty more marijuana than I had when I started.

For my birthday in April, I celebrated to a point that even scared me when I stopped and looked back at what I'd done. As usual for a Friday happy hour, I ended up getting there around five o'clock and closed the bar that night. I prided myself on being able to drink as much as I could while keeping my composure to be served. Drugs helped.

The next day, I bought two cases of beer to go to a picnic and party. One case was for the owner and anyone who came; the other was for me. I got there around one o'clock and stayed until just before midnight. All kinds of stuff was going on. An average of about twenty people were there all day, with many coming and going throughout the day.

There were grills going, games, and things to do to keep everyone occupied. The later into the evening it got, the louder it got. People who had been there for a while were visibly intoxicated, and some became a little rowdy.

The atmosphere changed. Jokes people had made earlier weren't as funny now. Words were said, but nothing happened. I felt it was time to go, though. There was another reason I decided to leave other than that I thought the police would be called soon: I had drunk the entire case of beer I'd brought. My cooler was empty. I kept the cooler in my truck the entire time, locking it every time I left it, because it was where I kept my stash of everything else I had with me. No one seemed to notice me going to my truck as often as I did.

I didn't say goodbye to anyone as I slipped off into the night. No doubt not in any shape to drive, I somehow found my way back to the bar I always went to. I closed the bar that night, seemingly feeling I was fine. I woke up obviously hungover the next day, but by noon, I was drinking again with a different group of friends and playing hockey.

Celebrating my birthday and feeling deserving of it, I took the weekend as a sign of a fun spring and summer yet to come. As much as I drank and used drugs, which I was able to get with ease, my recovery time from feeling bad never was a problem. I bragged to my friends about what happened and how much I could consume.

I didn't notice most of the reactions as bad. I could see disbelief in some people's faces as I proudly told others. One guy said to me in front of a couple other people, "Yeah, well, that's a normal thing to be able to do, huh?" He laughed, and soon after, the others did too. I played it off, as I did everything else. I didn't care.

One month later, my friends and I were playing hockey on a Sunday morning at nine o'clock. Everyone hated games at that time. Just being there on time was tough, let alone running around and trying to actually be competitive. It wasn't unheard of to see someone vomit after a shift or two from the night before. Sometimes people didn't show up at all for those games. Many times, having enough people to play was difficult.

The only good thing was that the other team had the same issue we did. No matter what, though, we always played to win. Some days we had it; others we didn't. The idea of going for a beer after was usually on the table too.

We'd found a bar around the corner to sponsor the team. They loved when we came in, especially on slow days, such as Sunday morning or afternoon. We had been there for a couple years, and they knew they would more than make their money back off of our drinking and eating there. We'd have guys from the opposing teams and even the referees come in with us.

A day in late May turned out differently than I'd planned. As expected, we had barely enough people to play. The previous night took a toll on how much everyone was running. After the game, we agreed to go to the bar to eat lunch and have one. *One* meant *one hundred.*

We opened the place at eleven o'clock that morning. I had breakfast, lunch, and dinner there and was overconfident in thinking I could replicate another twelve-hour-plus day of drinking. A few other guys stayed all day too. Plenty of extracurricular things were going on outside all day. Using the excuse of stretching our legs to the multiple bartenders we had, we witnessed a beautiful, warm, sunny day come and go.

One friend had a great connection who would deliver. He was never shy about sharing. He never asked for money; he just liked doing it. He and I got along great.

That day was no different with him. When we'd finished what he had on him, he made a call, and within a half hour, a friend of his rolled in and dropped something off for him.

While there all day, we played everything from darts to pool to poker machines. There were multiple sporting events on TV. There was never a dull moment as people we knew came and went. We were the only constant customers of the day.

It was after midnight when things finally broke up. We felt that doing one last shot on top of everything we'd already drunk was a necessity. Before we toasted the day to the shot and the last beer before we left, things had seemed fine. I still had my full faculties. After the shot we did, I was barely functional. I tried to cover my reaction as I made my goodbyes quickly to my friends. I needed some fresh air.

The cool night air helped me quickly refresh myself. Unfortunately, that refreshment didn't last long; everything I'd put into my body was now on blast. I knew it was going to be a difficult drive. I was in trouble: focusing was difficult, and my judgment wasn't there. I had roughly a fifteen-minute drive through four different police department localities.

I remember leaving the parking lot with the windows halfway down and my stinky hockey equipment in the bed of the truck. I could still shift the gears well enough to get out onto the road. I was a mess, though. It was as if I were learning to drive all over again. I passed a police station and decided to speed up to get away from it. However, I failed to remember to stop or even slow down at the next four red lights over the next few miles. I had gone through multiple intersections at ridiculously high speeds, when a police car saw me.

I never saw him or his lights. From what he said, he followed me for about a mile and a half before I finally pulled over. He said it was a miracle that I'd barely avoided a car at the biggest intersection as I went through it at full speed. Needless to say, he was pissed off.

The breathalyzer revealed a .27 reading for my blood-alcohol level. There was a half-smoked joint visible in the ashtray and a rolled-up bill on my passenger seat. I was immediately taken to the local jail and quickly processed into the county jail. I was arraigned by a judge and released on my own recognizance by seven o'clock the next morning.

The judge read me my charges, none of which were good: DUI, drug possession, multiple charges of speeding, and endangerment to others. The list he read seemed to keep going on. He didn't have to let me go either; he made that clear to me. He had my record in front of him. He saw the other DUIs I had. He told me about the changing laws to take people like me—multiple offenders—off the streets and the longer-term prison sentences they were now imposing.

"The laws have changed; society has become tired of people like you. You haven't learned that you can't do this. My recommendation is that you get a good attorney and prepare for the worst. Have a nice day. Get out of here." His words were to the point. He was serious.

I asked the clerk at the desk where I received my wallet, keys, cigarettes, and lighter where my truck was. It was at a garage on the other side of town. It would cost a couple hundred dollars to get it out of impound.

I took a bus to get it thirty minutes later. I had to wait another hour before the place opened. I called off work. I prayed my boss didn't pick up. Thankfully, he didn't.

After having little care about how people saw me before yesterday, now sober, I faced the serious reality of what I'd done to myself. I started to think about how I looked to others and what I'd been doing to achieve where I'd gotten myself.

The grim reality of who I had become was terrible. The judge's words about a prison sentence replayed in my mind. I thought about who I really was as a person. I didn't see much there.

After I got my truck out of impound, I drove to my mom's home and told her the news. She was devastated, but she had expected something like would happen. She was angry and even blamed my failure on herself. I apologized to her and made sure she knew it was on me, not her.

I dropped down onto my bed and pondered the undesirable situations going on in every phase of my life, including what I'd done to myself and how my family, friends, and coworkers would see me.

How would they see me? It wasn't going to be good. Reality hit me as plain as day: I was a mess. My life was so far out of control that I couldn't put the brakes on myself. It was all my own doing.

My mind couldn't let go of the idea of prison. There was no avoiding the situation; it just was. I started to sink into depression the more I processed it. Hope in my life was gone. I had done this to myself. I couldn't go back to change it now. I would've given anything to go back.

I realized all the pain and inconvenience I had caused so many people. I thought of the damage I'd caused and how I'd insisted it was never my fault. It was all my fault. I'd blamed so much on different people and made excuses for how I wanted to see life. I believed I was perfect, and the rest of the world was wrong.

The look on my mom's face when I told her stuck in my mind. She looked defeated and deflated, thinking she had failed. My issues hurt her deeply. I knew the pain would not lessen during the time period before I was sentenced. There was only one way I could avoid hurting her anymore, I decided. I was done. I was going to take my own life. I could only hurt her one more time.

She would be free of the burden of my messing up again. I'd be doing her a favor that way. Plus, it was an easy way out for me. I quickly became okay with the idea. A calm came over me. I believed that was the correct idea. There was only one question left: How?

I would do it on my terms. I was gonna do it the way I knew best: with alcohol and drugs. Unfortunately, my personal stash was gone, either confiscated by the police or used on Sunday. I had some weed the police hadn't found, which was a bonus. After I woke up from my long-overdue sleep, I decided that was the night. Why wait?

I slept until late afternoon. As I walked out the front door, I said to my mom in her kitchen, "I'll be back in a bit. I'm going to the store." She said something back, but I couldn't hear her reply. I jumped into my truck in the driveway and drove away quickly. I could see her in the doorway as I pulled away.

My first stop was to get a fifth of whiskey. My second stop was to get a bottle of sleeping pills. I was going to take the pills and drink the bottle after everyone went to sleep. I would end it all in my truck. Most of the damage I had done had been in a vehicle, and going out that way seemed fitting.

My sister was upset when she found out later that day about my arrest. She went on a tangent, telling me I could have changed things if I had only done this or that and not this or that. She actually reinforced my decision to end my life. I was going to hear the same thing countless times from everyone everywhere if I stuck around. I knew I had a problem. The problem was me.

After my mom and sister went to bed, I got into my truck, which I had parked in the garage that night. I smoked a little weed and started taking the sleeping pills one by one. I washed them down with some mixed drinks until I had put the bottle away. I positioned myself across the front seat of the small truck and stretched out as far as I could. I slowly drifted off to sleep. I thought I had finally done the job.

You can imagine the surprise I went through when I woke up sweating and in an uncomfortable position, cramped in my truck. I was plenty drunk and groggy but dismayed that I couldn't even kill myself. I was stunned I was still breathing.

I could hear my sister moving around, getting ready for work. The garage was located underneath the living room. No one was aware I was in the garage.

I made my way from my truck back into the downstairs part of the house and slipped into the shower to avoid seeing my sister leave for work. All the shower did was make me a wet drunk. I heard her leave, got out, and fell back into bed.

When my mom got up, I told her I was going to work but was going in later. It was a lie. I didn't go in at all. I didn't call off either.

I went to the same stores I had the day before. This time, I bought a bigger bottle of sleeping pills. I got a half gallon of whiskey this time. I decided to go to my dad's grave site to tell him I'd be there soon.

By the time I got there, it was midmorning, and I was fading fast. I was an emotional wreck at that point. It probably looked as if I were mourning a past loved one rather than preparing to join him.

It was probably around ten o'clock in the morning when I blacked out. I don't remember getting back into my truck, but I did. I came to when I ended up getting into an accident by rear-ending a minivan. I was more concerned about where I was than what I'd just done. The police there knew who I was. I'd been to that police station a few times before.

After I figured where I was, I had no idea how I'd gotten there. I wasn't anywhere near the cemetery I'd been to earlier. I was really drunk at that point too. Suddenly, my fear of getting caught kicked in again. The feeling that came over me was "Get out of here now!"

I motioned to the driver in front of me that she should pull up ahead, and I'd follow her. I could see the woman waving back as if to say, "Okay." As she pulled over off to the side, I made a quick right turn, and I was gone. I looked at the radio in my truck: it was a little after two o'clock.

That's the last thing I remember. I woke up in my truck. I'd passed out with the truck running in my mom's garage. The police were there with guns drawn on me, telling me to get out of the car. I could hear my brother's voice telling the police to put down their guns, as it was obvious I was fully incapacitated. I was incapacitated, but the police didn't know that. My only thought was *I wish I was dead now more than ever.*

After all the commotion I'd caused, I was removed from my truck with no problem. Because I'd passed out while leaning over toward the passenger seat—I guess to reach for the bottle—the police thought I had a weapon. For their own safety, they had their guns on me. My family understood afterward. The police were doing their job.

I was sure I'd had an accident that had damaged the front of my truck. I didn't know I'd been in another accident, though. I was made aware of damage all down the passenger side of my truck. I had no memory of hitting anything. Had I sideswiped something, such as a car or a guardrail? It was bad. The front looked fine.

Multiple police cars and an ambulance were in front of my mom's house. All eyes were on me. Handcuffed and struggling to walk, I was helped to the ambulance, where I was going to be checked out. I looked at the ambulance driver, and she looked at me. She asked, "Are you okay?"

Embarrassed by all that was happening, drunk, and exhausted, I finally gave in. "You know, I think I have a problem. Can you help me?"

We all stopped right there in the driveway. "Say that again—to them," she said, directing me to speak to the officer holding my arm, who had stopped too. The officer stared at me.

Looking at him, I said, "I think I have a problem. Can you help me?"

He had heard me say it to the EMT, but he needed me to ask him. The person who'd just had a gun pointed at me said, "Yes, we can. All you had to do was ask. I'm glad you did." I wasn't sure how or what I'd asked for, but relief came over me.

As I was directed to the ambulance with the EMT, the officer walked over to his partner. They had a conversation with my brother and my mom. I had no idea what they were saying. To be honest, I didn't really care.

Sitting down in the ambulance, I was told to relax. I finally lay back on the gurney inside. I was told everything would be okay. I passed out or blacked out again. I had no idea what would happen next. I just wanted to sleep. I was done. Whether I'd been caught or just given up didn't matter. I finally surrendered.

20

Ending Up in the Craziest Place

I remember entering the ambulance. It was as if time stopped after that. All that I had put into my body had taken over. I had no idea where I was. I had the worst headache I'd ever had.

I was lying flat on my back. I attempted to move my head to see where I was. One of my sisters noticed my slight movement and approached me, holding her daughter. I wasn't ready to talk to her, but I wasn't going anywhere quickly either.

It seemed as if she were yelling at me when she spoke. I could barely focus as she spoke about all I had to live for. She said her daughter needed me, and the rest of the family did too. She didn't let me lose sight of her; she made sure I was looking into her eyes. I saw tears in her eyes.

I later found out she'd never raised her voice at all. I perceived it that way because of how bad I felt. Every sound I heard was so punishing it was ridiculous. Never in twenty years of active drinking and drug use had I ever felt like that. On top of that feeling, I was also in some serious trouble over what I had just done.

I still wondered where I was. A woman behind my sister gently touched her on the shoulder and asked her to please step back. I figured the woman was a nurse. Behind the two of them, in background, was a big bald-headed man. At first, I thought he was a police officer. He stared at me, just looking down, watching me. A moment later, after the nurse and my sister shifted places, I saw that based on his clothing, he was either an orderly or a doctor.

I scanned the rest of the room to see where I was as my sister and the nurse spoke with their backs turned to me. To my left was a long window with bright sunlight streaming in above the image of trees and a beautiful day I normally would have been out in. To my right was an empty bed, and past that was a door to a bathroom. I knew I was in the hospital. The nurse then turned to me and said, "You're okay. The doctor is going to be here in a few minutes. He'll tell you everything that's going on."

I couldn't have moved if I'd wanted to. I knew if I tried, the large bald guy at the door wasn't going to let me anyway. The guy was big. He had the physical presence of someone I wouldn't have messed with even if sober. I noticed his hands were huge, and his forearms looked as if Popeye had nothing on him.

The doctor came in a minute later and cleared the room.

It was just the doctor and me. He asked how I felt and if I was having any bad thoughts or feelings of hurting myself. I said I wasn't. He knew I felt terrible physically, so he focused his line of questioning on my mental state. I finally asked him, "Hey, where am I at, man?"

Without any hesitation, he told me, "You're in the psychiatric ward. There was no bed available at any of the rehab centers in the area, so this was considered the safest place for you. The other alternative for you if you want to leave is the county jail." He stared at me, waiting for my reply.

"Oh, okay," I said as I looked outside. The fight in me to leave was gone. I was defeated. I didn't want to be in jail—that was for sure.

He said my family members were getting some things for me and would be there soon. The nurses were going to bring some food in soon. I could walk around if I wanted. If I wanted to shave, I could, though I would have to be supervised and couldn't keep the razor. I reached for my face to see if I needed to shave. I felt my chin and each side of my face. I could feel stubble all over. I hated the feeling of stubble on my face. Facial hair, when one was working outside, was always either itchy or hot. I tried to shave every day no matter what. I felt cleaner when freshly shaved.

I told the doctor that a shave would be great. He said it would be no problem. "I'll let Mike know, and he'll help you out. You and I will talk later. Get some rest."

I assumed Mike was the large bald man standing outside the door. I looked out the window, wondering how I'd gotten there. What all had gone wrong? What was going to happen? Being honest with myself wasn't my normal thing. The damage I'd done to myself and others seemed impossible to fix. I didn't have any idea where to start.

As I sat up in the bed, a nurse came in with a tray of food, some vitamins, and a drink. She didn't seem happy. She said directly, "Don't get used to this; the cafeteria is down the hall."

A thought then dawned on me: *How long have I been here?* I didn't even know the date or what day it was.

"What day is it?" I asked as she signaled for me to open my mouth to take the vitamins.

She smiled as I downed the vitamins and showed her I'd swallowed them. "It's May 26, 2004."

I replied, "Thanks. I knew the year. I guess I'm not gonna forget that date being here, huh?" I laughed off the reality of where I'd ended up. Inside, I wasn't laughing. I wasn't going to forget how bad I felt at that moment.

After she left, the big bald man walked in. "Hey, pal, heard you want to get a shave. I got you. Give me about thirty minutes. I've got to help some nurses right now, but I'll be back."

I finished eating the tray of food the nurse had brought. I couldn't remember when I'd eaten last. The food wasn't bad.

I had my back turned, looking out the window, when he spoke, taking me by surprise. I quietly said, "Sure, you got it." As I looked at him, I saw how big he was, easily six foot three or four, with really broad shoulders. Even wearing scrubs, he looked strong physically.

I had no concept of time while in the state of mind I was in. I could feel myself slipping into depression over how my life looked now. When the intimidating individual came back, he took me by surprise again. He walked in, said hello, and then turned and closed the door. He then walked toward me and stopped a couple feet in front of me. A sense of fear shot through me. I felt as if I were about to meet my judge, jury, and executioner. I was wrong—again.

In a relaxed, calm tone, he asked, "Can we talk—off the record?"

I hesitated for a moment before answering. "Yeah. Sure."

He began by saying, "I heard you're in some trouble. I've been in a similar situation. I got myself in some jams, all to do with drinking and stuff."

He said he'd been a Marine Recon. He'd been in scary situations himself, none of which had scared him more than a situation similar to what I was going through. My fear of him slowly went away.

He mentioned some things that had happened to him and affected him and some things he wasn't proud of. He'd been incarcerated due to his drinking. He'd lost it all. He'd been more than $100,000 in debt at one point.

He was now on his way to graduating medical school at night to become a pediatrician. He worked multiple jobs in order to pay for his education and repay the debt he owed. He was close to reaching his dream. His life had changed because he'd changed his life.

Hearing him say that was nice, but it didn't exactly solve the problems I had. He said once he'd quit drinking, things had seemed to come together—not exactly in the terms or time he would have liked them to, but he was coming back from the damage he'd created. He said he'd been sober for almost five years.

I told him I had gotten two DUIs within three days, so things probably weren't going to work out great for me. I explained that I had two prior DUIs and was afraid—about everything. He said he'd had a few of them also. He'd done the time and left that part behind him.

He said he'd found a way to remain sober by going to meetings and learning from and being around people with the same or similar habits he had. He used the information to handle daily life situations without relying on a drink or drug. He'd found his spiritual side and a way to see his life on his terms.

For the first time in a few days, a moment of calmness came over me. His message of hope was something I needed. I had the feeling he could see through my bullshit because he had been there. He didn't force anything on me, which was what I liked the most. He was there at the perfect time for me to listen.

I shaved, and he went on his way. He said he'd be around if I needed anything.

I went back to my spot, staring out the window. I heard my mom's voice outside the door a little later on. She was talking with someone, but I wasn't sure who. My mom is pretty small, maybe five feet tall, but she has a loud voice when need be. The place was so quiet that when anyone spoke at a normal volume, I could hear it perfectly if the person was near the doorway.

She and one of my sisters came in with a bag of clothes. They'd brought more than I'd thought they would. I had to question it. I didn't want to be there. My mom realized my angle quickly, and the chips fell onto the table with power and directness I hadn't expected.

My mom didn't hold back. "Look, if you leave, they call the police, and you go to jail. You have to be signed out by the doctor when you leave. After here, you go to a rehab facility. No questions. There aren't any beds available anywhere now, so here is where you have to stay. This isn't the worst place you could be in. You could be in jail."

She looked exhausted. She was getting a break from me. Knowing I was in a safe place helped her. Her voice then softened. "You asked for help; learn how to take it. You have a problem, and I don't mean the legal one. You have a life problem. It's time to get yourself straightened out. This has gone on entirely too long."

Tears welled up in her eyes, but she didn't cry. It would have been a sign of weakness. That wasn't her. I was on the verge of pushing her to a point she didn't deserve to go to. I realized I needed to back down.

Having to raise five kids by herself for a long time had taken a toll in ways I could only imagine. I wasn't making things easier with my questions. Fighting with her for caring made no sense. I knew the rest of my siblings weren't happy with me, although she said they'd be coming to support me.

Then she said something that made me laugh. She said she'd had a conversation with a big bald-headed man. "He was a big guy. His name is Mike. More like Big Mike," she said in astonishment. He was big to me, and he towered over her.

I smiled at her. "Yeah, I met him. He hooked me up with a razor." I didn't tell her about the conversation we'd had.

I gave up the idea of leaving. Worrying about how things would be with my sisters and brother was next up. My mom said that none of them had been prepared for me to do something like this. My brother wasn't happy about coming to visit me at all. I understood that. He and I were different in many ways.

One of my sisters came the next day, and I received another lecture out of love about how much I meant to them all and the need for me to change. My sisters were happy I was alive. Their love and concern poured out. Another day passed before my brother showed up. When he came in, I could see he had no real desire to be there. I knew it. I told him at one point, "You can leave."

We then had a discussion about what exactly I had done. It went on for quite some time. I knew how he saw me now and where I stood with him and he with me. He had every right to be upset. I asked him to leave after the conversation. My mom was visibly disappointed that her two sons couldn't be in the same room together and talk. He got up and left.

One nurse reminded me every day for what turned out to be nine days there that I was the only person in there who had a chance not to be on something in order to feel normal. I was the opposite of everyone else there. There were people with severe issues in there. I had a chance to change myself without using or consuming drugs or alcohol. She was right. She walked me out when it was time for me to finally leave.

My friendship with Big Mike grew stronger every day. Some things that happened there took me back to my most basic self, such as making a pizza from scratch with people whom life seemingly hadn't been fair to. There were things that made me smile—things I found gratitude in and needed to see and experience.

The turning point in all of it was when I broke down and cried. I let it go. I released the emotional feelings I'd stored inside my mind, heart, and soul. I let it all go in the physical form of tears. I got to the point that I couldn't cry any more over it.

There was only one way to go. I had hit rock bottom, and I was still there. The road ahead was unknown, and I was afraid of many things and worried about how everything would go. Leaving there was the next step.

My family were persistent about getting me into a rehab center, and it finally happened. After leaving the hospital at eleven o'clock in the morning, I had enough time to get a haircut and be at the rehab facility by three o'clock. My mom and one of my sisters drove me there.

As I was checking in, my mom asked the woman at the desk, "What else can we do now?" She and my sister waited for the next instruction.

The woman paused for a second and then smiled. "Well, it's all kind of up to him from here. You got him here."

The woman behind the desk told them family night was on Wednesday nights. I hugged my sister and mom and assured them I'd be okay. I told my mom I'd call her in the next few days. I laughed and told them, "Your parts are over. Thanks. Like she said, it's up to me." It made sense: it was up to me.

I ended up staying in that place for a total of twelve days. It was supposed to be twenty-eight. I had a hearing for the first DUI and hoped they'd consider dropping the charges. I also had to meet my attorney, whom my family had gotten through a family friend my dad had taught to swim as a kid. The friend handpicked the attorney to represent me. He said he was good.

The rehab center was a blessing. I met some interesting people. I learned that the percentages of success aren't that great. Depending on whom you believe, the rate is around 6 to 10 percent. For drug addiction, it's even lower. Jails, institutions, and death are the results for many who face addiction. It's not guaranteed that will happen, but the results from either can take its toll in other ways too. Relationships, careers, health, mental state and other things are all on the table to be lost, tainted or destroyed.

There was a roll call for all the people in the facility at every meal or function. There were roughly fifty to fifty-five people there at a time. That meant about three to five of the people there at any time had a chance of living a sober life. I made up my mind the first day I would be one of the three to five. I didn't care who the other two to four were.

The structure of the place made everyone accountable for many things I had taken for granted. There were people of all ages, different races, and different religions. Some people had been to multiple places multiple times. Like me, a few were in such a place for the first time. A couple people even had been in as much trouble as I was.

There was little downtime during the week. During the weekends, there was a fair amount of time for leisure. After a couple days there, it seemed everyone knew everyone. It was odd to me to see how many people took an interest in helping or motivating someone else to get clean or sober but had trouble doing it for themselves. I guess that explains the low percentages they spoke of.

When I received confirmation of my court date, I wanted to be there to face the situation head-on. I knew I was in trouble, and the longer I waited, the more bad thoughts I had about what could happen. I thought that at least if I knew the outcome, I could handle it better than not knowing.

In a weird way, I wanted to get back to work, even though I was sure everyone I worked with knew what had happened, along with my drinking and drug friends and the entire neighborhood where my mom lived. People were going to talk. I was sure they had already. It was time to get on with things.

21

Dealing with the Problem

The reality of things came to light quickly after I left rehab. I left on a Saturday afternoon. Leaving was something I'd imagined often while I was there, and now it was time. I thought about all the people I'd met and the info I'd been given. I also agreed to and signed on to an outpatient program for the next few months.

I decided to actually do what was recommended for the first time in my life. I promised myself I'd attend some meetings I probably should have attended a long time ago. I had learned more than I'd thought I would, much of which had come from the person I shared my room with. He was there because he was afraid he'd use heroin again. He'd been sober for many years but was having urges to use. He was afraid he'd lose everything again if he did, including his life.

It didn't take much to figure out it had happened to him before. I picked his brain about things I wouldn't have ever considered asking anyone before that. His honest answers were valuable. It was as if he were there especially for me. He listened to every question I asked. He too offered hope. Like Mike at the hospital, he'd been able to find hope in a situation I was unable to. They both felt that everything always happened for a reason, whether it was imposed upon or embraced by a person. Whatever happened, there was something behind it. Sometimes it was understood, and other times it wasn't.

One of the things I learned that stuck was the percentage of people who made it without falling back or relapsing. After seriously looking at myself, I came to the conclusion that I had relapsed every day for ten years or maybe even longer. My problem had been obvious enough for others to see, so what had made me deny it for so long?

The consistent answer was fear. I feared change, a new life, and a different way of thinking and living. I feared the future, past, and present. I feared people, how I was seen, and how I felt. I feared what I was, who I was, everything I had done, and, most of all, the unknown punishment that lay ahead. I had been clean and sober for twenty-one days, but all those fears lay ahead for me in day twenty-two, and it wasn't even there yet. My mind was already thinking it, though.

I had come to the conclusion that I was going to be at my first hearing, which meant leaving the facility a few days earlier than anticipated. Something said to me, *Get going, and be there.* I had to face it eventually, so why not get on with it?

I okayed things with the people at the rehab center and was released late on a Saturday afternoon. I'd made arrangements to be picked up, and everyone was on board with my doing the things I'd been asked to continue when I left there.

I had to execute the change. It was on me. I'd been clean for three weeks and knew a little, but I was afraid. I was entering into lions' den all over again. I was as uncomfortable as I'd ever been. I had learned some tools to use; it was now a question of using them.

On the drive back to my mom's house, I wondered how everyone I knew would view me. What would the neighbors think? How would I be received at work? What about my friends? The biggest common bond I had with many of my friends was the connection of drinking and, with a slightly lesser percentage of them, drugs. I knew that seeing them was unavoidable. A few of them had reached out to my family to see how I was doing. However, I couldn't place myself around many of those people anymore. I had to do it for myself. I still could be their friend; I just could not do what I'd been doing with them prior. None of them were bad people; we'd just done some things I couldn't afford to do anymore.

On Sunday morning, I got up around six o'clock. I was used to getting up that early from the regimented schedule of the past few weeks. I attended a twelve-step meeting, as promised, which I'd found before I left rehab. I'd found one for every day of the week.

I just wanted to blend in and say nothing. That didn't happen, though. I was like a deer in the headlights. My fear and discomfort were noticeable to everyone. I was told that every one of the people there had felt like I did at one time. It made sense and was kind of a relief.

A woman sitting next to me introduced herself and then quietly asked me if I was in trouble or was there voluntarily. I thought my story was unique, so I didn't think she'd understand. I gave her the abbreviated version: "I was in trouble with some DUIs, but I probably should have been here years ago. I just got out of rehab yesterday."

She smiled before speaking. "I had a bunch too—five total. I thought I'd go to jail, but somehow, it worked out that I didn't. It may look bad now, but you never know. I lost my license for a while, but I got it back. It took time, but it was okay. My life changed. It's better than I ever thought it could be. It hasn't always been easy, but it's better than it was."

I couldn't believe what she'd said. It sounded eerily similar to my story. She took away my fear of feeling that no one would understand. She not only understood but had gone through something similar. I suddenly felt maybe I was in the right place. It couldn't have been just a coincidence.

On Monday, I met my new attorney for coffee about an hour before my first court appearance on my original DUI charge. He explained that prosecutors would show the evidence they had against me and see if it was enough to file the case downtown and proceed with further action against me. He assured me that was going to happen. He told me not to worry because I wasn't going to jail that day, so I could relax.

He explained what was going to happen and the action he would take on my behalf. He was going to try to get the two DUIs in three days somehow put together. He was going to delay the sentencing as long as possible. He highly recommended I go to as many meetings as possible and have signed documentation for each one for multiple reasons: (1) it would show the court I was trying to work on myself; (2) I really needed to work on myself, as it was in my best interest as a person to learn to live a different way; and (c) it couldn't hurt.

He spoke about how the laws had changed and the stiffer penalties for the charges I faced. Five years was the minimum. He suggested I take a nice vacation of some sort before the sentencing.

We entered the court, and it seemed we were out as fast as we'd walked in. Everything went just as he'd said. He said I'd soon get a letter telling me when we would have the next court hearing. He said over and over that I should not stress out about the whole thing. He was honest about everything, and I liked that, but it was paralyzing to think about where I'd be in a year or so.

My return to work the next day felt awkward from the outset. Mostly, everyone was happy to see me back. I heard some jokes behind my back, but I had to take it. The people I'd done things with before didn't stop on account of my being back. It seemed I was being tested or pushed to see if I'd do something with them. It was brutal; I was right back in the middle of what wasn't good for me.

I found out quickly that I had little in common with many of the people I'd trained with, hung out with, or become friends with over the past years. I'd known some of them for double-digit years. I'd known Dave since the beginning. I felt as if something were off between us now.

My situation had a trickle-down effect on the entire crew. The energy of the place changed some more. I'm not sure what was said or by whom, but others had had to pick up my part while I was gone. I felt like they looked at me differently.

I'd also put my boss in a difficult position. He was disappointed in me too. He had every right to be upset. Again, he'd paid me while I was off. He wanted to see me change as much as my family did. I was hurting his business. I wouldn't have been mad if he'd fired me after that.

Expectations were placed on people to do more. Some stepped up. The ones who did had no problem. Blame, I felt, was put on me for the changes. My problem seemed to be others' problem now.

The rest of the summer work-wise was both good and bad. It was good in that I refocused on the business side of things. I looked at things as if I were doing them myself, from plants and design work to talking to people. I'd taken for granted how much I knew and how far I'd come in doing that work. That was a reward in itself.

I went to a meeting every night for the entire summer. I had a routine. It helped me block out the negative stuff going on around me and think more about the future. One of the entrepreneurs I worked with got in trouble some himself—way more than I had. He was into things pretty deep and got into a situation that went badly. Guns were involved. He shot at another man. The man pulled a woman in front of him as a shield. She was shot and died. My coworker was charged with third-degree murder.

No one could believe it. Just like in my situation, one thing had led to another. He'd never believed something like that could happen, but it ultimately did. Elements of his situation had been much the same as in mine: alcohol, drugs, and a weapon. Mine was a car. His was a gun. Add in some bad decisions, and things like that can happen.

My next visit with my attorney, during which we'd meet the judge who'd be sentencing me, came up a couple months later. Unfortunately for me, we learned I'd landed a judge whose daughter had been killed by a drunk driver.

My attorney, who got the sentencing delayed that day, said it was probably the worst-case scenario for him being able to help me. However, a few weeks later, something good happened.

In what my attorney considered a miracle, the woman I'd hit in the last DUI had heard about me and decided not to press charges. Since my truck hadn't been running and the keys somehow had not been in the ignition or on my person in my truck while I was passed out, somehow, the DUI charge was dismissed. No one really fought it, as they knew I was still up on the original DUI charge.

I got the call telling me the news while I was at the outpatient rehab facility. The counselor couldn't believe it. She said, "That never happens. That's amazing." She said to me and to the group, "Sometimes good things happen when we try to do the right thing and are grateful. Some might call it karma." I didn't care what it was called; it was good news for me.

My attorney kept pushing back the date when we were scheduled to appear before the judge. We could see she was ready to sentence me each time, but he stressed that I was doing rehab work, still employed, and helping maintain a business where I played a prominent role.

The judge asked me to step forward one particular time to make sure I knew exactly where things stood with her before she extended my case again. With a firm, strong voice, she made it clear how she felt. "When it is time and there are no more delays available, I will sentence you to the maximum that the law will allow me to."

I felt my heart in my throat. The only words I said were "Yes, ma'am." The grim reality for me was that it was her court, not mine. Any sense of hope for something positive in my direction deflated in that instant. My attorney knew it. He said the furthest he could push it out was May 2005. That was it.

I made it to Christmas, and he said he could extend it one last time in March when we met again. He recommended I plan a nice vacation for my birthday, go somewhere, not think about anything, and just enjoy the time I had.

I didn't want to ruin the holidays any more than I had already, so I didn't say anything to my family about it. I told them we were delaying the sentencing as long as possible. My mom was worried more than anyone, and it showed. It was terrible.

Physically, I was feeling better and looking better, and I had an outlook on life that I hadn't expected from myself. I prayed for a miracle to happen. I didn't think anyone heard me.

At work, we worked all winter again. Cold temperatures and snow weren't a big deal anymore. There were plenty of other things going on besides my issues. Dave ended up leaving. He moved to be closer to his family before Christmas—something he said he probably should've done a few years back. It was time for him to go. For me, his move was tough. He and I had been through a lot. He'd gotten me the landscaping job to start with fifteen years before. We'd had some great times together with a lot of different people in a lot of different places. I probably spent more time talking to him and doing things with him than anyone else over that time. We'd worked together, talked about women, both played and gone to see sports, and just laughed about things in general. It was as if I'd lost a best friend, which I kind of had. It had to be that way, though. Everyone knew he wanted to be closer to his family.

My boss was losing his top performer, who was moving, and his second was going to jail. I felt even worse after learning that. He'd always been there helping, teaching, and caring about us. I was letting him down with my actions.

He'd always known there was a possibility something like that could happen, but it was reality now. He had known Dave even longer than I had. Dave's last month was tough, as we knew he was leaving. The beginning of the next year wouldn't be the same.

One morning in early April, I was working near the shop on a rainy, cold day that was horrible to be out in. My boss insisted we stay and get the day in. Anyone in his right mind would not have been out that day. The guy I was with and I weren't happy about being out in the weather. It was miserable.

We knew why we were out: it was spring. My boss had the work booked up already. That was work in itself. We knew he couldn't get behind that early in the year. He eventually would, though, because he always did. Clients were upset when we weren't there on time. They wanted their homes to look nice for the upcoming year. They trusted him to make that happen. He trusted me.

I heard my phone ring and figured it was the boss calling to see if we were done with what we had hoped to accomplish for the morning. Maybe he would even say to call it a day if we were lucky. As it turned out, it was my attorney. I wondered what he wanted. Probably to remind me to take the vacation he'd spoken of months back, I thought.

"Jack! You won't believe it! You're not going to prison. I can't believe it!" he said. The guy I was working with could hear him from across the yard. My attorney finally regained his composure and asked if I could meet him at the coffee shop where we had originally met before the first court hearing.

"I'll meet you there around five," he said. "I'll explain everything then. You're not out of the woods, but you're not going to prison. We have to do some things, including going in front of the judge we have been in front of for the past year. We need her to sign off on your transfer from her court to a new court. You fit exactly what the program calls for. Can you meet there at five?"

I couldn't believe what he was saying. I didn't understand it all other than he'd said I wasn't going to prison. Stunned and now laughing, with tears in my eyes, ready to cry, I took a moment to answer. "Yes! Yes, I can meet you there at five o'clock. I'll be there." I took a deep breath and stared at my buddy I was working with. "That was good," I told him. "In fact, it was great. I'm not going prison!"

In feeling the emotions of the moment sink in, I no longer noticed the rain and cold I had felt a few minutes before. My coworker smiled from ear to ear, staring at me, waiting for the details of what had just happened.

I repeated the conversation. The relief that overcame my body was something I couldn't explain. Something was lifted from me. I had no idea what my attorney had done or agreed to, but I didn't care. I was going to do whatever was required of me. I would have walked on hot coals if I'd had to.

I wanted to tell everyone in my family immediately, but I decided to wait to tell my mom in person. I wanted to see her face. I owed it to her to tell her in person.

My boss pulled up fifteen minutes later to see what we had done in the not-so-nice weather. He saw us smiling as he pulled up. "What's so funny? You two actually look happy to be out in this stuff. What's going on?"

"I was gonna call you when we took lunch." I paused to collect myself, not believing what I was about to say. "Well, my attorney just called. He worked some kind of magic, and it looks like I'm not going to prison after all. I'll be in a program of some sort. I've got to meet him later today." I was beaming all over again.

His jaw dropped. He was speechless for a minute, looking at me and then the other guy. My coworker chimed in, laughing. "I heard him through the phone across the yard. His attorney was happier than him."

My boss finally spoke. "Really? That's unbelievable." He smiled and stared. He'd not ever thought I'd tell him that.

Before he could speak further, I broke in. "I don't know anything yet. I'll call you after I talk to him and get the details. I know nothing other than that. And I'm good with that." I sighed heavily as I finished speaking. His eyes scanned the yard and the project at hand. He went right back into work mode.

He saw that the two of us were making headway on the project. With the news I'd just received, we would definitely finish the project on time. Before he got back in his truck, he yelled over to me across the yard. "I guess miracles do happen, huh?"

I smiled back. "I think they do."

By the end of the day, my boss had told the other crews about my news. Some of the things said behind my back before were now being said to my face, including who had said what. No one could believe what had happened.

I caught up with my attorney late that day. He was still buzzing about the news. He said we had to go in front of the judge to transfer my case to a new court. That meant facing the judge who'd been ready to send me to jail months ago. I would be the first person to participate in the new program.

He became serious while describing what was expected. "There is no room for failure, or you'll go back to see the first judge again, and she will send you away for a long time."

I would be under a strict house-arrest program. I had to be employed, pay a fine and a house arrest payment, and go to meetings. I would lose my license for eighteen months and then have a breathalyzer machine in my truck for a year, which I had to pay for too. I'd also have to meet the judge in person every month for an update on my progress with a probation officer who could come see me or ask me to come to their office at any time. Finally, I would be tested for drugs and alcohol whenever they requested. They could come to my work and test there too.

After he'd finished explaining, I laughed. "That's it? I can handle that." It was a lot, but I kept thinking about the percentages I had learned about in rehab. I'd be in the small percentage of those who made it, I decided. My ace in the hole, in my mind, was the support of my family. I owed it to myself to succeed, but I wanted them to see me do it. I wanted to earn back from them what I'd lost.

He said he'd get back to me on the court date to transfer to the other court. "Have fun telling your family the good news," he said before we parted ways. That time, I hugged him when I left.

My mom had the best reaction of everyone I told. She was the happiest and most relieved I'd seen her in a long time. I told her about the stipulations, and she, like me, had no problems with any of it. She almost cried while telling me, "It was God, prayer, and asking your dad to help from wherever he is."

Her religious belief was the backbone of her faith. I had drifted away from religion, partly because of my drinking and drug use. The news, in my mind, was nothing short of a miracle.

I explained everything to my boss, and he was happy to have me. He couldn't have replaced me. As a bonus, I told him I'd make myself available to work on Saturdays if I could swing it with the court and probation. He was all for that.

In late May, I appeared in front of the judge to have my case moved to the new court. My attorney reminded me not to speak no matter what. He used selectively chosen words with her and thanked her for the court's patience.

She ripped me a new ass before she let me be signed off. She assured me she would be following my progress, and if there was a slip on my part, she would be there.

I turned to my attorney as we walked out and said under my breath, "I hope I never see her again anywhere in my life."

He smiled, barely nodding. "Don't let that happen then."

22

The Judge

After we pulled the proverbial rabbit out of the hat, everything was scheduled to start in the beginning of June with the new court. My attorney, my family, my boss, and a couple close friends encouraged me to continue doing everything I'd been doing so far. I couldn't afford any lapses.

It was weird for me to believe I was coming up on staying sober for a whole year. I'd met people, such as Big Mike, who'd been clean and sober for some years. I'd met some who had been sober for ten, fifteen, twenty, or twenty-five years or even more.

But this was me. I could believe other people doing it but not me. With all that had happened and the possibilities of what could have happened, I didn't fall back to the way I had been. Something changed.

I received a written copy of the stipulations and rules I had to abide by. Understanding them was not hard. The thought of not executing them all or of something going wrong made me uneasy, especially because of how little control I had over many things.

On May 26, my family had a surprise party for me. Some close friends, guys I played hockey with, and some people from work came. I was humbled and impressed. I'd had no clue it was going to happen until about two minutes before they all yelled, "Surprise!"

I never told anyone in my family, but many of the people they'd invited were the same people I'd drunk to excess with, bought drugs from, and done drugs with. There were around thirty people there. I was surprised. Everyone stayed for about two hours.

I excused myself at one point to go to the bathroom, and as I did, I heard voices out in the driveway. People were out front, laughing and carrying on. By the voices I heard, I knew who was out there. I looked out to see the same people celebrating my sobriety by drinking beer and smoking a joint in my mom's driveway. I was a little shocked, but then again, I wasn't. I shouldn't have been.

I heard about a plan to go to the bar after. It hit me right then and there: *I can't be around some of these people anymore.* I didn't need to be. I then heard my boss join the conversation and make a harsh comment about me. Everyone laughed. Many of the people didn't even know who he was.

It was hard to hear that from him. Whether he was trying to funny or really meant it, I didn't know. I wondered where I stood with him. I couldn't say anything. I couldn't get fired or quit because of the court's stipulation about my being employed. I just needed to get through the legal matter and on with my life. Looking at the big picture, I knew I needed to take it one day at a time.

Keeping up with the meetings had become second nature by then. I received a coin to commemorate my one-year accomplishment. After the meeting ended, I was filtering my way out, when a big bald man with a big smile on his face stopped me and said, "Hey, pal, how are you doing?"

My jaw dropped all the way to the floor. It was Mike. He reached out to shake my hand. My hand disappeared into his paw as he said, "How about that? A year for Jack. Crazy, huh?" He was smiling from ear to ear. He was standing next to man who I guessed was in his mid-sixties to early seventies. He was even taller than Mike. He congratulated me too. I had seen the guy before. He had a distinct European accent that stood out.

I thanked them both and told Mike about all that'd happened. Like everyone else, he couldn't believe it. The other man said goodbye to Mike and shook my hand again before he drifted into the crowd. Mike said if I needed anything, I could call him, and he'd offer his help in any way he could. He handed me his phone number.

"But for the grace of God," he said. "It's amazing. You just have to do whatever is asked of you there. Don't get upset over what you can't control, and find some gratitude for the whole thing, even if you get frustrated. I'm sure it'll have its moments. I'm happy for you."

We spoke for a few more minutes about things that had happened since we'd first met. His being there made the moment more meaningful. I shook his hand and gave him a hug. He wished me good luck. I told him, "Thanks. I know I'll see you again."

I was fitted with a house-arrest ankle bracelet the following weekend, and I met my probation officer for the first time. He pulled no punches about how the situation would be. I was given work times and meeting times, and I'd be confined at my mom's house for the rest of the time. After that, if I didn't screw up by being late for anything or not paying off my house-arrest monthly fee and, on top that, a $5,600 fine, and then after 5 years, I had the opportunity to have my freedom back. I had plenty of doubters. Myself included. It just seemed so far away.

The state didn't suspend my license for three-plus months after the system started, which meant I could legally drive and still be under house arrest. It bugged the probation people. I loved it. I could drive to work, meetings, and court for the first few months. I would still lose the license for eighteen months, though.

When my license finally was suspended, the one thing I had going for me was that my family members were willing to help in any way they could. They all made sacrifices to get me to the places I needed to be. I was able to walk or ride my mountain bike to work if it came to it. I'd just have whoever was driving at work take me directly home if I was short on time.

The morning when I was to meet the judge in the new court system arrived. My attorney, the DA, and probation were there. It was a packed house that day. The program's goal was an intensive rehabilitation for nonviolent offenders. The restrictions, time constraints, fines, and intensive outpatient work were far better than the idea of wasting time in a prison cell. I was glad the opportunity was available to me.

All those who'd brought the program to fruition were there to document the program's beginning. I had to prove I was visibly hooked to the bracket and agree to the conditions. That would be my attorney's only visit to the court. After that day, only the judge, probation, and I would be there.

I had to report monthly after that and every month was given a subpoena telling me when my next court appearance was. The judge wasn't a big man height-wise, but he looked big when sitting up in his seat in the courtroom. He asked me questions each time about how I was doing, how I felt, how work was, where things were in my life, and what I did in my free time. He actually seemed to care. He always acknowledged that he was hearing good things about me from probation. I was paying my fine; I wasn't late for anything; and most of all, I passed all my breathalyzer and urine tests. He always said before I left, "Jack, remember, I don't want to have to do my job, and if you do what's asked of you, I don't have to." He would wish me good luck and say, "I'll see you in a month."

After four months, seven more people came into the program. Like me, they were like deer in the headlights when it started. The judge would call all of us individually to see how we were and go over the progress we were making.

After a few more months, there were more people in the program. The judge started to call groups of five people at a time to go over things. Eventually, as a reward, I had to visit him only every two months. There were so many people in the program by then that they had to have more probation officers and bracelets to handle the offenders.

The judge, after not seeing me for two months, would call me down by myself and address me in front of the group who were there that day. He remembered everything we talked about during each visit. In fact, he knew everything about everyone. He did, on occasion, have to send people to jail for violating the program's rules. He was working within the parameters of the program. It was his job; he didn't enjoy that part. He enjoyed seeing the successes.

Unbelievably to me, a handful of people continually violated the rules of the program. Knowing what would happen and that they could be tested at any time, they tested positive for drinking or drugs.

They were sent to a state facility to serve the full amount of time they originally had been sentenced to.

Exactly one year after I went on house-arrest monitoring, I appeared in court, and my leg monitor was removed. I hadn't been late at all over the year and had paid off the entire fine. I'd also won two $1,000 scratch-off tickets, which had helped me to pay off the fine completely. (You could place that under the term *miracle.*) I'd completed all the requirements to be released on time.

The judge made a big deal about congratulating me for my accomplishment. I made sure he knew it hadn't all been my doing; many other people had made it possible. Also, I'd needed the time to heal some wounds with my family and create trust again. I thanked him and all the people who'd been involved in the program and allowed me to accomplish what I had.

I enjoyed seeing the judge and telling him I was good. I'd never expected that could happen. One day a few months later, he asked me a question as I stood alone in front of him, though the question was really for everyone. He stared down at me and then looked over into the jury box, where everyone else in the program sat. "Well, so what's next, Jack?"

I didn't have an answer. I wasn't sure what he meant. He'd asked me, but he'd meant the question to be for everyone there. What was our plan next?

He knew I didn't have an answer right then, but he wanted me to think about what was next in my life. We agreed the first year had sort of blown by. I told him I'd think about it. I didn't see it right away, but he wanted me to succeed as much as I wanted to. The entire program was built to help participants succeed.

What's next, Jack? His words played over and over in my mind for the next two months until I saw him again. By the time Thanksgiving came around, I got the courage to tell him I was going to start a landscape business the following year. He was surprised when I stated my intention. He didn't know how much he'd influenced it either, but he had.

I dropped a few hints to a couple people I worked with that the next couple weeks would be my last. The first time I said it, I'm sure it sounded as if I were just frustrated.

It was time for me to leave. I knew it. I didn't care how anyone felt or what anyone said about my decision either. I didn't care what it would be like when I wasn't there.

I laughed to myself while thinking about how happy some people would be when I left. There'd be some.

As Mike had said to me, I had to find gratitude in my experience, even if it was tough. Things became frustrating with my limited abilities and with some of the people I worked with. There were lessons from each, though. Sometimes it was hard to see while in the moment.

A lot of people had taken the time to teach me about work over the years. I'd learned a lot about things that didn't always have to do with work either. My last month there, I made it a point before I started each day to reflect on the good times. I decided to appreciate my experience. I figured I had worked with as many as 150 people during my time there. There had been obvious changes between my first and sixteenth years there. Physical, mental, emotional, and, as I now recognize, spiritual changes had taken place within me. I was ending a chapter and feeling happy about my decision. I also felt fear. The good times outweighed the bad, although people tend to focus on the bad ones more. All of them together made up the entire time.

Besides the question "What's next?" something else was driving me away from there, and I was more than okay with it. My question to myself was "What is it?"

The Monday after Thanksgiving, I made the announcement to my boss and my coworkers that a couple days before Christmas would be my last day with the company. I only told a friend I'd worked with every day for the past three or four years that I was going to start my own business. I didn't tell everyone else because of the unknown response it might create.

I was surprised by his answer. "You should have done that years ago. You're ready to do it now, though. You'll be fine," he said, laughing. That reaffirmed my decision.

On my last day, my boss called it an early day, and we had a Christmas party and going-away party for me. There was a catered meal and a cake. I reminisced with many about some of the places we had worked and all of the people we had worked with over the years. The return to yesteryear brought back some funny memories and things we couldn't believe had happened.

It then hit me like a punch in the face as I panned the room: almost everyone there that night had been at my one-year-sobriety party. I had now been sober for more than two and a half years. I remembered some of those same people drinking in the driveway at my mom's house and speaking unkindly about me. I remembered exactly who'd said what too. I'd proven them wrong. I had to let the feeling that was coming over me go before I left there. I couldn't leave like that. It was more of what I proved to myself that helped me say nothing. I had changed.

I was given a watch as a sign of thanks and appreciation for my sixteen years there. I appreciated it. I asked the friend who had picked me up if we could get going soon. He was talking with another guy and quickly stopped talking to him to answer me. He leaned toward me and whispered, "Whenever you're ready, I'm ready."

I made it around to say merry Christmas and thanks to everyone. Some I hoped never to see again. I'm not being mean; it's just that my time in their lives was over. New things lay ahead. Some people I just didn't enjoy being around anymore. Some felt the same way toward me. There was no hate or anger toward anyone. It was over; that's it.

I thanked my now former boss one last time. Saying goodbye was harder than I'd thought. He'd taught me so much over so long a time, and I was grateful beyond words. He and I, along with a few others, had become part of a family, so to speak. He was always there for us. He warned us of things that might happen and helped us get through them after they did. We all got upset with each other at times but found a way to go on. We learned from mistakes and turned most of them into better things than we expected. He was a good guy. He wasn't perfect, but who is?

I gave him a hug and shook his hand. I walked out the door with my head up, knowing all I'd accomplished and what I hoped to do with my future. I was anything but sure of it, but I had to start somewhere. Leaving that part of my past right there, I allowed the next to begin.

23

The Doctor

I decided to ask a friend of mine to go in with me on starting the business. My fear of doing it by myself overtook the desire I had to be successful on my own. We'd split everything down the middle as far as both work and profit. We had guidelines on bidding jobs, and in most cases, we planned to do it together to keep things straight.

I also had to keep up with the stipulations of the court program. I needed to be employed at all times. Because I left my job and didn't go to another, I technically violated my agreement. I butted heads with probation on not being permanently employed through the winter months. They weren't okay with my taking the time to get a business started and threatened to put me back under house arrest, which would have set everything back and returned me to square one. They suggested I go to the church my mom attended and ask about doing some volunteer work. I made an appointment to see if that was a possibility.

I sat down with the priest and explained all that had happened up to then. Not only he did agree to help me, but he also signed off by writing a letter directly to the judge. I was to paint the office and other rooms that needed cleaning up and a new coat of paint. It was considered volunteer work, which was legal for me to do.

Not only did the pastor get me out of a tight spot, but he also said there was no hurry to get the work done. He said if I was there for a couple hours each morning, then I would have time to take care of the things I needed to do to get the business started. He gave me a number for the people at probation to call so they could verify my hours, intentions, and production for each week. He also said it was time the front of the building got changed around some. Knowing my partner and I would be looking for work, he asked me to do a design for it. It was a paying job and free advertising at the same time. Plenty of people would be asking who'd done the work.

By the time my next court appearance came up, I was ready. The judge was impressed that I'd made the time to set up a business and do the volunteer work. The letter from the church made out personally to the judge was the final touch on things.

I hadn't let the people at probation know I had the letter. They were surprised. Some might say they were angry. I made a copy for them to have. I circled the phone number on their copy as a little added shot on my part.

My partner and I lined up a fair amount of work for the first couple months based on work we had done on our own previously and some word of mouth. Going in, we knew it was going to be different, having to do everything we needed to do to be successful.

My business partner had gotten married the year before. He and his new wife were excited and optimistic about what we could accomplish. We had a powerful feeling that positive things were about to happen.

I'd gotten my driving privileges back with the agreement to have a breathalyzer installed in my vehicle. It was a necessity for me to start the business. The breathalyzer would show if I tried to drive with alcohol in my system. That was the last thing on my mind. I'd learned my lesson.

Working with my friend that year was more difficult than I could have imagined. Sadly, his marriage didn't work out. Sometimes it just happens that way. I was now seeing a troubling situation from the other side. I started to feel the way my old boss might've with me. I realized I probably wasn't invested fully in my job enough with all I had going on. It was tough to stay focused; my mind wandered.

Over the following few months, things were a roller coaster some days. There wasn't much I could say to my partner to move him out of the funk he was in. I tried to remind him of what others had told me:

getting through might be harder than he thought, but time would still go on.

With all that was happening with work, I thought I was experiencing karma for my past actions. I was living through it with him—something I needed to go through for my actions in the past.

I was working harder physically. I was dealing more with the clients because my partner wasn't as focused all the time. At the end of the workday, he didn't want much to do with anything other than trying to fix a problem that was unfixable. All of that made him more frustrated. Everything seemed to compound day in and day out. He knew it too, and he apologized to me often about how things were turning out.

We'd been friends for a long time and had worked together years before. We knew each other well. I got frustrated at times with the situation, and he knew it. That being said, there wasn't any way I could have hated him or anything like that. I felt bad for him. I was able to see different versions of similar events and the results of them. My friend was living his own nightmare. He hadn't expected that to happen. I saw up close how his family and close friends went through it too.

Thankfully, he didn't get in trouble with the law or anything like that. I told him that other people went through similar things, and he eventually would heal and go on. However, my words still didn't stop the way he felt.

I knew I needed to separate myself from him in terms of working with him or running a business with him. The last few months of the year were not as either one of us had wanted them to be. I wanted to see him less and less each day. I still liked him; he was a friend before anything. I just wanted the year to end. The bright spot for me was that I knew it eventually would end. We both agreed it was best if we ended our partnership. We would still be friends. There were no hard feelings at all.

The best thing that happened before the year ended was a huge surprise I received right before Thanksgiving: I was one of the first eight people to be released from the new court program. I was released two and a half years earlier than expected. I had proven myself. I was now free to live my own life again. It was like an early Christmas gift.

The year ended on a good note that way. I looked back on what had happened, and I decided that the next year, I was going to do the business on my own. I'd done a large part of it for the last five months anyway, so what would it matter? I was going to focus on some higher-income neighborhoods.

The break over winter was much needed. I had to heal physically. I had to get ready to run a business by myself. I needed to set new goals and see myself hit them.

During that break, I decided the last thing I wanted to think about was work. I took time to myself and caught up with some old friends. I hadn't had time to see anybody, as the past year had been so busy. Being able to drive again was a welcome relief.

The wife of a friend of mine and I were talking in between Christmas and New Year's. She told me she'd met a man who was able to tell one's future. He did it by shuffling a regular deck of cards. She was skeptical of what he said, because why wouldn't you be?

She and a friend had gone out of curiosity. He'd told her some things that would occur and said she should be ready. He hadn't tried to scare her; he'd just been relaying what he got out of the cards. She said I should go check him out; maybe I could find out something about my business.

A few days after New Year's, I decided, *Why not?* I met him in his office. I shuffled a regular deck of cards, and he flipped them over one by one, telling me the story of what he saw. One thing that stuck out was his claim that in the next two and a half months, I'd have a brand-new black truck. He said it was funny because I couldn't drive it.

I'd never said a word about having a breathalyzer in my current truck or that it would be there for three more months. He assured me that would happen. He told me not to worry about getting work for my business. He said if I did my best work, it'd be there. He told me lastly about a doctor I would work for. Money was important, but it was not all about money with him, although he said the money was there and I should not worry about that either. He said I'd learn something bigger that I'd use later on.

He also told me I would come into a small lump sum of money some years in the future. "It's not by any means enough to retire on or anything like that, but it comes to you. The only thing is, you might not enjoy how it comes to you, but it will help you. That's just what I'm getting." He was as puzzled as I was at hearing him say that.

I told my friend's wife about my visit. We were both curious to see if the truck statement came true.

Two months later exactly, my mom, who knew my plan to take my business to some places where I might make some more money, told me how proud she was of me for how far I'd come in the past few years. She said I couldn't go into the places I wanted and drive up in the truck I had. She was going to give me $10,000 to help buy a truck to make my job easier and make me look good doing it.

I was floored by her act of kindness. It wasn't a spare $10,000 either. She worked hard for everything she had. Her gesture was a commitment of the faith she had in me. I made it a point to say I'd pay her back, but she said it was not necessary right away. She wanted me to get my business going. "Pay me back when you get it," she said.

In mid-March, she and I went to a car dealership where I knew one of the salesmen. I'd met him a few years back. I hadn't seen him in a year or so, but he knew what had happened with me. He was happy to see me. I told him I was hoping to get something for the beat-up truck I was driving. If I got $500, I felt that would be good enough for me. It was that bad.

He laughed when I said that to him. Leaning into my ear, he said, "I can't do that."

I explained I'd just put new tires on it, and they'd cost $300. "How about three hundred?" I said, hoping to get the tire investment back.

"I know the truck you want; don't worry." He directed me outside and positioned me to look up on top of a hill where a bunch of new trucks sat. "The black one." He pointed directly at it. "I'm gonna give you twenty-five hundred dollars for your truck. Are you okay with that?" He laughed. "Let's go test-drive it."

I couldn't believe what was happening. My mom had heard him and was as stunned as I was. She loved the truck.

Walking toward it, I realized I couldn't do the test drive. "You have to drive it; I'm not legal to drive it for another two weeks." I thought about what the card reader had told me two and a half months ago. It was happening right in front of me.

"That's okay. I can keep it here for a couple weeks; that's not a problem," he said, still laughing.

I ended up getting it at a great price with a warranty that lasted a year longer than I'd be paying for it. The payments were easy to handle. None of it made sense, but it was fantastic. I'd gotten the truck I wanted. I was ready to get the season started.

After that, I went to the nursery and spoke to the owners there. I'd known them since I started landscaping. They all knew what had happened. They also knew I worked hard, and they were willing to help me.

A man named Frank and his brother and parents owned it. I'd gotten along with Frank the best over the years. He was always willing to help with any questions I had; plus, he gave me a deal on plants and materials. I told them I was on my own that year. Frank's parents said if I stayed on the path I was on and didn't screw up, they'd refer me to anyone who asked. I knew what she meant by screwing up: the drinking and drugs. I said I'd appreciate anything they could offer, and of course, I'd do my best work.

Starting April 1 was always a goal. Finishing a week before Christmas was one too. Everything in between was about working. That was exactly what happened. With my regular clients there already, Frank and his family kept me busy all year long. It was great.

Frank mentioned that as a favor to him, I should go see someone if I had time. He was a doctor. Frank said he spent a fair amount of money at the nursery and liked for his home to look nicer than anyone else's in the neighborhood. Frank also said, "He's fired the last eight companies he's had there. He's kind of particular about stuff."

Frank and I had become friends outside of work too. On Mondays, we'd go get wings at a bar on his way home. I usually tried to make Monday a day not to kill myself with working because there was a full week ahead. I learned to try to balance each week all the way through if I could. There were times when it didn't always go that way, but that was my intention.

I set Saturday mornings aside to finish up loose ends I hadn't gotten to during the week. Saturday afternoons were when I tried to set appointments. That way, I could meet with people who worked later or had stuff to do during weeknights. Sometimes I didn't have time, or I was just too tired to meet them, so I tried to take advantage of time the best I could.

I told Frank over wings that I was meeting the doctor he'd talked about on Saturday at noon. He was the last scheduled person I had that day. I was finally going to get an early day. Frank was jealous about my being done at noon on a Saturday.

On Saturday, I pulled up to the doctor's house a few minutes before noon to scope the place out. It was an odd-shaped house set the opposite way from the other houses on the street. It was the biggest house on the street due to an addition over the garage. A narrow driveway went up to the house and ended up opening up into a wider parking area with a two-car garage. Halfway up the driveway was the front door, located on the left side. Huge trees were all around the yard, with open areas of sunlight. Multiple varieties of plants lined the entire property. It was a nice place with lots of room to add some different ideas to. I liked it a lot.

As I surveyed as much as I could see without wandering around the yard without introducing myself, I heard little voices yelling for their dad inside. "Someone's here!"

A moment later, a man came out to the driveway to meet me. "Hey, you must be Jack."

We shook hands and introduced ourselves. He had the firmest, hardest handshake of any person I'd met before. I was not ready for that; I thought he was gonna break my hand.

His daughters came out behind him one by one. The youngest ones, identical three-year-old twins, clutched either leg. The other two stood behind him. The other two's ages were six and five. He had them all introduce themselves.

We took a tour of the outside, going over every stitch of the yard, from the lawn to the flowers, trees, and other plants, including the smallest details of what he liked and didn't like and why. He spoke about what his wife liked too. I asked him questions, and he asked me questions. It took about thirty minutes to go over everything. Overall, it went pretty smoothly.

I told him what I thought. I quoted him a price and explained what I would do and why—mostly trimming stuff up, edging the beds, and doing some other small things that weren't anything out of the ordinary. I told him I'd flip a couple things around on my schedule and get to his home early the following week.

When I felt we'd covered everything and were on the same page, he mentioned he wouldn't be in town when I planned on doing the work. I could feel he wasn't sure I'd do all I'd said I would if he wasn't there. He seemed skeptical of me without knowing me and what I could do. He had every right to feel that way.

His concern wasn't anything new. I decided to ask him some questions to help him trust me on what I was going to do. "I understand where you're coming from, but do you think Frank would lead you in the wrong direction? You trusted him to ask for a person to make your yard the way you want it. Now you have to trust me to do it, or you don't. I have one thing to tell you before I leave today. Remember the house number. It will not look the same."

My confidence in myself might have sounded arrogant, but it was true. It wouldn't be hard for me to do all I'd said. He didn't get the concept that I could do it. I then asked him about himself to turn the tables and manipulate the situation. He just didn't think he could be wrong.

"You're a doctor, right? How many people don't believe you when you diagnose what's wrong and tell them how you're going to help them? How many trust you right away? Let me do what I do, and if you're not happy, I don't even want your money. I know I'll have done my best, though. I can also walk away right now, and you can find someone else. I will not even be upset either way."

I didn't think he would stiff me on the bill even if he didn't like my work, but it was a chance I was willing to take. Inside, I knew deep down he was going to like what I did, so I was confident enough to say it. By that time, his daughters wanted his full attention back on them on his day off. We shook hands and agreed I'd be there in the next few days.

As I walked back down the driveway toward my truck, I looked back and said, "Just remember that house number, okay?" I laughed as I said it.

I went to see Frank and thanked him for yet another job. Frank was swamped with a busy rush of weekend shoppers, so my visit was a good reason for him to slip out back to escape the chaos. To his family, it looked as if he were getting materials for me.

"How did it go?" he asked, leaning up against the back wall.

I replied, "Pretty good. He knows what he's talking about. I also think he'd like to do it himself, but he doesn't have the time."

Frank had known that before I said it. "He asks a lot of questions when he comes in. When are you going to do it?" Frank obviously knew I had the job since I'd said things had gone pretty well.

"Next week. I'll need a couple things from you, but I'll tell you Monday."

A few days later, I started to work at the doctor's house. As I'd promised, it took two days to complete the project. There was no strain or anything too difficult that prevented me from completing it. The doctor's wife was in and out both days. She seemed amazed at how quickly I completed all we had spoken about on Saturday. She knew exactly what the plan was and what I was going to do. She had no problem handing me a check at the end of the second day. I asked her to have the doctor call me when he got back in town.

I found out from Frank that the doctor worked with people who had concussions. He'd actually treated my niece, who'd been in a car accident a couple years back.

A few days later, I received a call from him. He was impressed with what I'd done. He wanted more stuff done. He asked if he and I could meet again to discuss other sections of his yard. Of course I agreed; it was a no-brainer.

Before he hung up, he said something that allowed me to help him with his yard and home: "Jack, I trust you." He offered his ideas and listened to mine, and we came up with some nice solutions for each part of the project.

Trust is a huge factor in anything and everything. I ended up doing yet another project there and the fall cleanup of his yard. After that, the following year, he was the first job of the year. He told his neighbors about me, and I ended up with more work than I ever could've imagined. He told me in the spring to come by every few weeks just to see if anything needed to be done, fixed, or added to make the yard better. It was a tremendous compliment. It was a great place to work. His wife was nice, and his daughters were comfortable with me working there. I was comfortable being there. I got another reward a few weeks after that.

I was working across the street at one of his neighbors' homes, which allowed me to look at what I had created in the doctor's yard. I hadn't looked at things that way often. That was another thing I learned by being there: things always looked different depending on where you were standing. New plants were always blooming, while others had run through their cycle. I hadn't seen the place from where I was seeing it at that moment. I'd impressed myself. It felt good.

24

Some Other Talented People

My business the following year took off early. I'd rested up and prepared myself based on what I'd experienced the year past. I had new goals set. Being more organized was the first goal. Getting the amount of rest needed to go at a continual rate was next. Last was being prepared for what I couldn't control. Unfortunately, there are things we can't control in almost everything we encounter.

As far as maintaining my sobriety, I figured if it wasn't broken, I shouldn't try to fix it—the judge used that saying often. I kept doing the things I needed to do. I started playing hockey again with some new people. Mike and I spoke more regularly. He'd become sick. He had to use an oxygen tank to help him breathe. It was going to be a permanent thing for him. It didn't seem fair. It had happened in the blink of an eye.

He had been two classes away from receiving his pediatric degree, when polyps were found. That news would have torn apart anyone else I knew, but he was at peace with it somehow. Or he hid his true feelings well. I'm sure he went through the natural reaction of "Why me?" Who wouldn't have?

I tried not to pry into how he felt. I knew if he wanted to talk about it, he would. Over the winter, he asked me to go with him to look at some homes. He was looking at buying one. He wanted my opinion on what I thought of the yards and plants at each one and what I could do with them.

Seeing him with the tank of oxygen was a completely different sight, unlike the person who'd helped me just a few years back. He'd seen me at rock bottom and extended his hand in a way that I see now was meant to be.

I promised I'd help him when the time came when he needed me. Seeing him that way was tough. I could only imagine how he felt. I would've been complaining, I'm sure, but to whom?

The doctor's home was first again when the year started. Many other clients from the past year called, hoping I could get to them as soon as I could. I had told a few people if they didn't give me a referral to a friend, I wouldn't come back next year. I'd been kidding, but many people had told their friends. Frank was feeding work to me too.

I really enjoyed working for some clients. Some I had known for years. I knew a couple of the families from working for my old boss. When they heard I'd left, they brought me back to work on their houses. I'd been working at some homes for a long time by then, and they knew I would do what they liked. I'd known some of the families since I started when I was nineteen. One woman and her husband I got along with extremely well. He'd done the same type of work for years and now worked from home. His wife worked part-time from home. I was at their house a few times during the year. It was another good place to be. She and I were talking one day about one of her sons, and she mentioned he was having some learning issues at school. I told her about the man I'd met over the winter and how, with a simple deck of cards, he'd been able to see ahead of time somehow and had told me about the truck I was now driving.

I wasn't sure how she'd take it, but I thought a visit with him might be helpful in finding out what the issue with her son was. She had nothing to lose, and who knew if he could help her? I didn't want to scare her, but I knew the idea might.

Little did I know how much she liked the idea. She'd had an experience earlier in life with a person who was able to connect with something on another level or in another dimension. The person had predicted some things that had happened.

I gave her the number to contact the man, and she met him the following week. I ran into her at Frank's nursery weeks later. The results she'd gotten from the man had been spot on. He'd said her son was dyslexic. She'd been able to take the necessary action to get him the help he needed.

She'd told another person about her experience, and the person had recommended she meet some people able to do something unique of their own: two women who could connect to people who'd passed on or over, depending on how one saw it. She wondered if I'd like to meet them if she set something up. I thought about it and decided to do it. It might be interesting, I thought.

I agreed, but I was so busy that I wouldn't have time until fall at the earliest. She understood. That gave her time to find some other people interested in meeting with the women too.

She and I stayed in touch about it, and three months later, I met the two women at the home of a friend of hers. The day was November 3, 2008. I'll never forget it. It was one of the best days of my life, if not the best. I had only one person I wanted to speak with. I was nervous, a little afraid, and a little puzzled about how it worked, but most of all, I was excited and hoped to somehow hear from my dad.

He'd passed away almost forty years before. I had few memories of him. I'd thought so much about him for so long. I was mad at him in a way. I'd missed a lifetime without him. I'd heard about him from my older sisters, my grandparents before they passed, and, most of all, my mom. She missed him in more ways than I did. I think part of my anger stemmed from being mad at God for taking him. He'd been taken from my entire family.

When I sat down with the two women, my anger left me—for a little bit at least. They said some prayers and invited whoever was there to come forth. They could see my dad and hear him perfectly. I saw them staring somewhere behind me. They then said my grandparents and others were there. People I'd had relationships with who had died were now speaking through the two women.

My dad somehow seemingly knew how I felt and spoke through the women in the most gracious way toward me. They were able to communicate with him and relay his and the others' words with ease.

The women told me things about my past that they couldn't have known.

He first told them to thank me for meeting him in that format. He told them to ask me if it was okay with me if he did most of the talking. There was so much he wanted to say.

At that point, from there on, my mouth was wide open, but no words were able to come out. Through the two women, he was able to describe things about my life that no one ever would have known. He brought up my new truck and a small scratch I'd put in it that had made me mad. I couldn't believe what I was hearing. He was right. I was mad about the scratch. Where was my dad that he could see that?

I was able to talk to my grandparents. Remembering them and the many great times with them brought me to tears. I didn't want the time to end, but I knew I didn't have much more time. There were other people scheduled to meet the women that afternoon and evening. Each person got fifteen minutes, and my time seemed to go by too fast.

I couldn't believe what had happened and what I'd just experienced. I'd learned so much in fifteen minutes that I'd never known. My dad had always been there—or he is there, I should say. My allowing him to speak was what he'd needed, but I had more questions that I hadn't gotten to ask. I needed to meet with the women again.

Six months later, exactly two days after my five-year sobriety anniversary I had an appointment to meet them, and him, again.

On May 28, 2009, I had an hour scheduled. I took the day off, something I wouldn't have considered for something else. I was early, and I was nervous. I had many questions I wanted to ask, but it seemed as if I forgot them all as I opened the front door of the place where we were meeting.

A few minutes after I arrived, the two women arrived. They asked for a few moments to prepare, and then they'd be ready for me. They recognized me from the previous visit. A few minutes later, it was on.

I entered the room they had prepared and sat down. A feeling of calmness surrounded the room. They did everything they had done before: said a few prayers, held my hands, and asked for protection from the archangels and the Holy Spirit.

It wasn't scary or anything like that. The next almost hour and a half was mine—my time to laugh, cry, and learn about someone I missed who I'd thought wasn't there. He had been there in the way that was available to him, one I still didn't understand.

I did get some answers but not all the ones I wanted. My time there that day changed my perspective of life in ways I had to accept. In many ways, I'd thought I was getting away with things for so long.

I learned there is no way to get away with anything. My actions are always seen, even if no one else is around. Something bigger than me that I can't explain is watching over all of us. Whatever it is, it's a part of us all, whether or not we know it or believe it. Trying to understand it isn't something that can be done in an hour.

One more thing happened that afternoon that I was not prepared for. One of the two women started to write something down on a piece of paper. When she'd finished writing what she was told, she handed me the piece of paper. "Your dad asked me to give you this. He wants you to write a book. This is the title of the book he'd like you to write."

I started to laugh as I answered, "What the hell are you talking about? Write a book? Me? You're kidding. I can't write a book." I was baffled by the request.

The other woman smiled and said, "If you want to do it, do it. There will be a reason for it, I'm sure. We don't have it for you now, though."

I paused once more, contemplating what I had just been asked to do. "Why not ask why?" I started to laugh again. "I don't know how to do it. I hardly have the time."

The woman called me on my words. She replied, "You have the winter off; you can work on it then if you want. There isn't any hurry. Just do it at your own time."

Again, I froze up. "I'm not making any promises. We'll see what happens."

When I left, I was on top of the world. I had just had another conversation with my dad and my grandparents. It seemed the time had flown by, but the session gave me a renewed feeling about my own life.

I wondered how the two women could connect with the dead. Where did that skill come from, and how did people handle it when they found out they could do it? It amazed me.

My forty-five-minute drive seemed like fifteen minutes on the way back. My dad also had asked me to pick up roses for my mom on my return. What was I gonna say about that? I stopped by a store and grabbed a dozen red roses. I also bought a scratch-off lottery ticket at the store next door. I won $100 on it, which easily covered the price of the roses. Coincidence or luck? I wasn't sure which way to go on that one.

My mom was both surprised and delighted by the roses. Her voice showed her disbelief. "Your dad always got me roses. Wow, it's been a long time."

I didn't mention that it hadn't been my idea. I just said, "I felt like getting them."

My mom hadn't been feeling physically well for a few weeks, and the surprise was like a small shot in the arm. It took her back to a place in time almost, a time she'd forgotten.

I went back to work and focused on that as much as possible, sprinkling some hockey into a couple nights a week. I was starting to get back to enjoying myself in life. I told both Frank and Mike about meeting the two women again and how fascinating it was.

Then there was the book thing. Both of them told me to only do it if I wanted to; if not, then I should leave it behind. I thought about it more and more.

By the time August came around, I decided I needed to get away for a vacation. I was going to drive until I didn't want to, get a hotel room, and head to the beach the next day. I'd stay a few days and then make my way back in one whole day of driving. I was my own boss, so I had no one to answer to if I took an extra day either. I liked that more than anything.

The experience I'd had in late May was on my mind from time to time, and the drive on the first day was no different. I wondered how my sister and brother would react if I told them and asked if they wanted to go meet the ladies to experience what I had. I had no idea how either would take my offer or if they'd believe what I told them.

Something amazing happened.

As I pulled up to the hotel, the same two women I had met in May were standing right in front of me. They immediately recognized me.

No one could believe it. We were so far away from home, standing in front of each other.

After the hellos and "What are you doing here?" questions, I knew the meeting was no coincidence. I asked them if it was a good idea if I brought my brother and sister to meet my dad. One smiled and said, "He just said he'd like that. He's with you when you're in your truck."

The other woman then mentioned a rainstorm I'd driven through on the way down. "He just said you had a close call on the way here."

My jaw dropped. On the way, a car had passed me going way too fast and created a rooster tail of water that, combined with the storm, made me lose total vision, and for a moment, I'd felt I lost control of my truck. How could she have known that other than something or someone telling her?

She then said, "Don't worry; they'll do it for you," referring to my brother and sister. "Just ask them. You don't have to be afraid."

What were the odds of meeting those two women three hundred miles away at a particular moment in time to answer a question I'd wondered about for the last five hours?

I said goodbye to them and told them I'd be in touch in the next couple weeks. I knew our meeting wasn't a coincidence. It happened for a reason.

When I got home, I was nervous when I spoke to my brother and sister and told them about everything from the last year until the past weekend. Neither one of them ran away screaming, but I could sense a little skepticism in each. They both agreed to go with me without hesitation. I couldn't believe it. I faced no resistance at all. I still couldn't tell my mom, but I knew I would have to. I wanted to; I just didn't know how to bring it up to her.

A few days after Halloween, I put in my regular day. It was darker earlier due to daylight savings. I was playing hockey after work that night. I was running a little behind. I didn't want to be late, but I was caught up in traffic. Losing an hour of light cut into the time available to get things done, which meant I had to use my time more effectively.

My plan was to take a quick shower, grab some food on the way, and get something after the game. I wanted to check on my mom too. She'd been experiencing more health issues, which seemed to be related to the medications she'd been taking. I'd taken her to all of her doctor appointments due to my ability to set my schedule. She was feeling well again.

She was in a great mood when I caught up to her. She had been listening to the radio, which was turned up louder than usual. She turned up the volume if she was working around the house. She had been fascinated by two women who were able to connect with spirits. They were on the show because it was almost Halloween, and they dealt with ghosts and that sort of thing. She said she'd been listening for an hour, and the two women were amazing.

I knew exactly whom she was talking about. It was them. I then noticed the date: November 3, 2009—one year to the day after I'd met them. It was the perfect opportunity to put everything on the table, I thought.

She stood at the top of the steps, looking down at me, telling me who the women were and what they could do. Over the next few minutes, I explained how I knew them firsthand, including my meeting with them a year ago to the day and whom I'd met when I spoke with them. She said nothing at all. It was the last thing she'd expected to hear from me.

I explained that I'd wanted to tell her earlier but hadn't known how to. I hadn't been sure how she'd take the news. Then, for good measure, I took it one step further. She still hadn't replied to anything I had said, so I just kept going. I told her I was taking my sister and brother to meet the women in the next couple months. I wondered what she was thinking. I could see her processing what I'd just shared with her. I'd stopped her in her tracks.

I was running way behind on being on time for my game by then. I felt bad about what I had just dropped on her, but my leaving would give her time to think and give me time to think about how I could talk to her about what I'd experienced.

When I returned later, we had a nice talk about how things had changed since she'd lost my dad. She remembered the good and the bad—the bad being the pain she'd felt in having to handle all she had.

The emotions that came forward and the stories she told me were things she hadn't let out for a long time. I sat there listening to stories

I'd never heard. I smiled, cried, and took it all in. I explained that before that day, I hadn't known how to tell her about my experience, but it was the right time. The fact that it was a year later to the day had us both shaking our heads.

I explained my times with the women she'd heard on the radio. She was interested, but I could sense she was apprehensive to ask more questions. It seemed the experience scared her in a way, so I didn't push any more on her.

She was surprised when I told her my brother and sister both had agreed to meet the women in the near future. Usually not one to hold back on how she felt, she said only, "Really? When?" It was as if she couldn't believe all I'd told her, but it was real. It was a lot for one day.

My sister agreed to go after the holidays, and my brother would go before I started work again. I slowly let it be known I was going to start to write the book I'd been asked to write. Of all the things I had told my family about, the book was the thing that made them look at me as if I were crazy. They were okay with the stuff about meeting the two women.

When the time came to go, I prepped my sister to ask questions and be open. I sensed she was skeptical or maybe nervous. About ten minutes after we sat down together, the ladies did their thing. My sister was resistant at first, but what they told her about things and people she had known proved to her the skill, talent, and abilities the women possessed.

My sister surprised me when her husband's grandmother came through. My sister later revealed that she had asked on her own for his grandmother to come forth. The little woman graciously had taken to her when they first met and even more after she was married. I hadn't known how much my sister missed her after she passed on. Her mother-in-law, who'd passed after a battle with cancer, also came through, and they communicated about her daughters.

I watched my younger sister go through emotions of love and happiness. All the while, I was speaking with the other woman to my dad and grandparents. At the end of our time, I felt I'd given a gift to my sister, my dad, and all the others. The ride back was great. Of course I stopped for roses. That time, my mom figured out the reason.

A month later, I took my brother. I was hoping for something close to or maybe even better than the experience I'd shared with my sister. I found out it didn't work that way sometimes. The best plan can fall short. The whole experience with him went sideways from the start.

My brother and I were different in many more ways than we were the same. My brother was gay. I was not. There were other things too. I was wrongly critical of him. I had no reason to be that way. My drug and alcohol addiction fueled my feelings toward that. I couldn't get the why part of it.

When I got sober, changing and rebuilding my relationship with him was the most important thing to me. It took time, but it came back. Our relationship was special because of how different we were and what each of us had gone through and done to become who we were. He'd gone through his own battles to find himself. I was proud of him, and he was proud of me. The biggest things he taught me were forgiveness, kindness, keeping a sense of humor, and unconditional love. We also found we didn't always have to agree. That was okay too.

The day we were to go, he was late to meet me to start with. I hated being late, and he knew it. On the ride there, he told me about what he'd done on the previous Saturday and the great time he'd had. I said I'd stayed home all day Saturday, as I hadn't been feeling well. He pinpointed everything he'd done and described it so vividly that I felt as if I'd been there. After he was done, I tried to prepare him the way I had my sister. He shrugged off everything I said, which added a little fuel to the fire, so to speak.

I was pushing it to be on time. When we were ready to walk in, he decided he was going to go smoke. I just stared at him. As he walked back outside, when the door closed, I said to myself out loud, "What an ass." No one was anywhere near me to hear me say that. I was alone.

I'd quit smoking about sixteen months after I quit drinking. Rational thinking tells you smoking is the dumbest thing you can do. When you initially start, your lungs reject it. It makes you sick to your stomach. You have to willingly do it to make yourself not cough, and you still do. It takes away from your physical life in many ways, and it can even kill you. To top it off, cigarettes are a waste of money, and smelling like an ashtray isn't good for anyone.

It pissed me off that my brother still smoked. He said it calmed his nerves. That was BS; it's just another form of addiction. He didn't want to quit, and he wouldn't unless something made him want to. I knew that all too well from my own experiences.

He walked in a few minutes later as if nothing were wrong. The receptionist had told me the women were ready, and we could come up when he was done. We were now late because he had to smoke.

When we were in the room with the women, one brought up exactly what my brother had talked about on the way there about the previous Saturday. It sounded to me as if my dad had been with him the entire evening. It was cool. My brother didn't see it that way, though.

Out of nowhere, my brother looked at the ladies and denied that it had happened at all. I couldn't believe it. The rest of our time there was about as awkward as it could've been. I couldn't understand what was happening. The rest of the time after that felt like a waste of time. I was embarrassed by the whole thing.

It was a quiet ride back. I thought about saying something but didn't. I also thought about pushing him out of the moving truck, but I didn't do that either. I barely stopped to let him out at his car. I did go get roses for my mom. It was the least I could do. The gift I'd thought I was giving my brother never materialized that day.

I called the ladies the next day to apologize. They said it happened, though not often. I didn't understand why it hadn't worked the way it had for me and my sister. It frustrated me and made me angry. I never brought up the topic with him again one on one. It wasn't worth it.

25

The Teacher

I decided I'd put the time into writing this book, as I'd been asked to. With no idea who would help me with editing it, publishing it, or anything like that, I trusted it would happen. It took a total of sixteen months to write. Everything fell into place as one thing led to another. I met a beautiful woman in the process. A wonderful relationship with her came from it.

She found a woman to help me who knew things I had no idea about. I wrote it all by hand. She typed it out and edited it in the process. She warned me never to write something like that again; I should use a computer.

You can imagine how my family looked at me for writing the book. They thought I was off my rocker when I told them why I'd made the decision to do it. I even thought it was crazy from time to time. I didn't understand why I'd been asked to do it. I just did it.

I learned some things about myself in doing it. The good and bad experiences I'd had were all still vivid in my mind, including the feelings that came from certain people, places, and things; feelings about myself; and how I'd made others feel with my actions. I saw that miracles had occurred, and I'd taken a lot of life for granted. Writing the book was a cleansing experience for me in many ways.

Of course, I didn't see it that way when I'd completed it. I went back to the women who connected with my dad and asked them what was next. "What do I do with it now?" I had put time, energy, emotions, and a financial investment in the book. Could they at least tell me where to go? I didn't get the answer I wanted to hear from them.

They told me to let it go. The book was about releasing the events and emotions so I could move forward and be free from my past. Their reply made me upset. I felt alone with what I had just done. I felt duped into what I'd been asked to do.

Through the woman who did the editing, I met a man who was working with her also. He was writing a book on astrology. He had been involved with astrology for thirty-some years or so. I knew little about it, but I found interesting what I learned from her about him.

Using a person's time, date, and place of birth, he compiled the person's chart. It was based on the position of the planets, sun, and moon and other factors. I didn't understand it. I thought it was like an in-depth look at a person's horoscope. At the time, I was at a point where I was interested in any kind of help to tell me where things were going, so I decided I'd like to meet him.

I contacted him by phone. He'd been expecting my call, and I gave him my info. He said it would take a little time to analyze my chart. We met the following week. It worked out nicely because I'd scheduled work near his office that week.

I met him at eleven o'clock in the morning at his office. He immediately asked me not to tell him anything about myself. He was confident in what he saw in my chart based on the little information I'd given him. He turned on a cassette tape to make sure I had documentation of the hour we had.

As he started to speak, looking at his computer and then looking at me, he explained how everything in the sky had been the moment I was born, including the characteristics of what each planet did, the cycles and retrogrades, and things I wasn't familiar with.

As he looked at his computer, his next statement blew my mind and made me sit up straight on the couch I was sitting on. "You're coming up on an anniversary of some sort, huh?" he asked.

I wasn't sure if he had spoken to the woman who'd referred me to him or what. “Yes, I am. I’m a couple weeks shy of my sobriety anniversary.”

He leaned over and looked at me face-to-face. “You attempted suicide, I take it?”

I slowly answered, “Well, yeah, I did.”

He then said the date May 25, 2004. I stopped him there. “My sober day is May 26, 2004.” I said it as if I were telling him he was wrong. “I blacked out. I have no idea where I was.”

He then pointed to the computer and said, “Well, you actually died that day. You were gone. You’re still here for something. This mark here shows that. I’m positive. I’ve been doing this a long time.”

I stared at him in disbelief. I couldn’t explain how he knew what he did when he said, “You have another one of these marks back in your chart. Does March 15, 1973, have any significance?”

He had just picked out the exact day of my dad’s death. I paused before I answered. “How did you know that?” I asked in shock. He knew he’d hit a cord with me on that one.

He had my full attention. He explained plenty more things over the remaining hour, and the tape he made was a bonus. He mentioned that I’d come into a window of luck in the next few weeks. “Throw a couple bucks down on the lottery if you think about it. You might get lucky.”

He mentioned a few things about where my path wanted to go and the reason my soul was there. He explained everything easily. He explained that all people, places, and things experience life and death. What one experiences at different points is different for all people. Each planet and combinations of them affect certain points in time for persons, places, and things. The effect might be good sometimes and difficult other times.

We also talked about free will, the ability to change our own paths to create the destiny we make for ourselves. We talked about different references to and beliefs about what God was in life. It had nothing to with religion. God is different for everyone. Time isn’t.

Ultimately, though, God, or something greater than us, depending on where you’re from or what your belief system is, is in control of it all. When I left, I felt I’d learned something new, and it was worth my visit.

How had he known the day my dad passed on? That was the one

thing that really got me, not to mention about my own situation, and had me scratching my head. On top of that, two weeks after I sat down with him, I won on some scratch-off tickets—$1,000 and $500—and I hit on some daily picks for another $500 and $200. How had he seen that coming by just looking at a computer? Maybe it was just luck, but he called it.

Feeling that things didn't make sense about writing the book, I put my full focus back on work. It was my own outlet to sanity. My relationship with the woman I'd met who'd helped me find the woman to work with on my book had gone from hot to cold. It just didn't seem to work.

My mom had some more issues with her health, and things weren't going well there. I felt it was a blessing that I was able to help my mom after she had helped me.

Being aware of the tendencies I knew about myself, I spoke with Mike as much as always. I kept going to meetings. I also was legally required to now. I never forgot what was working for me. I couldn't allow myself to fail after all I had gone through.

One Saturday morning, I had an appointment set up for ten o'clock with a couple regarding some possible work. Almost there, I received a call from the woman, who said her husband had had an unexpected issue come up, and they wouldn't be available until one o'clock. She asked if I could meet them then. That had happened before, so it wasn't a problem. Still, I was frustrated by it.

I realized I was close to the location of the meeting where I'd met Mike years back. I would be late, but I decided to go anyway. The group was so big it usually split into two groups. I enjoyed the group and its open topics. It was held in a church, in a big back room used as a children's library. Anywhere from twenty to forty people were there.

I'd never spoken at that place before, but that day was different. I'm not sure what the topic was, and I'm probably right by saying I wasn't anywhere near it when I spoke. I just went off. I was upset with how everything had been going lately. I'm not even sure what I said, but I felt better on the inside after getting it out. I let it go. I released what was inside me.

When it was over, the group broke up fairly quickly if the meeting was finished on the other side. Occasionally, there was a wait, and everyone would quietly hang out until the other group finished. That day was one of those days. I wasn't in a hurry, so it didn't matter much to me.

A man came over to me. He raised his hand toward me and nodded to me as he neared. I'd met him a few years back. It was the tall guy with the accent who'd been speaking with Mike when I got my anniversary coin. To get to me, he politely moved aside a woman who was coming up to speak to him.

He had a smile on his face as he reached out to shake my hand. "I needed to hear your voice today. Thank you." That was the first thing he said, not "Hello" or "How are you?" or "Nice to see you." I was puzzled by what he meant. I wondered what the hell I'd said now. He caught me off guard.

We made small talk, and he asked how I'd been. He hadn't seen me in quite a while. He remembered the conversation with Mike years back about the court system I was entering into. He laughed while saying, "I don't see a shackle on your leg anymore," referring to my house-arrest bracelet.

I said I'd started my own business and been busy lately. I explained that I was there kind of by accident that day. He said, "I never really had a green thumb. Books have always been my thing. I have so many books, and I can say I've read them all too."

After hearing him say that, I surprised him by saying, "I just wrote a book not all that long ago too. I've got a copy in my truck outside." I knew he was going to be surprised, which he was.

"Really? What's it about? When did you do this? How long is it?" He fired questions off in amazement, just as I'd expected.

"If you want, I'll go get it from my truck. If you have some time, maybe we could go get a coffee down the street, and I'll tell you about it."

After processing the idea that I'd really written a book, a second or so later, he replied, "I have some time; I'd love to see your book. There's a coffee shop right down the street from here we could go to."

I agreed that was a good idea. I went to my truck and then met him a few minutes later in front of the church. We walked down the sidewalk a little ways to, ironically, the coffee shop where I'd met my attorney for the first time before court. I laughed as I told him that. He read the back cover. Then he looked at the front again. He finally started to read the first page as we slowly maneuvered our way into the coffee shop line, which was backed up five or so people deep.

He asked about the reason and inspiration behind my writing the book. He flipped through it and asked more questions about how long it had taken to write, my emotions and feelings about it when I'd started, and how I felt now. He was politely grilling me about my work with greater interest than I'd thought he might. I enjoyed the conversation a lot. The more he asked me, the more questions I wanted to ask him.

When we sat down at a table, I answered his questions one by one. I saved the part about meeting the two women who could connect to the other side or the afterlife until last. I was afraid of how he might react.

Surprisingly, he was intrigued by my experiences and the people I'd met, from the man who read the deck of cards to the two women to the astrologer. He was curious about them all and wanted to know more.

I interrupted his questioning of me and asked him some questions of my own. "What do you do?"

"I was a third-grade teacher in my first job. Then I taught high school. I ended up coming here with a few degrees and became a professor and ultimately the dean of literature at a college." He had been recently forced into retirement. He didn't like it.

We talked for a little longer that morning, and around noon, I told him I had to go. I said he could keep the book if he paid me for it next week. He said, "If you're going to be here, then yes, I will. Maybe we can do this again."

Without hesitation, I agreed. "That would be great. That's the bonus about being the boss-making your schedule. I like that part of it."

I attended the same meeting the following week, and the two of us went out for coffee again. Our conversation was like a feeling-out process for two people who had a twenty-five-year age difference but were similar in many ways. I simply enjoyed talking to him. We agreed to meet again the following week and then the following week and so on.

For more than a year, we had coffee together until noon after that meeting, aside from maybe five or six times when we didn't meet due to a holiday or vacation or something like that.

As it turned out, he had started that meeting more than twenty years ago. It was like his baby. He was twenty-five-plus years sober when I met him. I enjoyed picking his brain and talking to him about all types of things. He was well versed in so much. We came to a point where we both opened up about some things that were pretty personal.

Like others, including me, he had regrets about some of the things he'd done. He'd been married a couple times, and with each, there had been some mistakes. He said he had changed his religion four times. I thought that was amazing. Our relationship grew to the point where there wasn't any offense in asking certain questions. It took some time to get there, but when I felt comfortable enough to ask about the religion thing, I couldn't hold back.

"Who the hell were you looking for anyway? Four times. I've got a God, and at certain times, I've doubted he exists at all. I don't necessarily feel that way now, but four times?"

He understood what I was asking. He'd been born into one religion through his family; he had changed to two others with his marriages; and the last religion, as he put it, had found him. I won't explain further because it doesn't matter. He reminded me of the twelve-step program's idea of "God as you understand him or her." All people are spiritual in their own way.

We came to the conclusion that maybe we were not capable of understanding or supposed to understand God. We had a difficult time understanding ourselves.

Most of our other conversations were much lighter. Some I really enjoyed. Each week, I felt I was there to learn something or find a way of looking at things.

I told Mike about my meetings with the older man, whom he had known for a few years. Mike said I didn't yet know how valuable it was to just sit and talk with the man. I wasn't sure what that meant.

Time went by. I had been doing my landscaping business for six years since leaving my old job. I felt myself physically breaking down. I'd also lost some of the desire to do it. Frank was leaving the nursery business at the end of the year, which probably played a little part in my decision. I was done. It was time for something else, something new.

No one could understand my decision to get out, not my family, clients, or friends. It was like déjà vu all over again, like when I'd told them about writing my book. Few understood what it took. Some said to hire people, but seeing what had happened with my old job didn't leave me much faith in doing that.

Due to what happened next, I had to tell my English friend I could no longer meet on Saturday mornings anymore. He'd shared with me an amount of knowledge that, combined with the knowledge of the judge and the doctor, was essential in allowing me to find success at something I didn't necessarily see coming.

The judge had asked continually, "What's next?" The doctor had said, "I trust you." The teacher had said, "I needed to hear your voice." I repeated all of those much-needed words over and over when facing what I encountered next.

I would find myself in one of the most uncomfortable places I'd ever imagined, yet somehow, things made sense—but of course, not at first. It just doesn't happen that way sometimes.

26

Sometimes You Have to Eat Your Words

When the end of the year came, I was physically exhausted, but this time, I wasn't coming back. I told my clients they would need to find someone else to take care of their property the following year.

Twenty-two years had taken a toll on my body. I was still heathy, but physical labor breaks your body down over time. The recovery time is harder. Suddenly, knees don't bend, the sore back is always sore, and arthritis sets in. The physical pain becomes uncomfortable and unbearable. Many times, the breakdown doesn't happen overnight. It takes time.

Many people I knew, from family and friends to clients, found it difficult to understand why I was getting out of the business. I looked crazy—again—to most. I was okay with that. It helped that I didn't have to answer about what I would do next. I didn't even know myself. I knew what I didn't want to do, though.

The person who did understand was Frank. He knew from his own firsthand experience how hard landscaping was. He'd done it himself before he started to work in the family store and business. He'd seen it break people down quickly and over time too.

I'd made enough money to take a little time off. That was a good feeling. I was able to be there for my mom too, and my family was aware of it. They were glad I could be there to take her to her appointments.

Without telling her, I was keeping an eye on her. I watched how she did things and asked how she felt. Asking what and how she felt after taking certain medications was always what the doctor did, so why not? I tried to make it look like I wasn't watching.

Knowing she didn't enjoy taking some of the medications, my family and I were afraid she'd tell the doctor what he wanted to hear so she could get off of them. She didn't enjoy going to the doctor; it made her feel as if she were sick. I tried to constantly explain that she wasn't sick. Her body just needed medication to make her life easier. The plan was to find the right combination.

I'd sit behind her at the appointments and nod to the doctor if I thought she was telling him the truth, based on what she'd told me. To her, I was just driving her there. My family asked her to allow me to go into her appointments as a precaution. It was funny how it worked.

My on-off relationship with the woman from before was now on again. She, like everyone else, didn't understand my leaving my business. The topic led to many uneasy discussions. No one could see it my way, but I was at peace with my choice.

I understood how people saw me. I came to the conclusion that rushing into a new career or something like that was what everyone else wanted or expected. People expect you to do whatever they would do. I wanted to do something I wanted to do, not what someone else thought I should do.

Everyone thought I needed to be doing something. The thing is, I was. I was waiting to see where *it* was. Sometimes you have to go find it, and sometimes it finds you.

As spring came, things started to bloom, and the grass started to grow. I could sense that those close to me thought I was just being lazy. I found it funny what people thought I should or shouldn't have been doing. It was the first time in more than twenty years that I wasn't being told what to do or committed on where to be. I wasn't feeling tired or sore at the end of the day.

Those close to me wondered when I would do something. By late May, everyone was growing more and more impatient. I stuck to my guns about finding or being put into the right place. Few, if any, could understand that I was relaxed and calm about how things were going. Had I felt an immediate need to do something, I would've.

I was having coffee one morning, when I got an email from my astrologer friend. He was doing a presentation in the next week or so. I kind of had forgotten about him. I thought it would be nice to see him in person.

It had been almost two years since I'd met him in his office. Reading the email, I knew I was definitely going to go see him. I'd been in contact with him via text after taking his advice to play the lottery and winning. His reply to that had been "Told you."

As I read the email further, I had second thoughts. The event was at a place I'd vowed never to go to again: a library connected to a police department. I'd visited many times; I just couldn't go there. Even though the jail and the library weren't the same, they were connected to the place where he was speaking. It was all under one roof. It sounds dumb, I'm sure, but that was how I felt.

For the next week or so after that, I flip-flopped on my decision to go or not. Something inside me said I needed to go. I convinced myself something would come of it.

It had been a hot day, and the sun was slowly going down, but the humidity was still high. It was uncomfortable. I felt the same way as I pulled up and saw the entrance to the police department. I decided to park as far from the entrance as I could. Parking on the opposite side of the building meant I would have to walk around the front in order to go inside. Walking around the corner from the parking lot, I could feel the heat of the blacktop parking lot rising upward. I felt the warm breeze of cars passing me as I walked on the sidewalk.

I took a deep breath as I looked at my phone and saw that I was about ten minutes early; it started at six o'clock. I noticed my friend as I walked up. He was speaking with a woman. He saw me through the glass windows and doors and pointed to me. Then he smiled and walked to the door to open it. He gave me a handshake and then a hug. "I can't believe you're here. How the hell have you been?" he asked loudly.

I was relieved to see him first thing. With a smile, I replied, "I'm doing pretty good. I decided to get out of the landscape stuff; it just became too much. It was time. Look at you, though. You look good. Did you lose some weight?" I wasn't sure if he had; he just looked better overall, as if he were happy about doing something he enjoyed.

He then went back over to the woman he'd been talking with. He introduced us to each other. Her name was Donna. We said hello to each other, and she then excused herself to go to the bathroom before the event started.

He and I walked toward the big room where he'd be doing his presentation. I peeked in to see about twenty-five people inside already. There were some empty seats still available.

He had stopped while I kept walking, and I hadn't noticed. I heard him say to the woman who'd just excused herself, "Hey, Donna, you and this guy have to get together and talk."

I looked over at her. She was about to enter the ladies' room and had no idea what he was talking about. She walked back toward us to have him repeat what he'd said. "What?" she asked.

He said the same thing again but much slower. "You and this guy need to talk. I think you could help each other."

She looked at him, looked at me, and said, "Sure." She still had no idea why, and I wondered why he wanted us to talk too.

He reached out and pulled me face-to-face with him. "Trust me. You need to talk to her. You'll see. And if you don't, I'm not doing another reading for either of you." Then he laughed. I just smiled and looked at him, having no idea what he meant, but I agreed I would. Before I went to use the bathroom before the presentation started, I told him I had to leave around seven thirty because I had a hockey game. He understood and was fine with it. He was just happy I'd come to see him.

He knew just about everyone who was there. He said hello to a few people and said we would be starting soon. "Get a coffee or cold drink before we start." It was obvious to everyone he liked doing this—teaching it, promoting it, and living it.

I returned a minute or so later. The room he was speaking in had filled up quickly. I dipped into the room and sat in one of the last remaining empty seats. There was a purse sitting in the chair next to me. A moment later, Donna walked in and sat next to me. Before it started, I shook hands with her and introduced myself again. "Hi, Donna. I'm Jack. So why do we have to talk? What do you do?"

She said hello again and then told me, "I have some Suboxone clinics. Here, in Baltimore, in St. Louis, and in a couple other cities. Suboxone is a drug that lessens the withdrawal from heroin and opiates so people can wean themselves off and be completely drug free. It depends on the person, though, and how quickly he or she wants to get off of it."

I was aware of the drug somewhat. I knew it was given to people who went into rehab centers for extended stays, usually only for the first few days.

I told her a little about myself as quickly as I could before the presentation started. I mentioned that I'd just hit another anniversary recently. I proceeded to tell her about the book I'd written and my connection to our mutual friend.

We knew our friend was about to start, and we also knew he was going to ask us if we had spoken yet. It was just what he did. We laughed about that for a moment and agreed we should have coffee and talk more the following week. As my buddy walked in, he stopped and saw us next to each other.

Out loud in front of everyone, he asked, "Did you two talk yet?"

Without hesitation, I replied, "Next week we're meeting for coffee."

He smiled at both of us. "Okay, that's good. Let me know how it turns out." He jumped right into his presentation and didn't miss a beat, knowing what he had just done. I had a feeling I was there specifically to meet that woman.

She and I both excused ourselves just before seven thirty. Before we went our own ways, we spoke for a minute again. I told her I almost hadn't come there at all. Donna told me, "I drove by the place by ten minutes, and I was almost home, but something told me to turn around." That kind of sold both of us about being there.

The following week, we met late in the afternoon at a coffee shop. Donna talked about the clinics, including the groups, the doctors, and the weekly drug tests required to be able to make the place work. It sounded like an intense place.

I told her about the two women I'd met and my reason for writing the book. I told her about being in the legal program and its requirements and then starting my own business.

We spoke for about an hour. Donna asked if I'd like to come check out her clinic and maybe sit in and talk to the groups there. "Bring your book too. That'll get their attention for sure."

I agreed without even thinking about it. All that had happened had led us to meet each other, and I had the feeling I was meant to go there.

27

I Never Planned for This

The next week seemed to go by quickly leading up to my trip to the facility Donna had invited me to. I drove in and parked in the same garage I had parked in for my court days. It was where all the judges parked. The lower level was full when I pulled in that morning. I drove up a ramp to the next level.

The attendant on duty waved me over and asked me how long I would be. His name was Clayton. I wasn't sure, so I told him, "No later than two o'clock, I think. It may be earlier. I honestly don't know."

Clayton was easily six foot four and maybe 250 pounds or so. He was a large black man. He paused for a minute and then spoke to a person crossing the garage, reminding the person to leave the keys in the car so he could move it if he had to. He focused back on me a second later. "You can park over there behind the cones if you're not gonna be all day."

Without thinking, I said, "Oh, you got it!" I looked over and saw the one spot. I told him, "Thanks." I weaved around the cones and backed into the spot, blocking the car parked all the way in.

He said, "Leave your keys in it, and leave the door unlocked. I'll be here until three. Your keys will be downstairs in the box if you're not back by then."

Clayton walked back over to me. I assured him the keys were in it. I thanked him again for giving me the spot. He asked, "Where are you going?" I told him I was going to the Suboxone facility. I briefly told him about meeting Donna and being invited by her to talk to some of the people there. I then flashed him my book. Surprised, he asked, "You wrote that?"

I nodded. I walked over and showed it to him. I showed him the back with my picture on it. He was stunned and asked, "How long did that take to do?"

I laughed. "Forever. I have to go to this place now, but I'll tell you about it if I see you later. It'll take more than a minute to explain."

He laughed. "Okay, that's fair. Hopefully I'll see you later then."

I shook his hand and thanked him again for the parking spot.

I walked by the courthouse I'd been in many times before. I smiled as I went by. That was the past. Since then, for the past five years, the court and the people who ran the program had asked me to come back every year to speak to the newest graduating classes. I did without question. I made it a point to remind each group not to forget what they'd experienced and how their lives had changed. Graduating from the program meant their lives had indeed changed. Sometimes when we're in the middle of something, due to our emotions at the time, we can't always see the progress we've made.

Going back allowed me to talk to the judge, which I enjoyed, even if it was for just a few minutes. I felt that my talking with him let him know that the program was worth it and that the effort the court had put into me was still working. It showed me he really cared about everyone.

The clinic I had to go to was about five or so blocks away, on the ninth floor. I'd gone by it many times before but never known the place existed. It was right by the bus stop I'd used when I went to college more than twenty years before.

From the parking garage, it only took me a little more than five minutes to get there. Even the elevator ride was quick. I didn't have to ask for directions. I found the office by simply following some of the unhappiest people I'd ever seen before.

I walked in behind the two people I'd shared the elevator with, trying to blend in, as if I were there for the reasons they were. I immediately felt the energy of the place. It didn't feel good. The people there weren't happy about being there. Many were there only to get something to ease the uncomfortable feeling of withdrawal.

I quietly introduced myself at the desk to the nurse. I could hear behind me in the waiting room people complaining about having to wait; they were in a hurry to leave already. "Where is the doctor? I can't be here all day," one woman said.

The place gave off a negative feeling.

The nurse in the office unlocked the door to enter the waiting room. She locked it behind her and said to everyone that she'd be right back. "Follow me, please. Donna said you were coming." Her demeanor changed as we walked into the hallway toward the offices in the back. She seemed relaxed once away from her office and the waiting room.

I could hear voices coming from another room. I assumed that was where the groups met. The room was separated from the hallway by a ten-foot wall, the last four feet of which were plexiglass at the top. I had to stand on my tiptoes to see into it, and I'm six feet tall. I saw people sitting inside, talking among themselves.

I saw Donna after we cleared the corner and entered another hallway. She saw me walk in. She came over and shook my hand. "You made it. That's great. I'm a little busy, but I'll be there in a bit to see how things are going. I told the group leader you were coming in; he can get you up to speed."

I said, "Okay, see you in a little." She went the other way into her office, closing the door behind her.

The nurse looked at me and said, "It's like that a lot here. She doesn't stop. She makes this place go. I'll take you to the group now."

The nurse brought me back to the door we'd passed earlier. She went in, excused herself to the group, and asked the man in charge to come out to meet me.

We introduced ourselves, and he gave me the lowdown about how things went. He explained that the participants all gave urine samples first. They then joined the group. When ready, the nurses called them back out to do blood-pressure tests. They then went back to the group. Lastly, they met with the doctor. The doctor would give them a prescription if everything was good. If they failed the drug test, they were subject to being released from the program. The test showed how much of what was in their systems and if they were taking what was prescribed to them.

There were three groups, with twelve to eighteen people in each group. He estimated the last group that day should be done around one thirty to two o'clock. He said every week, each group had a paper printed about what they would discuss that week. Getting people to participate was tough sometimes. Some people had been there and been prescribed for years and shared little at all.

Some people, though not many, had used the program the way it was intended: taking lower and lower dosages of the drug until they were past the withdrawal part altogether. They were able to be free of the Suboxone and of drugs completely.

Not many people were willing to go to that extreme. They were handcuffed to Suboxone in the same sense they'd been handcuffed to their drugs of choice before. Suboxone was legal, though.

He said some of the people had insurance to pay for the treatment, while others paid out of pocket. It seemed to be a big issue with the ones who paid out of pocket. One woman felt that since she paid out of pocket, she shouldn't have to do the group. She believed she should just get her prescription and leave. It didn't work that way. Sadly, she was unable to understand the severity of the addiction she had to another drug. She'd forgotten she had once lived a life that wasn't dependent on being on any type of drug. She had no desire to change or listen to how others had changed. She had become complacent and adjusted to life that way. But she didn't like it.

After the short talk outside, he introduced me to the group. I heard exactly what I'd thought I might. "He's a cop," someone in the group said. To me, the comment was funny. I'd expected it. I'd gotten my hair cut a day before, and it was short on top with no hair on the sides. My being a cop was the furthest thing from the truth.

The people I'd passed earlier while walking in had joined the group. I think they had a hard time believing me until I pulled out the book I'd written. Passing it around the room, I reminded them to look at the picture on the back, which verified without question that I'd written it.

I explained about my past, including the suicide attempt, the court system, the judge, and all the players in it. I talked about starting my own business, getting away from the people I'd surrounded myself with before, and changing my life.

The man running the group had not known about any of that, and he started asking questions. One person made a snide remark or two about what I was telling them. I turned the attention on him and why he was there. Calmly, I asked him how he was going to get out of where he was now. There was no problem after that.

Donna told me later, in between the first and second groups, that I'd gotten a few nice compliments. I also found out that one particular person was really mad at me. I knew exactly who it was. I told Donna who I thought it was, and she said I was right. She told me to be aware of a couple people in the next group. She also felt that group could be a little more difficult with me than the first group. It was nice to know what to expect. She said one person would have a reaction to me just based on how I looked. She said I'd know who right away. In the controlled chaos I was in, people were funneling into the chairs, staring at me, wondering who I was and why I was there. I said hello to each one as he or she came in.

The room was tightly packed with around eighteen seats in it. Men and women from eighteen to sixty-plus years of age sat in the room together. They huddled next to people they knew or felt comfortable talking to or being near. I was the elephant in the room.

People looked at me but said nothing to me, until one particular man walked in—the person Donna had made me aware of earlier. Some, it seemed, were waiting to see his reaction.

The guy was around five foot eight. I couldn't gauge his weight because of the baggy way he wore his clothes. He wore one distinctive color. He had on a shirt and hat of the same color, with shoes to match. His blue jeans were the only thing different. He was a young black man. The color he was wearing didn't represent the sports teams in the area we were in. He was proud of the color he wore. Everyone knew it too.

He didn't hold back as he and I locked eyes. He spoke loudly to make his point. "My God, they got a cop in here! What is going on now here?" Some people in the room laughed and commented outwardly on my being there. It was as if the room started to come to life.

I just smiled at him. Donna came in a few moments after he did. She walked up behind him and stood just inside the door. She let the group finish their comments and the stir he had created. I just smiled at them.

"Hold on!" Donna said. "None of you have a clue who this is. He's here to talk to you. How about having some respect and letting him talk for a minute? You can ask some questions after if you'd like. Maybe he'll ask you some too." She knew from the first group that I wasn't going to hold back if they tried to get one over on me. I just couldn't be mean in doing it.

I knew I was there to help them, not embarrass anyone. I did not want to defeat the purpose of being there. I was ready for them compared to the first group. The first person I needed to address was the young man in obvious gang colors who'd called me a cop. Donna stood there waiting to see what would happen. I doubted anyone would say anything out of line with Donna outside the door, still though I chose my words carefully not to mislead anyone.

"Well, for starters, I'm not who or what you think I am." I panned the room and then focused my attention on the one young man. "My name is Jack. How are all of you today? I've been invited by Donna to come share my experiences with you. I'm glad you proved one of the things I've found out: we can be wrong sometimes. I don't know you, so I can't judge you, and I'm not going to assume that you're something you're not either.

"As a matter of fact, I'll bet I've been in more trouble than you in life. Probably more trouble than the entire room combined. I'm not bragging about that either. It just is that way. Five DUIs and multiple drug arrests. The first person in a court system. Can anyone top that here? Anybody at all? I'm also nine years clean and sober. I started my own landscaping business and spent six years doing that. I spent twenty-two years in that business total. I've also written this book here."

I handed the book to the person next to me. "My picture is on the back if you don't believe it's me," I said with sarcasm. The room fell silent, even Donna. "Donna and I met last week through a mutual friend. She invited me to come talk to you guys."

Donna saw I had control of the room and excused herself. Before she left, she said, "You might want to listen to what he has to say. It may help you."

When the book came to the man who'd questioned me earlier, he spoke again. "That's you all right." He had another question for me. "Who was the judge you had?"

I told him and then asked, "Do you know him? Have you met him before?"

He replied, nodding, "Yeah, I've heard of him. He can be tough."

I validated his reply. "Yes, he can. He taught me a lot. It was me who made him do his job, though. He was protecting everyone else from me based on my actions. He's actually a nice guy if you don't do the wrong thing."

I told them about myself, my addiction and its progression, the people I'd worked with, and the people I'd associated with. I pointed out that I'd relapsed every day for ten years. I'd known I had a problem and done nothing about it. I'd allowed it to take me. I spoke about the percentages I'd learned and said I'd made the decision for myself that I was going to make it. No else had done that. I'd kept to it. I was proud of that.

The man from earlier tried one last time to be funny and crack one more joke. He was trying to take over the room after his earlier failed attempt. I figured he had done that before, and it probably worked wherever he went. I knew I had to slow him down. I wanted him to tell the others his reason for being there.

"Well, now you know why I'm here. Why are you here today? I don't mean to put you on the spot, but it seems like you like to talk a little bit. How'd you get caught up in what you did, and what got you here?" I called him out, and to my surprise, he didn't disappoint. He went into a story about being shot in a gunfight with his brother against another group of people.

He glorified the story, but he didn't ever answer the question. He was saved by the fact that it was his turn to see the doctor. I asked him to come back before he left the building, and he promised he would. He surprised me when he did.

I admired him for keeping his word and returning after seeing the doctor. I asked to speak to him alone outside the doorway. He agreed with hesitation. He also got in a funny line to amuse the group. He said, "I'm going that way, so why not?" I even had to laugh a little bit.

Outside the doorway, no one was around. "What's your name?" I asked. "I didn't catch it inside." I knew I caught him off guard with the simplest of questions. He wondered why I was asking it. He finally answered after a second or two.

"My name is J. C. Why are you asking?"

I replied quickly, "I just wanted to know to say thanks for participating in there. I wanted to wish you the best of luck in getting out of here soon. I mean it. I was serious about all the stuff I went through. If you know the judge I had, then you probably know what it's like to be in trouble. I hope things work out for you."

I also couldn't pass up taking a last shot at him too. "I guess J. C. is short for Jesus Christ, huh?"

He smiled and laughed.

Maybe it is, I thought to myself, staring at him. *It's kind of who he thinks he is, though.*

We shook hands and said goodbye. I told him it was my pleasure to meet him. I'd never expected to be standing in the hallway with him when he'd walked in earlier. Crazy things happen, I guess.

It appeared to me Donna had made sure he was one of the last people to see the doctor that day. Donna and I spoke again for a few minutes before the last group started. "He's something, huh?" she asked.

I chose my answer carefully. "Yes, he is. He comes off as trying to command everything in the room. I wish he would've answered my question, though. He dodged it the entire time."

The last group went pretty smoothly. Donna and I talked a little more after the last group ended, and she offered me a job with the same group the following week.

I'd enjoyed the day, and the idea of spending one day a week there wasn't bad either. Who knew what would become of it? I needed a job anyway, so I agreed and told Donna I'd be back next week. Funny how it worked out. I was surprised it worked out that way.

I texted my friend who'd said Donna and I needed to talk and told him what had transpired. I knew what his reply would be before he sent it: "Told you!"

28

Keeping Them All Happy

Part of people pleasing is trying to make everyone happy. It's something people can do in many ways. At times, it can hurt, backfire, or be taken advantage of too. Sometimes it can prevent the results of what needs to happen in life.

Some people make it a full-time job and never get paid for it. It's just who they are. I've seen and experienced it many times in my life. People can also feel pressured to do things they don't want to in order to appease others. Anytime I tried to take advantage of someone doing it or do it for others, it caught up to me and bit me harder.

Having met Donna the way I had, my spiritual side or my intuition told me I was being put in the place where I was supposed to be. Yes, I could've kept doing the landscaping business and made certain adjustments, but I didn't. I was opening myself up to something new. No one understood that.

As I explained the situation to the people close to me, they still failed to see the way things had worked out. Some told me I should've started looking in that direction before I'd left the other profession. "How would I have known this months ago?" I asked many of them. I explained to them that something bigger than I was had put the opportunity there at the time it was meant to happen. It was time for the next experience.

My taking the new job got some of those people off my back. It was also something I felt I could enjoy, and it was only one day a week.

I was able to keep an eye on my mom. Her health seemed to have leveled off and seemed to be improving. The medications she'd been taking had finally acclimated to her body. She was happier and more level-headed, and her physical pain was kept at bay.

I also had time to visit my friend Mike on a regular basis. His health wasn't getting better. One doctor had told him that because of his current health, he probably wouldn't live much longer. He could've taken the news badly, as some people might have. Instead, he took it as a sign it was time to find a new doctor. He wanted someone who was looking for a solution, not conceding an end result.

Years back, Mike had been on a mission trip to Haiti. He'd met a woman who was a doctor from El Salvador. His relationship with her was magnetic. They'd gotten married a little while after meeting. He always said it was destiny. He'd had to leave the country to find her. The funny thing was, he had a doctor with him at all times.

I spoke to Mike about what I was going to do on my first day there. I knew what I was going to do, but in running it by him, I knew I'd get something more—and of course, I did. My approach was simple, direct, and to the point: have control of the room, try to make it fun, make it worth everyone's time, and be prepared for anything. *Let them see that we're all the same. There's a solution for anyone to change; you just have to find yours*, I repeated in my mind.

I was ready for the first day. My first group started at nine o'clock in the morning. Donna asked me to be a few minutes early. I took a gamble at parking in the same place I'd parked the week before. Clayton smiled as he saw me pull up. "Hey! You're back. It must have gone well," he said, kind of surprised to see me again. I had missed him when leaving last week.

I replied that it had gone well. "They offered me a job one day a week. I should be back here by two o'clock today. I would've been back last week, but I ended up talking with everyone in the place last week."

Clayton said, "That's great. Park in the same spot as last week. Just leave the keys in it. We'll talk later."

What a relief, I thought, seeing three cars behind me backed up and not seeing a place to park on the level I was on. I drove around the coned-off area and backed in again. I waved to Clayton as I slipped down the flight of steps that put me right on the street.

I saw some people from the last week's first group when I walked into the place. A couple of them were surprised to see me again, based on their expressions. I walked around the corner to the office area and found Donna to let her know I was there.

She was on the phone. She saw me and gave me a smile, wave, and thumbs up. That was all I needed. I signaled the nurse in the waiting room by holding up my open hand to say, "Give me five minutes." She nodded without anyone noticing.

I could see the waiting room filling with almost the entire first group. I took a moment to myself to set my intentions on what I wanted to do. It felt like a minute later when they all rolled in. It certainly wasn't five minutes. There were some comments, as I'd expected.

I asked everyone to remain calm before we started. It wasn't going to be as it had been. Two people said they needed to leave early for reasons that I laughed off after hearing them. I passed a sheet of paper around, asking them to sign their names along with the time they'd entered the room. Half of them wrote down the time they'd come into the office. I called BS on that right away, and no one liked it at all.

I made my rules clear. I wasn't there to babysit anyone. "I'm here to help you. I'm not here to judge you. Don't put me in that position. I've probably been where you are, have been, or are headed. I've changed my life with the help of others. I made a decision. I've made both good and bad choices since. I know myself and my tendencies. I can't change my past. I can only learn from it."

They had no idea what hit them; my approach was different from what they knew.

I took a second to retrieve the attendance sheet. I scoured the names and read them all aloud to make sure I pronounced each correctly. I again laughed at the times they'd written down. How could they all walk into the same room at the same time and write down different times? Some had a thirty-minute difference. It said a lot about where some people were at with the truth.

I went into the reasons why I did things differently. "First of all, I want you to speak with respect for everyone in the group. There is no glorifying past drug use. I will need you to trust me. That may take some time; I understand that. I need to hear your voice. That means participate. There is nothing to be afraid of. I heard everyone talking in the waiting room, so I know you can talk."

Some people said they wouldn't participate, as I'd expected. I asked those people, "What are you afraid of? The truth? Getting better and finding a solution to why you're here? Seeing that you're like everyone else? You're all here for the same reason, if you haven't put two and two together. It's called addiction. Some of you will not like me, I'm sure, and to be honest with you, I'm fine with that. The sun will still rise and set, and I will sleep well."

Silence fell over the room. I noticed Donna standing outside the door, holding her phone to her ear. Whether she was on it or just listening to me, I didn't know.

I asked them all to introduce themselves again so I could learn their names quicker and so they knew whom they were talking to. Some of them had been there for a long time and never spoken to each other. After that, I gave them a final round of my expectations.

"I don't care what you tell the doctor. The staff and I will talk afterward to see who's failed a drug test this week. You all knew the rules on being dismissed from the program before you came in. Lastly, before I dismiss you from group, you need to tell me three things you learned from the group that day. It shows that you're paying attention and that we aren't wasting each other's time," I calmly said. "I need to hear your voice."

The same people who'd complained before were up in arms about my last comments. I looked over to see Donna laughing outside. She then came in and backed up all I had said. "He's doing this for you—to help you fix some things in your own lives. You don't want to be coming to places like this for the rest of your life, do you?"

What I had asked of them was so uncomfortable and over the top for some that I understood their fear of saying anything. They were used to looking at a piece paper every week that explained some stuff they hardly ever talked about. Knowing that, I asked, "What's next?" It was the same question the judge had asked me. Time wasn't on my side, as people were now going off with the nurse for their doctor visits, so I decided the "What's next?" question would be the topic for next week.

We went around the room with everyone saying everyone in the group's name over and over. It helped everyone, myself included.

Before the second group came in, I could hear some people talking to Donna about what I was asking them to do. I saw some people talking to the second group, preparing them for what I was going to say. At that moment, I liked what I was doing. With the next group, I changed one thing: I shook every person's hand to welcome the person as he or she entered the room. I did it when they left too. I thanked each person for his or her participation and patience with me that day.

J. C. was back in the second group. He was skeptical from the beginning. However, his group took my rules and plan much better than the early group. Maybe the others just weren't morning people. They were miserable compared to those in the second group.

Donna came in again and backed up my statements. She had a better time talking with the second group. She liked everyone. Donna liked the people; she didn't like their addiction, what it did to them, the effects it had on them, and what it turned them into.

She liked J. C. too. It was obvious what he was involved in, and he did nothing to downplay it either. The things that seemed to work on him were respect and some good old sarcasm. He liked to laugh. He was an intelligent man in the street-wise sense.

I found out he was twenty-nine years old. That was a relatively high age for a person in his field not to be in jail. I had a pretty good idea he was a well-respected member of the group he associated with.

I wanted to know more about how he'd ended up in a gang and then in the clinic. He'd steered around answering that question the last week, and I hadn't forgotten. I knew the way to go about it.

He was polite with the group, although his ego came through at times. He smooth-talked Donna outside, or at least tried to. She wanted him to get his life straight and not be in that place. She saw where his current path was going to end up. The thing was, he did too. Their talk outside the doorway ended with her saying, "You will participate in anything you're asked."

I could hear him reply, "Yes, Miss Donna."

His group was fun. They participated without any pressure from me. Like the previous week, the last group was pretty much a breeze too, with exception of a couple people who, in all honesty, didn't have a chance. It was obvious there was some mental illness with one man. Drug use had taken a toll on him in many ways. It was sad.

There was one twenty-something-year-old kid who was heading down a path that was going to take him places he couldn't imagine. Hope for him wasn't there. I'd been to that place emotionally, but at an older age, and it was horrible. He hadn't lived it yet.

The drugs he was still doing had a stranglehold on him. He was only there to use the Suboxone as a withdrawal prevention. He was honest about it at least. He'd lost his family over his using. He'd failed out of school. Jail, an institution, or death was next. He was aware of it; he just didn't care about the outcome. I wondered if I'd see him next week.

When I returned to my car, the garage parking lot now had plenty of open spots available where cars had left already. It was just before two o'clock, when I saw Clayton walking back toward the office where he had a chair and radio. He asked how my day had gone.

I explained to him how everything had come about to my getting there. I told him a little about my experience that day and how awkward it had been at certain points, though I never mentioned any names or anything like that. He could relate because he had known people with the same type of issues. The people were all the same.

We talked for fifteen minutes or so. He said that next week, I could have the same parking spot again. That was a relief. It was one thing I didn't have to think about. I didn't say it to him, but I felt I could talk to him about what I was seeing and the reactions I was getting. I was going to talk to Mike about my day anyway, but I figured another opinion from another unbiased source might be a good thing for me to use. Whether I used any input or extra ideas I was given was up to me. I had learned that in listening to others, I might hear a message that needed to be delivered. I just had to receive it and use it in the correct way.

By the end of the day, I realized I had to be direct and honest with everyone there as need be, Donna included. I needed to do things in a way that would make the most of my time there. My way was a combination of things I'd learned and my own skills, talents, and abilities. I hoped to get a positive result from at least one person a day if I could. In doing so, I needed them to fully trust me. I needed them to feel comfortable so they could understand more than they did now. The unknown factor was whether or not they were willing to listen and let me help them.

Part of gaining the trust I was looking to earn from them meant I had to be honest in answering their questions. The following week, I allowed each group to ask me questions or bring up a topic to discuss.

During my first visit, I'd told the group about myself, and I'd thought I covered my story fairly well. I guess I hadn't, though. In each group, people asked the same three questions in slightly different ways. One was "How have you stayed clean and sober for so long?" Another was "Are you afraid a moment or feeling might come up that will make you want to use again? The third was "If you made the choice to do it again and no one would know, would you do it?"

I explained again that I changed the people, places, and things, including whom I was doing it with and where I was doing it, but the hardest part was working on my thinking. My brain was programmed to think a certain way. I changed how I reacted to things in life and what I needed or thought I needed. Using was me chasing a feeling, urge, or desire, but drugs didn't allow me to feel anything, whether I considered it good or bad. Using ultimately took me to a place I didn't need to go to or experience again. I couldn't successfully do it and live a normal life. Drinking for twelve-plus hours and doing drugs in a day wasn't normal. Functioning with a 0.27 blood-alcohol level wasn't either.

I explained that because it took a good bit of time to get that way, the changes needed might not be easy. For me, though, it actually was easy in a way. I had nothing left; I was lifeless with my addiction. Total surrender on my part was the only way to go for me.

I told them, "It also helped me to learn from people who were successful in what I was trying to learn how to do on a one-day basis. Work on an hourly basis, a minute-to-minute basis, or a moment-to-moment basis. Once you figure that out, do it again the next day. Ultimately, if you want it badly enough, you can. Others have done it. Why not you?

"I learned that if I do feel like I may want to use, then I should call someone. If that person's not available, call someone else. Repeat it until you find someone. It's also okay to say you feel that way. Anyone can at any time."

The last question I couldn't explain exactly the way I wanted to fully. That day would come eventually. I told them that if I got to a mind-set or place where I thought I was going to use, wanted or needed to use, or felt it was justifiable to do so, I still couldn't do it. I knew something was watching.

I said, "I'd be disrespecting God, or whoever is in charge, who has given me so many chances and loved me until I learned to love myself. I thought I did. I didn't, though. I was ashamed of what I'd become. Trying to commit suicide was really me hating myself. Hating my life. It's what addiction can do: it can take control or terrorize anyone.

"I wasn't born that way. I've been blessed to overcome it with the help of others from all walks of life, including people from different places with issues similar to mine and others without them.

I thought the question about whether I'd do it if I could get away with it without anyone knowing was funny. I said, "I'd know I was living another lie. I don't have to lie today about anything." I told them what I thought would happen if I did make that choice. "I believe that if I do, whether I'm inside or outside, I'll somehow be struck by lightning. I'll end up living, but the pain I take from it will last the rest of my life." They laughed at that, but I still didn't want to test the waters on that.

I stressed to everyone, "I'm this way today only for me. It's not about being greedy in any way. Everyone around me benefits, myself included. Even people I don't know. That chaos I created by doing what I did doesn't exist. I'm in a better frame of mind to handle what's going on in life. It's not perfect, but it is certainly better than it was.

"Time has allowed different forms of healing to begin in physical, emotional, spiritual, and even financial ways. None of those changed overnight, but little by little, they all changed in some way. It wasn't always easy, but I learned that change doesn't have to be bad, though sometimes it's uncomfortable."

There was one thing I couldn't deny that was true for me: I hadn't been arrested or in any sort of legal trouble since I'd made the decision to change. The common denominator was undeniable to everyone who knew me too.

29

Put the Plan in Action

Over the next eight weeks, things changed slowly but dramatically in different ways. Each group changed. The early morning group was still much more combative verbally than the other two groups combined. Two or three people were carrying heavy emotional baggage. They were stuck, which prevented them from receiving the help that others were getting.

My intent was never to insult anyone, but in my pointing out facts, some felt that I was. Donna knew what was happening. She took up a position outside the door, listening to it all. The same people each week caused problems. She calmed them down.

It was evident to me that some of the replies I received showed people were listening. Listening led to thinking, and thinking led to answers. The answers led to possible solutions. They were only possible, though, if they were attempted. That was where some people stopped. There were those with a willingness, though.

The middle group became my favorite. They started to participate with each other in sharing and built an inner circle among themselves. They listened to each other, and they called each other's bullshit. They fed off each other. It was easy to talk with them.

Two people had worked with the doctors and weaned themselves off substances to become completely drug free. They came back every week to support the others. They were like gold to me. They gave a lot of credit to the group, and in return, the group admired what they'd done.

The third group was the easiest. They got along well. They were the quietest out of the three. One young girl brought her infant baby in every week. She was battling issues with a bad relationship. She was handling it, though; she found strength to keep going on for her baby.

As different as all three groups were, they were all seeing the same doctor. They all gave the same answers. The ones who were still using gave the same excuses. When they realized they were more similar than they'd thought, their connection grew.

Every week after the first one, I had different topics that sounded horrible to them at first until we broke them down. One week, I said, "Tell the group three things you would change about yourself. But it can't have anything to do with your financial situation, where you live, or any relationship you have or are in. It has to be internal about you." As you might imagine, when people got honest with themselves, tears began to flow, for both men and women.

To ease the situation, I said, "Now tell the group one specific thing you really like about yourself." They had no idea I was asking them to do an abbreviated moral inventory of themselves.

The topics each week were different. One was about changing the people, places, and things. One was about living with what they'd done in the past, as no one could change the past. A person had to learn how to change the future by not making the same mistakes made in the past.

Fear, denial, and forgiveness were fun topics. We talked about believing and knowing they were important, special, and worthy. We dealt with self-esteem issues, money, legal issues, personal records, emotions, physical pain, and death. Redemption was a good one, and so was asking for help.

One topic that came up more than any was judgment, including how they felt others looked at or thought of them, whether or not it was true, and how they felt about themselves. Judgment paralyzed some people from going, doing, and being in many different ways. It was terrible. It was probably the biggest hurdle each group needed to overcome.

With every one of the topics I brought to the forefront week in and week out, I had to explain how I had gone through the same things. It was the only way I could gain their trust. I could see it was working. People weren't complaining all the time; the energy of each group changed slowly but surely.

A few people didn't come back from week to week, so new people replaced them. They were either kicked out or arrested, or they went to a different place altogether. Some weaned themselves off drugs too.

In each group, I had the group members explain to the new people who came in what was going on. Donna was happy about that. She would come in and ask questions; she knew everyone there. I loved that she was direct.

Anyone who had any issues with me complained to Donna. Those numbers went down over a short period of time. Don't get me wrong: there was plenty of stuff I could have done better. I'm more critical of myself than anyone else is. But things definitely changed. One person in particular changed in a way I never would have guessed.

J. C. was in the middle group. He was a big reason why I enjoyed his group the most. He slowly opened up every week. I shook his hand and welcomed him in every week. He started to shake mine before he left.

He made sure he told me and the group what he'd learned each week without my asking. He had insight into some things, and when he shared, he helped others make sense of the topic and understand when I had trouble doing it. He was nice to be around.

By the way he dressed, everyone knew what he was affiliated with, although it didn't seem to matter in the group. He was just J. C.; he had the same issues everyone else did. His relationship with everyone in the building was good too. When we checked his drug tests, he failed some weeks, and other weeks, he was good. It didn't make sense.

J. C. did have a small issue one week. A white man walked in with a bandana on his belt loop. It was a color different from the color J. C. always wore. His eyes immediately went to it and locked in on the man.

The man sat next to me and signed the check-in sheet. He apologized for being early. He was in the last group but was leaving out of town to work, so he'd come at that time. He'd told me the week before, and I'd okayed it. I had forgotten until then.

J. C. reacted as if he were staring at an enemy directly in front of him. Seeing that, I introduced the man to the group and explained his reason for joining the group. J. C. spoke up quickly. "Welcome to the group. What's up with your bandana? Who are you with?"

The man, who was maybe twenty-five to thirty years old, was stunned by the unwelcoming question. "Ah, it's my lucky bandana. I always take it when I'm leaving town for work."

The question from J. C. was awkward enough, but the look on J. C.'s face said volumes. He'd been programmed to react that way from his past experiences. He noticed everyone in the room staring at him. I tried to deflect the moment by thanking J. C. for welcoming the man into the group. It was the only time something like that happened.

In sharing my experiences with the legal system, I explained the importance of going to twelve set meetings, finding a spiritual side if possible, and finding someone with similar issues and clean time to help with staying clean and sober. That hardly went over well with everyone. Some people did go to meetings, though. A few even had a sponsor.

One day in group conversation, the topic of why I'd decided to write the book came up. I knew Donna was aware of it, and she understood. She'd met people in her life who did that sort of thing, and she understood there were people who could connect to higher dimensions or different spiritual worlds to speak to those who'd passed.

I knew that when I tried to explain that to heroin and opiate addicts—well, let's just say I'd have some skeptics. Every persons relationships with God or a higher power or whatever spiritual beliefs they had were different for all of them. That also applies to the entire world. Some felt condemned for what they'd done. Others didn't believe in the possibility of it all.

A person in the last group of the day asked the question, and I promised I'd answer it the following week. I decided to make it the topic for an entire day with all three groups. I told them the topic would be "Things we might not understand."

Since I'd been there, in talking about my writing the book, I'd been asked that question a couple times before. Each time, I tried to push it off and talk about something else. I wasn't sure how some would take it, based on my own family's responses.

In speaking to those people about it, I expected some interesting responses—and that was what I got. I realized it was great because I was able to use the responses I received in a way I hadn't thought about before. It finally made sense to me. I just had to make it make sense to them.

I warned them of what I thought might happen before I got started: some people were not going to take it well. Some might, I said. With everything I'd spoken of before, I had used my personal examples to show them we all, in some way, had the same feelings, emotions, and beliefs in many different forms and experiences.

Because I knew that what I was about to tell them might be tough to believe, I explained it by saying maybe they had not put it in the perspective I was about to tell them regarding how it had occurred. I started by saying, "Some of you may think I'm a little crazy, but this the truth about how it went down. In my opinion, it was the best day of my life."

I first mentioned the man who'd used a deck of cards to tell me of some things in my life three months out and even further. I then mentioned meeting the two women who'd introduced me to my dad, grandparents, and aunts and uncles.

Some of them just stared at me without speaking. I'm sure some were wondering if I was back on drugs or had been drinking that day. Some said it wasn't possible. But most of them wanted to know more.

One young girl in the first group understood better than anyone else. She had met some people like the ones I had described. She validated my story to the ones who had a problem believing. It helped to have someone who could corroborate my story with similar experiences.

I told them first it was my choice to what I did as much it was to make the changes I did to have me experience what I did and meet the people I had. At any point things could've been different. I saw it today that I was blessed the way it had worked out. That was the easy part.

I told them how some of my family and friends thought I was a little nuts for doing it at all, although again, if not for that experience, I wouldn't have been there that day. All three groups agreed my experience might come off as crazy to some. I'd doubted what I was doing plenty of times myself. I just kept doing it, and when I was done, it made even less sense—until I met Donna.

Because I couldn't explain the answers to all their questions, the conclusion I was left with and had to become okay with was that the experience I had with people I met was simply some sort of God thing. They same way I was in their lives in the position I was now instead of years before. Some of the people I'd met, well I couldn't explain how they did what they did?

I had the full attention of the room in each group of the day, and I tried to take advantage of that. I asked them to think of the things they had done to get them to that exact point, with us having that conversation. "What is or was the equation? What's the answer to this part? How does it work out with the knowledge you have now about yourself, about others, and about life? Can you do it? How will you do it? Will you do it? When does it happen?" I ran off a few more questions, daring them to think about the personal answers to each. I could see the wheels turning in almost everyone's head. Silence took over for a few moments in each group when I asked those questions. Silence is good sometimes. The answers weren't there yet, but the seeds to the ones that mattered were planted.

I said it had almost become an obsession for me to find out more. I was curious about how different people could have such abilities. I figured that aside from the man who read cards and the two women who connected to the other side and had brought the book idea forward, I had met more people like them since. There was my astrologer friend who'd introduced me to Donna. He also had recommended another woman who connected with and spoke to the other side and did astrology too. Then there was a woman who read tarot cards and could connect to whatever dimension people go to when they pass over. I enjoyed her help. She explained things so I could understand them. I became aware of much more. I had met a woman who read palms. I'd even met a woman who looked into a crystal ball. It surprised me that they all had similar feelings toward many things in many ways.

With the ones who connected to the other side, I was always skeptical at first, so before I met them, I'd ask my dad before we started to have them say something particular. Every time I did, it worked. The people I met with understood my doubts and insecurities regarding such a delicate experience. It was an icebreaker in a way. They gained my trust rather quickly.

All of those people had a skill I didn't. I was amazed by it. In a way, I became consumed by it. I wasn't living my own life. I was worrying about what my future was without living in the present.

I explained to all the groups that there was no need for me to meet with someone like that anymore, but if anyone else was curious about it, there were people out there with unique abilities. I was never afraid of any of the people I met, and they all were excellent at what they did.

I could see that some people were taking more time to process what I'd just shared than others. I asked all the groups to think about certain points in their own lives when something that happened could've turned out much worse than it really did, whether in a physical, spiritual, or emotional way.

My example was Thanksgiving at my sister's house a few years back. My full attention was on finishing up my landscaping season as quickly and painlessly as possible before the predicted weather made it more unpleasant. It had happened almost every year. Working in a yard and trying to clean it up when it was cold and snowing sucked. Instead of staying and enjoying the holiday with my family, I decided to cut out a day early. The weather was beautiful there. It was also decent at home. I left my sister's home at six o'clock in the morning and got on the highway. I was wearing shorts and a T-shirt in sixty-degree weather. The weather I was driving into was predicted to be in the upper forties with a slight possibility of rain.

I'd made it more than halfway and was going through the mountains, when I came across a snowstorm. I'd never expected it. There were two accidents on the other side of the road. One car had flipped onto its roof. I said to myself out loud, "What kind of idiot does that?" I was stunned to see that, but I kept driving faster, thinking, *I'll be out of this soon.* I'd seen storms like that before many times.

My brother had left about an hour behind me that morning. Because we'd both left, my mom and sister, who were driving together, decided to come back early too. They slept in and were going to spend the morning with my other sister. I called each to warn them about the snow.

Maybe thirty seconds after leaving the messages, I noticed I was flying down a hill that swept to the right. As I turned, I hit a patch of ice and lost control of my truck. For a moment, I experienced what I can only explain as the most complete calm sense of weightlessness. It is something I can still go back to in my mind anytime I want.

When that split second ended, however, the moment the truck caught ground again was the most violent experience I'd ever had before or have had since. I barrel-rolled up the side of the mountain and came back down the same way. I landed on my roof with the truck still running. The truck was destroyed. I was also one foot from being back on the highway. People in a car behind me stopped to help me out of the truck. When it came to rest, I was suspended upside down in my seat belt, with a pillow I'd taken with me lying under my head. I fell onto it when I undid the seat belt. In the truck were tools I'd forgotten to take out before I left: a saw, knives, and a shovel. I was unscathed, though—not a bump, scratch, or bruise.

A woman and her son and daughter helped me out. The doors were jammed shut by the ground. I unlocked the door, and the young kid pulled while I pushed with my feet to open it up. The woman said I'd rolled at least five times up and down the hill. My bumper was way back where the roll had started. My vehicle didn't even look like a truck anymore.

I called 911 to tell them I'd wrecked in the snow but was fine. I told them about the wreck on the other side of the road and said they should send someone there first. A little later, a trooper pulled up, and I gave him my information. He said, "It happens. The weather comes out of nowhere." He was stunned to see me walking around okay.

A huge wrecker came and picked the tattered truck off the side of the road. People had stopped to see what had happened, including a nurse. She asked me if I was okay. She couldn't believe I was. While riding with the tow truck driver, I contacted my brother, and he picked me up at the exit before the spot where I had wrecked.

The tow truck driver said that in fourteen years, he'd only seen one other wreck like mine in which some had walked away unhurt. He stared at me and my truck when we got out to meet my brother. He got a call about the other wreck. The driver had been scalped by a hockey skate. He was in trouble. They were hoping he made it to the hospital in time. With the tools I had with me, I'm not sure how I wasn't hurt at all.

During the moment of calmness I spoke of earlier, it was almost as if something pulled me into the middle of the vehicle. I was restrained by the seat belt. I didn't going flying around or anything. The sounds of crunching metal and the impact were so powerful it was unreal. Something saved me. Who or what that something was or is I still don't know.

When talking about the experience with all three groups, I learned that others had had similar things happen to them—maybe not to the extent I had but scary stuff or stuff they couldn't explain. I asked them to think about how close they all had been to dying, either because of their drug use or because of other events. I told them, "That's a pretty good indication you should get over this stuff, put it behind you, and find out what you're really here for."

It was a good way to open up some minds to think about God, a higher power, angels, or whatever one believed in. That day showed me the truck was replaceable, and I was not. I was still angry about losing the truck, though.

After the groups cleared out, Donna said that in the next couple weeks, she had more doctors coming on. She told me she had more days for me and new groups. I told her I was okay with that happening; I just needed to know the days. She also told me one doctor was coming on next week to replace the one I was working with. He was bringing his wife, who had been a counselor too. She was eighty-five years old, weighed eighty pounds, and had a walker. She would be working there too.

We came to the solution that the woman would run the groups, but I would do a one-on-one meeting with everyone in the groups. At the time, I had no idea how that would change everything.

30

One on One

The format of individual meetings was a good thing. I was able to get the people who hadn't shared much before to open up about how things were going. Unfortunately, for some of them, things weren't always good.

Everyone knew I received the results of the people who'd failed the drug test. Some of those people were at least honest about it. Others entertained me with some of the best bullshit stories I'd ever heard. Some I played along with just to see how far they would go. Many felt dumb after I told them I'd known. I never judged anyone for it, though. I'd done the same things in different ways. I said they were just lying to themselves. It didn't matter if they lied to me. The drug test said it all. Some had to be dismissed from the facility. It was part of the process, though. They still wanted to use drugs for reasons of their own.

Many were battling themselves as much as they were the situations that seemed out of their control. For some, life wasn't bad, or at least they didn't have as many hardships. There were others who had it much worse. One wouldn't have wanted to be in their shoes in a million years. I was amazed some people made it from week to week.

It was a diverse group of men and women of all races and ages and from all over the city and outlying areas, which proved to everyone that the disease didn't discriminate.

I felt the person who took the most advantage of the one-on-one was J. C. It was as if that format were made for him. He treated me with more respect than the others in all my groups combined. Little by little, he opened up more and more. There was a point where it stopped, though. I could tell he wanted to say more, just not there.

I did the one-on-one meetings in a small conference room. Many people came through it. One time, I did some of them in the back end of the kitchen. Nurses came through, and people who worked in the office came through. Donna would come through.

The trust J. C. had in me was lost every time the door opened. It was as if he had built-in paranoia within him. He would start to talk and then shut down, worried about who might be listening.

I enjoyed talking with him. I saw that being up front with him was finally allowing him to be that way with me. Because I had his weekly results, he couldn't lie about still doing some drugs. He said, "I'm in a tough spot sometimes. I can't really say why, though."

I was stunned to hear those words come out of his mouth. I wanted to know why. I hoped to get the information out of him in the time we had each week, but he got to a point where he just turned it off. I knew where that point was with him now, so I had to be delicate in how I approached the topic. Figuring him out was something I was trying to do in my spare time now.

Then the day came when he flipped the switch on me. He locked me up.

The conference room I was in had padded, reclining high-backed seats with soft cushions and wheels on them. That particular morning, I was getting near the point where he always shut down about whatever we were talking about that day, so I took a shot at a different approach.

I held up my hand with one finger up. "Hold it one second." I pushed my feet to slide myself in the chair toward the door. I then locked it. "Okay, go ahead. What were you gonna say?" I returned to the table, spinning the seat and pushing myself backward.

He froze for a second and then fell back into the chair, relaxed. "Can I call you, and we can just talk? I'd really like that. You get it; other people don't. You say you do it with your friend Mike. Can we do the same thing?" Right there he got me.

His request was as genuine as one person asking for help could get. I couldn't believe what I was hearing. I froze the same way he had earlier. I didn't have an answer right away.

I didn't want to say yes, but then again, I did. I took a second and tried to give the politically correct answer. "You know I can't do that. Everyone else would want my number, and I'd be on the phone all day after I left here." I laughed to make it seem as if I understood his request but felt it wouldn't be fair. I then told him in a more serious tone, "How it's perceived with our being in the same group may be a problem. I'm not sure they'll go for that. I don't want to get either one of us in trouble." I could feel myself backpedaling in saying that.

I didn't want to say no to him, though. I thought about how hard it must have been for him to ask for my help outside of that place. He trusted me far beyond what I'd ever considered. He'd had to do some serious soul searching to get to that point in time.

I couldn't say no, but I couldn't say yes. I continued to make excuses for why I couldn't do it. "If you were in another group, then I guess I would be okay with it. That's where I've got to be with it."

He smiled and said, "Okay, I understand where you're coming from. I don't want to get you in trouble. I couldn't do that." He was a good read of people, so I wasn't sure if he thought I was bullshitting him. I was off my game now; he'd gotten me.

I was relieved that he understood and wasn't mad. After that, we shook hands, and he said thanks, as he always did. I asked him to send the next person in before he went to see the doctor. He agreed and then said, "I'll catch up with you before I leave here today." He smiled and closed the door.

The next person came in, and we started to talk. Things seemed to go back to normal. Then, a few minutes later, out of nowhere, there was a commotion out in the hallway. People were yelling. I knew both voices immediately. It was J. C. and the doctor.

By the time I got out into the hallway, Donna was in the middle of the argument, trying to separate the two with her arms extended out toward each. It wasn't physical, just some loud yelling. The doctor said, "I'm not putting up with him. He's gone!"

J. C. yelled back a profanity and said, "He doesn't know anything!"

Donna put a quick halt to everything. Everyone in the place was watching the three of them. She pointed at J. C. "You! In my office right now." She then pointed to the doctor. "The next person is coming in a second. I'll handle this, and we'll talk later. Everyone get back to what you were doing; it's over."

She walked into the conference room and said to me, "What's going on with those two? J. C. was doing pretty good, right?"

With the other person still standing there, I couldn't tell her what he and I had just spoken about. "We'll talk later. I'm trying to get finished up here."

Donna said okay and headed back toward her office in the back. She knew something was up.

I couldn't believe what had just happened as I spoke to the next few people I saw. I wondered how much I was responsible for what had happened.

About twenty minutes later, J. C. came back into the conference room. "Hey, Mr. Jack. Well, I got kicked out by the doctor. We didn't get along anyway. I spoke to Miss Donna, though, and she's letting me see another doctor."

I was relieved to hear that he hadn't been kicked out, but I knew what he was going to say next. I'd been watching a master manipulator at work. I smiled, and he knew I knew.

"So I'm not in your group anymore. So I guess it'd be okay to call you then." He smiled. He'd pulled off his plan with perfection.

I agreed to it, laughing along with him for a moment, and then I got serious with him. "It's like this, with no exceptions: if you screw this up, I'm out. I'll block your number if I have to. We talk every day. If we can't talk, I expect a text saying why you can't. You can't get in trouble. No more drugs. I check your tests. If you want to do this, I'll help. Don't screw it up."

His smile disappeared. "Whatever you say I'll do."

We shook hands and gave a half hug, agreeing to the terms set. I looked at him and started to laugh again. "What the hell did you say to the doctor, man? And what did you say to Donna after that?"

He started to laugh too. "I told that doctor what he was. You know, he and I never got along from the beginning." He was trying to justify his behavior now.

What J. C. had done showed me he was thinking about changing who he was. However, I was worried about what he was. I said, "Whatever promise you made to Donna, you'd better keep it, and I expect you to tell me the truth too." He and I then exchanged numbers and texted each other to make sure they were real.

I couldn't believe he'd worked me the way he had. I told him I'd call him when I left. He said he would be there when I did. I talked to Donna after he left. She said he was right about the doctor. He had had problems with other people too. When I told her what had happened with his and my agreement, she was in disbelief. She couldn't believe the extent he'd gone to in order to get what he wanted. She warned me to be careful and to either call or text her after each time we contacted each other. We were both convinced it was a huge step forward in many ways. If I had any problems with him, she said the next move would be to dismiss him.

I walked back to my car. My friend Clayton saw the smile on my face and seemingly knew something had happened during the day. I told him about the blowup between J. C. and the doctor, though I didn't use names.

His eyes opened wider as he processed what I had said. "You got through to him. That's amazing. Congratulations on that. What's next?"

I was as curious about that as he was. I noticed he'd asked the "What's next?" question I'd been asked years before and now asked people at the clinic. I shook my head. "I guess we're gonna talk and see where he really is. I'm not sure what all he wants out of me either. For him to ask for my help, I do agree he has come a long way."

I often thought I could take Clayton to the group with me, and he'd do as well as anyone in getting through to some of those people. Clay was good at finding the right question or the right answer whenever we spoke about the reactions to the questions I proposed every day.

He pointed at me before speaking. "You have his respect; you have his trust. That's probably more than anyone has gotten from him in his entire life. You know he's seeing something in you that you can do something for him. That's a lot already."

I was humbled by his words. "I'm not here to save him, though. I'm here to help him save himself. I wonder every week if I'm going to see him the following one. He's opened up a little bit on some things. He stops before it's too far, though. He's referred a little bit to how things are for him. It's normal to him. And it's all okay."

The smile left his face, and his tone changed. "I know. I see it all around. Some of these young people are damaged severely by the time they're twenty-one or even before then. Their lives are over—either wasted in jail, or they end up dead. So how do you help him help himself?"

I shrugged before I answered. "One question at a time, I guess. I need to know him, but I don't want to hear his confessions or something like that. I'm not here to absolve him of his sins. I'm pretty sure he'll be straight up, though. Plus, he's come this far already. I think he's looking for answers to help him get out of it altogether. He's been in this since he was thirteen or fourteen, and he's almost thirty—that's over half his life. I guess I'll find out soon. I'm calling him after I get out of here."

I shook Clayton's hand, and he wished me luck. "I'll see you soon. I can only imagine what you're going to talk about. It'll be okay, though. Look how far you've come. This is bigger than you, and it's bigger than him now. It's about you and him."

I hit some traffic and had to go into a tunnel, so I couldn't call J. C. until I made it through that. It gave me time to collect my thoughts. When I called, he picked up on the first ring. "Mr. Jack, what's up? You outta there?" He was upbeat, as usual.

"Yes, I am. How are you doing?" Before he could answer, I said, "I was impressed with your work today. You're pretty smooth. I'm quite impressed by how quickly you managed to be booted out and let back in like nothing happened. What the hell happened there?"

Knowing I was calling him out in a way, he laughed a little. "Oh, you liked that? Well, the doctor and me never really got along. Miss Donna knows that. He said something, and I didn't agree with him, and I'd had enough. He's done it before. I probably should have just went and found Donna and worked it out, but you know."

I wasn't sure if he was giving me the answer I wanted to hear or was being as honest as he could be after he'd thought about how it played out. I thought of what Clayton had said: *This is bigger than just me.* It was about helping J. C. as others had helped me.

We made some small talk over the next few minutes. I asked where he lived and things like that. I knew he worked for a moving company, but I wasn't sure where he worked out of. When he told me where he lived, I realized he lived about ten minutes from my mom's house and about one minute from where Frank and I ate wings on Monday nights. That kind of freaked me out, but I didn't tell him anything other than saying I knew the area well. When he told me the location of his moving company, I almost wrecked my car: it was two doors down from the place my old boss had rented out years before.

When I told him that, we realized we had been next to each other every week for almost two years. Each of us knew the name of the other's employer because of the advertising on the trucks. We could not believe it. That was a little weird for both of us.

J. C. made my traffic-filled ride seem like a breeze that day. We laughed about a lot of things. As I got closer to my mom's home, I passed the bar I'd told him about in group. I told him I could have had my mail delivered there because I'd been there so much. I'd bought things other than alcohol there too.

He said he was aware of the place. Then, without realizing it, I opened up about the resentment I had toward the place. "I kind of hope that place gets what's coming to it. I know about some things personally, and I've heard some other stuff. I know it's been under investigation for quite some time. Something will happen; there will be a crack in the armor somewhere sometime, and it'll all come out. Karma will even it out. I'm glad I've washed my hands of the place."

J. C. didn't comment on that, but why would he have? After my little rant, he said he had to go. He was about to get off the trolley he was on. I knew exactly where he was. The stop was right across from the restaurant where Frank and I went for wings.

Lastly, before we hung up, I told him how our deal was going to go. "Here's how it has to work. You call me every day, or I'll call you. We'll text in the morning to figure out that time. We may talk for one minute or an hour—it doesn't matter. No using drugs. If you fail your drug tests at Donna's, that's not gonna cut it. Don't do anything illegal either. We can talk about anything, and I'll help you any way I can. I promise. You're also gonna meet my friend Mike. He's the best. He's where I go to talk. He's been there from the beginning for me. You and I are also going to go to a meeting of some sort too. I want you to experience it for a couple different reasons, but we'll talk about that later."

Without trying to negotiate any of the terms I'd just put out, he agreed instantly. "I'm fine with that, Mr. Jack. I'll call you tomorrow around five. Is that okay with you?"

His response was another surprise of the day. I didn't argue it all. "That sounds fantastic, my friend. Have a good night. By the way, J. C., thank you."

He sounded surprised as he asked, "Thank you for what?"

I told him, "I appreciate all you're doing. You've come a long way since we met. I appreciate you asking me for help."

"Well, thanks then. I'll call you tomorrow. If something comes up, I'll text you." It seemed everything I'd asked of him was sinking in. He said goodbye and hung up.

I texted Donna after I hung up with him: "It went better than expected. I'll give you the details later."

I called her the next morning. She couldn't believe it. She also said there were more doctors coming aboard next week, so I'd be working five days if I wanted. We weren't going to do the one-on-one meetings anymore. The timing of what had happened with J. C. was weird. It might not have happened a week later.

31

It All Speeds Up

J. C. kept his word about calling every day. We texted in the morning to set up the call time. We spoke sometimes in the morning while driving in, sometimes after work, and sometimes at night. We spoke about everything: family, work, sports, drugs, and whatever else was going on.

If anyone had told me when I started that I'd be speaking to J. C. daily, there was no way I would've believed it. I told him about the new groups I had coming up. I asked him what I should do as far as the topics I brought up with the new groups and what ones he'd liked. His input was a big help. I started to sense he might even be enjoying our talks.

The more J. C. and I interacted, the more I watched my relationship with the woman I was seeing again slip away. She was upset that he and I were talking at all, let alone as much as we did. I didn't hide my phone from her, and she knew my password, so she could see that we spoke a lot. One day she overheard a comment I said to him and was upset. She went through the roof when I got off the phone with him.

He was comfortable enough to talk to me about his intentions of planning some sort of way to get out of the situation he was in. He wasn't sure he could. He could be in serious trouble for even thinking about it, let alone asking about it. That was an obvious sign to me that he wanted to get out of the group he was with. He never called it a gang. It was just his group of friends to him. They were people he'd known half his life. They'd probably saved him many times. He was now hoping to leave without something bad happening. He wanted to change his life. I understood because I'd had to learn how to change myself, and it wasn't easy. His situation, to me, was way harder.

My girlfriend was mad. She had every right to be. It led to some bad arguments. Over the course of the next few weeks, the relationship ended again—for the third time. It was on me. I understood she was scared and didn't deserve to be on my account. She was right to feel the way she did.

It was a tough time for me. It was harder than I'd thought it would be. I was a little depressed because of it. But it also made me wonder if I was supposed to be with that woman after all.

Like my landscaping business, my job served as an outlet to avoid thinking about it as much as I could. I played hockey with some old friends again too. The physical outlet for me was a blessing, and I'd forgotten I enjoyed it as much as I did. It was as if I were twenty years old all over again in a forty-something-year-old body. But I still loved it.

J. C. sometimes worked out of town for weeks at a time, but he called every day. I could sense a change in his voice, so I thought it was a good time for him to meet Mike soon. Mike agreed without hesitation. J. C. was a little reluctant at first but agreed after a little persistence from me.

Before we all met, I told Donna what was happening. She was happy about it. She pointed out to me that J. C.'s drug tests hadn't been good for the past few weeks. They'd given him the benefit of the doubt since he was out of town working so much. Before that, he'd been doing great.

I didn't want to come down on him too hard, but I wanted him to know I was concerned because he'd been doing well recently. The next time we spoke, I asked him a few questions to lead into the ones I needed answers on. He knew all along where the conversation was going.

As I started to broach the topic, he stopped me. "Can we just talk about this when we get together with Mike?"

He took me by surprise with that question. I was proud of him. He was willing to talk about it—and face-to-face. He wasn't trying to hide things from me. Plus, he'd just agreed to meet Mike. I wasn't going to argue with him or ride him about it. "You got it, buddy. When you get back in town, we'll figure something out."

I heard relief in his voice as he said, "Thanks. It's not what you might think either." He then asked me how I was handling my breakup from a few weeks ago.

"I'm doing okay. We'll talk about that later. I appreciate you asking." It hit me then that he was concerned about me. It was humbling to me that he'd asked me that. We both had come a long way.

Over the next couple days, I spoke to Mike. He was fine with meeting J. C. Neither knew how much I'd told each about the other, but I had no doubt they would see the same things in each other that I had. I knew that Mike was one of my best resources to make another impact in a positive way on J. C. That was just who Mike was.

I spoke to J. C. and said Mike was looking forward to meeting him. J. C. got back in town on a Thursday, so we set up a meeting at a coffee shop for Friday night. I was to pick J. C. up at his house at six forty-five, and we would meet Mike at seven. I called Mike as I was arriving to pick up J. C. Mike was just pulling up to the coffee shop. He said it was pretty empty. It was kind of perfect, we both thought. There weren't any distractions there.

I was nervous while pulling up. I hung up with Mike and walked toward the front door. I knocked a couple times and heard someone approach the door and then unlock it before opening it. It was J. C.'s wife. "Hi. You must be Mr. Jack. He isn't here. He's down the street, helping a friend of his with a TV."

She saw by the look on my face that I wasn't sure what I was supposed to do next. She said, "If you go down the street here, you'll run right into him." She pointed in the direction of my car. "Just right down that way. He'll be at the end of the road."

I was in a state of disbelief. She saw it and said, "I told him not to go, but you know how he is. Just go down the street; he's at the end. You can't miss him."

I laughed, shaking my head. "Okay, I'll find him." I started to turn back down the steps, when she spoke again.

"You know, he likes you a lot. He thinks you're a good guy."

I stopped at the bottom, turning to look at her. "I like him too. I think he's a good guy too. He's killing me right now, though." I laughed.

I could see in her eyes that she was already seeing some of the changes he was making. My voice became serious again. "I wouldn't be here if I didn't. He and I are alike in many ways. He's come a long way so far, so let's keep our fingers crossed we can keep doing what we're doing." I hoped to reassure her that I cared.

I then laughed while walking across the yard. "I'll definitely be back if I can't find him."

She laughed too. "He's at the end of the road; you can't miss him. Trust me."

Just outside of my car, I called Mike before I got back in. "He's not here, Mike. He's down the street, helping a friend with a TV. He's supposedly waiting for me at the end of his street, but all I can see is complete darkness. And before you ask, I'm not sure if they stole the TV or what the deal is with that."

Mike laughed. "Okay. Just take your time, and be careful. I'll see you when you get here. Call me in a few minutes to let me know what's happening."

I sat in my car for a moment, laughing to myself. It was a late fall evening. It was already dark outside, and a light mist of rain was falling. Other than the one streetlight in front of J. C.'s, there wasn't another light on the entire road. I'd been on that road before. It was around a quarter-mile long. In the day, one could see down the entire road. There was complete darkness now. I couldn't see anything. Hardly any lights were on in any of the houses either.

I slowly drove down the street and noticed a few people sitting out on their porches. They stared at me as I looked at them. I drove slowly, trying to see if I could see J. C. I realized how awkward I probably looked to the people who lived there. At the end of the street, J. C. was waiting for me, just as his wife had told me.

"Hey, Mr. Jack. Pull up to the house with the lights on and the front door open. I'll be right up behind you."

I called Mike as I drove up. "I've found him, and the TV seems like it hasn't moved yet."

Mike laughed hysterically and said, "See you when you get here."

J. C. walked by me and up to the back of the truck I'd parked behind. His friend was there, pulling out the TV—a big flat screen in a box covered by a piece of plastic to protect it from the increasing mist. He introduced me to his friend while they maneuvered the TV off the truck, down a set of steps, and into the house.

It was impressive how quickly the two had the TV unloaded, moved inside, opened, and in its place inside the home. The house smelled as if someone had just smoked a joint or two in it. J. C. said from the other room, "Mr. Jack, I didn't smoke anything—just so you know."

His friend then verified that. "He didn't at all."

J. C. explained a little about me to his friend. J. C. said his friend was the only person he could really talk to about what had happened over the past few months. His friend added, "We've been talking about a lot of things." He was aware of who I was.

They didn't say exactly what they'd talked about, but I guessed they were ready to get out of the situation they were in. If it was meant to be or he wanted my help further, he had to bring it up. I just wanted to get on the way to meet Mike, who was still waiting.

A few minutes after they'd moved the TV inside and hooked it up, J. C. and I were in my car and on our way to meet Mike. It was about a ten-minute drive to catch up to Mike. He met us in the parking lot, and we all walked in together.

I introduced them to each other as we sat down at a table. I excused myself and went to get a few drinks at the counter. I had no problem with leaving them alone. I felt I knew what Mike was going to do. He'd done it to me years ago. He would assess the situation and say the right thing. He had the unique ability to do that.

After I ordered three drinks, I just stood back and watched. I watched them both and their interactions. Almost immediately, there was laughter and an exchange, as I had expected. By the time I got over to the table, I almost felt as if I were intruding. I never asked either what they'd been taking about. I didn't need to do that. It was between them.

Mike jokingly asked J. C. if the TV was stolen. J. C. looked at me and said, "You told him!" He was now laughing too. "I guess it could've looked that way."

Over the next almost hour and a half, I heard stories from each of them that I had never heard before. I was blessed to be a part of the energy at that table that night. I had a feeling the meeting could help J. C. take another step. Mike and I spoke to him about going with me to a twelve-step meeting—only one. He didn't have to go to any more if he didn't want to. He needed to see it and might learn something else there.

The evening came to an end with Mike asking J. C. one last question as we stood under the awning out front, preparing to run into the light rain. "Do you believe in God?"

J. C. smiled at him, looking puzzled. Before J. C. could answer, Mike explained his question. "What else other than God could bring together two white guys and a black guy fifteen and twenty-some years apart in age on a rainy Friday night to talk about all the stuff we just did? All the experiences—the good and bad, different highs and lows, the ability to change. There has to be a God."

J. C. took in Mike's words and, with both of them laughing, replied, "Well, I guess there has to be, huh?"

I knew what Mike had meant but didn't think J. C. took it that way. It was about finding your own answer and the way life works for you within your own world. Something bigger than us brings us together at the right time if we allow it to.

Mike walked over to J. C. and shook his hand. "It was my pleasure to meet you. Good luck in all you do. I'm glad I can put a face to your name now." He then turned to me. "Thanks, pal. I'll talk to you soon." He gave me a hug, and he was on his way.

J. C. and I ran to my car. "He's a pretty cool guy. You're lucky to have him in your life, Mr. Jack."

I started the car and pulled away. "Oh, I know that. He's taught me a lot. He's never told me anything directly to do or not to do. He's only asked me to think about what I'm doing and why I'm doing it. He doesn't force anything or try to intimidate but tries to have me solve many situations with my heart and my head."

The drive back was quick; there was no traffic at all. When we returned to J. C.'s home, he invited me in to meet his wife and children. As we entered, I could hear his kids running around upstairs, excited that their dad was home. He yelled up to his wife that we were coming up. He wanted to show me his home.

In that moment, certain things started to make sense. Things he hadn't told me about suddenly seemed obvious to me. He saw on my face what I was taking in. After going up the stairs, he called for his son and daughter to come out to meet me. They came flying out and latched on to him tightly. They were naturally nervous of a stranger in their home.

He explained I was his friend and said it was okay. He had them show me each of their bedrooms. They used another as a playroom. His wife was in their bedroom. He led me in there, and his wife was lying on the bed. She looked terrible compared to the person I'd met a couple hours ago at the front door.

He knew I knew something was wrong. She complained about how she was feeling and asked him to get her something for it. He slid into the bathroom and then back into their room. He handed her something and a glass of water. He then told her we would be checking out the rest of the house. We'd be downstairs if she needed him. I said it was nice to meet her. I was surprised when she said, "Me too. We didn't think you were for real at first."

He laughed as we went down the stairs. At the bottom, he said to me, "I guess you can understand that, huh?"

Smiling, I nodded at him. "Yes, I can."

Downstairs, he showed me the kitchen, living room, and dining room. There was another bathroom. He then yelled back upstairs to ask his wife, "Is the dog in his cage?"

Her reply was the sound of someone in pain. "Yes. Don't let him bark too much. The kids are going to bed soon."

He looked at me and said, "Let me check first." He opened the basement door and descended the stairs quickly. He said it was okay to come on down. Before I got to the bottom, his dog went nuts, barking. J. C. yelled at the dog to be quiet. It didn't work. The dog was the biggest rottweiler I'd ever seen in my life. The cage he was in was huge. It shook as the dog stared at the intruder in his home.

J. C. yelled at the dog until it finally calmed down. After a minute so, the dog lay there in the cage as if nothing had happened. I looked around the room and saw a washer and dryer, a pool table, and more toys for the kids. There were clothes hanging up and a table with laundry baskets on it. He then pointed out his pride and joy of the room: a recording studio he'd constructed in another smaller room. It wasn't big, but it worked for him. He lit up while describing how much he and his friends enjoyed being down in that room. He asked me if I wanted to record something while I was there, and he was serious.

I laughed. "I gave up recording music when I quit drinking. You understand how that is, huh?"

He laughed too. "Oh, I get it. That could be a trigger for you or something." He showed me all the tricks of his studio, none of which I understood, before we went back upstairs and sat in the living room.

He got a bottle of water for each of us. Sitting in a chair, I complimented him on his home and his family, and then I got right to the point. In the same calm voice I'd always used with him, I said, "Okay, man, one question. How high up are you in this thing you're in?" I didn't want to say *gang*, but that was exactly what it was.

He looked at me for a second, took a deep breath, and finally answered. What he said left me in a state of shock, although I couldn't let him see that. "Well, in the city, number-wise, I'm about three. I'm up there. I've been in this over half my life. I know it. I live it."

My heart went into my stomach. I tried not to show any emotion and stayed completely still while staring at him. I needed a moment to think this over. It suddenly came to me. "Okay. Nobody knows you're downtown at that place then. Nobody knows anything about me except your wife, your mom, and the guy we met earlier tonight, huh? No one knows you've got an addiction issue either?"

He nodded. "Mr. Jack, you're good. You're right on everything. I'd give all this back to just be able to be with my family and walk away from what I'm into. There is no future in this. I'll either be killed or end up in jail. I don't want either of those to happen."

My mind went to the guy we'd met earlier. J. C. knew it, as if he were reading my mind. "Don't worry about the guy you met tonight. He sees it the same way as me. It's a scary life anymore. These young kids are trying to make names for themselves, and they'll do anything. They're trying to climb the ladder too."

I smiled and tried to break up the seriousness of the moment. "Well, thank God for that man!"

His smile lit up again. "Or we'd both be in trouble."

After a few seconds of silence during which we stared at each other, I asked another question. "Your wife—does she have an addiction too?"

"Wow! How did you figure that out? She had a back problem. It started from there."

His honesty led to another guess from me. "Does she split your prescription with you? She was going through the withdrawal thing earlier, huh?"

My assumptions impressed J. C. "You're all over it now. You got me."

It was a relief he wasn't hiding it from me. I took a moment to think about how to handle what he'd revealed. "I think that first and foremost, you and your wife need to get off the stuff as quick as possible. That may solve problem one. Wow, man, the other thing—I don't have an answer for you. I wish I did. One thing at a time, I guess."

I thanked him for trusting me in meeting Mike. We agreed that no one downtown should know about that night. I did tell him I would tell Donna we'd met but not about the situation with his wife. However, he and his wife had to agree to make an effort to get off the Suboxone.

Thinking about the whole evening on my way home, I couldn't believe so much had taken place. I thought of J. C.'s expression when Mike asked him if the TV was stolen. It was a good evening. Something bigger than all of us had brought it together to make it work. At the end of the night, the uncomfortable had become a little more comfortable. That other thing, not even close.

32

Keep the Wheels Turning

I called Mike the following morning to thank him again. He downplayed his part in the whole thing. I knew differently, though. J. C. had really listened to him and opened up to him even more than I'd thought he would. I told Mike about going to J. C.'s house afterward for a little bit. What I'd learned about the situation was beneficial to know.

I asked Mike what his original opinion of J. C. had been and what he'd thought after we talked. Mike had seen and experienced things I had no need to ever know about. He had left his past in the past and become at peace with it. Still, I wasn't ready for his answer about how he felt about J. C.

"My honest opinion is that he scares the shit out of me. I got that feeling almost immediately. I haven't gotten that feeling in a long time. I'm not judging him by any means whatsoever, but he carries an energy around him as if he feels indestructible. He doesn't seem like he fears anything. He was very respectful, though. That being said, I did like him."

I'd felt the same way Mike did when I first met him.

He said, "You know, it's more than amazing how far you've gotten with him, but you have to consider that something could go wrong at any time with the whole situation. It's like with everyone else. We'll all go through different things. He has some things going on that not many can say they're prepared to handle. I don't think he's always ready for what can happen."

Mike was worried about my safety more than anything else. I knew he was right. I knew it because in all the time I'd been working at the clinic, I hadn't said much to my family about working so closely with J. C. What could I have said to anyone close to me about being around someone with his background? There was no way that would have gone over well with anyone in my family.

I couldn't deny that mentoring J. C. had already cost me one relationship. I felt as if I were walking on eggshells in not telling my family about it. It had crossed over the boundary of being just a work thing. It was on my own time now. Learning what I had made me nervous about how things really were. That being said, I was glad to know the truth.

The next following months went surprisingly smoothly. J. C. and I spoke every day. He passed his drug tests, with the occasional marijuana positive in his system. I felt comfortable enough to ask J. C. to come into my new group I had on the day he was there. I was still seeing about thirty-five to forty-five people a day but now was doing it five days a week.

Having J. C. come in to talk to everyone not only helped me out but also showed the new people there was hope. I was impressed with him. I knew I had a resource with him to use to help others. He had experienced a fair amount of the topics I'd brought up with his group, so he was well versed in adding to what I was attempting to get across with the newer groups.

We would try to talk about the day's topic the morning or night before if possible. He was comfortable with what I had asked of him. He was an excellent communicator when he wanted to be. It seemed to the new groups that he just walked in and was ready to go. He would stay for ten minutes and then go back to his group. He was helping someone else now, which made him accountable to do his best. He never bragged about it either.

He still had some issues, but compared to where he had been, he was a new person. He had even quit wearing his colors. He wore gray.

He said it was neutral. That was when I was convinced he had turned the corner.

I wasn't sure how the change in him was seen in his other world he lived in, but it made me worry about him more. Little did I know that in between Christmas and New Year's, something would happen that would change the entire dynamic of what was going to play out.

It was a rainy forty-plus-degree day—not a normal winter day. I was leaving the parking lot of a supermarket, when I saw I was getting a call from J. C. I thought it would be a normal conversation like the ones we'd had for the past few months. It was anything but.

"What's up, buddy? How are you doing?" I asked. "You getting ready for New Year's Eve?"

"Hey, Mr. Jack. Well, I'm okay, but I'm starting to see where things are at." I could sense in his voice he was starting to get angry about whatever had happened. "I was walking home through the field near my house last night, and a guy I knew from the past was standing there. I hadn't seen this guy in years. He just got out of prison. I'd heard he was out, but I never expected to see him there."

I asked, "What time did this happen, and where were you coming from?"

He slowed himself down. "I was at my buddy's. It was a little after midnight." His voice picked up again. "I was wondering, *What the hell is he doing here confronting me?* Then he pulled a gun on me! I asked, 'What are you doing?' He replied, 'You got a price, and I'm getting it.'"

I was glad I wasn't driving while he told me that. I couldn't believe what he was saying. However, the fact that he was alive to tell me meant that something had happened to prevent a fatality.

"Mr. Jack, he pulled the gun up and aimed it at my face. I looked right down the barrel. It was a full moon too; it was as bright as could be. Then the bastard pulled the trigger, but the gun jammed. He lowered it for a second, so I punched him in the face. It gave me enough time to get away. This was a couple hundred feet from my house!

"I ran as fast as I could. Then, this morning, I heard from my buddy that the police got the guy last night to top it off. He got pulled over in a car with a busted taillight. He's going away for good now. He's on parole, and they found him with a gun. He's gone!"

The way he saw what had happened surprised me even more.

"Mr. Jack, it reminds me of you wrecking in your truck. Something didn't let me get shot. Something protected me. There is no way I shouldn't be dead right now. I guess somebody is watching out for me." His voice had changed again. He sounded relieved he was alive.

Now, my first thought about what he'd said wasn't the same as his. Mine was *Somebody wants you dead. You were being hunted by someone.* The more I thought about it, the more I realized he was right. In the face of certain death, he'd survived. He'd dodged death.

I had to ask him some questions to ease my own thinking. "Do you have any idea who set this attempt out on you?"

I didn't expect his answer. His voice was calm again. "I actually think it could be my own people. This guy knew me. It wasn't one of those things that one of my enemies would try to do quickly and get away. This was personal. He found out where I was and waited. He knew I'd be coming that way."

I knew he already had been thinking about who was behind it. "Well, are you afraid of something happening again to you or to your family? What's your next move? I guess that's what I'm asking. I'm really happy to know you're okay. I mean that. I'm just taking in all you've said so far. You've reinforced in me the 'something bigger' aspect of this."

For him, being afraid was different. He wasn't. "I'm not afraid of anything—well, maybe my mom and my wife." He laughed. "Seriously, I'm not afraid of anything. It's either good or bad, and I don't put up with bad stuff for me or my family. Someone will pay if anything happens to my family."

I asked more questions, and as always, he was straight up with his answers. He said, "I do think someone will try something again. It may be tonight, or it may not be for a while. I just have to be on point like I always am. Even with my own. There aren't many people I trust now."

The two of us had developed an interesting friendship. We had the ability to learn from each other and also help each other. We could also make each other laugh, so that was what I tried to do before I hung up with him.

"Just remember one more thing, man: I'm not the one coming after you." I laughed.

He laughed too. "I know that, Mr. Jack. I know that."

I told him to be careful and maybe lie low for New Year's. We wished each other a happy New Year and decided to text tomorrow.

I contacted Donna immediately and let her know what all had gone down. She was and wasn't surprised. She, like me, thought he had some sort of guardian angel with him. He'd had his share of close calls in the past, especially after being shot, which had led him to her facility.

Over the next few weeks, J. C. changed toward everything around him. He explained more things to me, including how he'd gotten involved in the gang and the grooming that had taken place. He shared with me how some things worked in the group. He was keeping himself sharp and on guard at all times.

He'd also been working out of town more, which took him away from his family. He didn't like that. It was obvious it was eating at him.

Things had also changed for me at the clinic. I felt I was seeing way too many people a week. Sadly, it was a job that didn't seem to run out of clients. They were turning people away because of lack of availability. The energy of the place had become difficult to be in. The energy, from the people there for treatment to the people working there, seemed to change. It was wearing me down in many ways.

There were people who did want to get clean. Many others didn't. Their excuses were exhausting. Dealing with their lying, denial, and anger was tough sometimes. I tried to do everything in my power to leave the work there when I left. It was essential to make sure I left it behind before I got into my car. My way of doing it was prayer.

I was required to make reports on every person I saw. I had to do that after I got home, because it was too loud and busy to concentrate at the clinic. Doing the reports took an extra two hours of my day. I was losing time for myself. My notes were given to the doctors each day for the next visit to assist in the progress of each person.

As tough as things had become, J. C.'s tests showed he would do well for a couple weeks and then have a spike in drug use. I asked him what was going on with that.

He said he and his associates were required to meet at certain times to have discussions about how things were going. He had to be at the meetings and participate in certain social activities that came up each time. If he didn't participate, the others would feel he wasn't on board with everyone else. He knew he had a bull's-eye on his back, so drawing any more attention would raise more eyebrows.

It seemed to me he was worn out by that life. He wanted to leave it behind him. He was aware of where things were going. He was locked into it, though. It was as if it were a career he couldn't change.

In early April, around midnight one night, my phone suddenly rang. I was startled and had no idea who was calling. The caller ID showed it was J. C. Immediately, a sick feeling came over me. I feared something bad had happened.

I answered on the second ring. "Hey, buddy, what's going on? Are you okay?" I immediately knew something was wrong by his voice.

"Mr. Jack, I need your help. I want you to take this name down. Do you have a piece of paper near you?"

I grabbed a piece of paper and a pen and told him I did.

"Okay, Mr. Jack, if you don't hear from me by one o'clock in the morning, I want you to go to the police department, give them this name, and tell them I'm probably dead. They'll know where to go to find him."

I said, "Yes, okay, I've got it. I'll do it." He gave me the name, and I wrote it down and slid the paper into my wallet. I then asked, "Are you okay, man?"

His answer was quick. "I'm gonna pay this guy some money, and hopefully things can change tonight or real soon. Thanks, Mr. Jack."

I then went to speak with my mom and came clean about the call I'd just received. I said it had been from someone I worked with. I explained to her that I had to go to a particular police station and do what I'd been asked if I didn't hear from the person in an hour.

As you might expect, she was in disbelief at what I was saying. Explaining it to her took almost until one o'clock. I didn't tell her the whole truth because I was trying to make the situation sound less severe. I hadn't heard anything from him yet, and it was almost time to go. I made my way to my car and started it.

Before I pulled out of the driveway, I said a prayer out loud that I would hear from him before I got to the station. As I reached down to put the car into reverse, I saw a text from J. C. flash in: "Mr. Jack, I'm okay. I'll see you tomorrow."

It was 12:59 according to my phone. *Prayer answered*, I thought.

I walked back into my mom's house and explained that he was fine. I knew she hadn't been ready to hear what'd I'd just spoken to her about, but she was proud of me for helping another, no matter how difficult it was. The stuff I'd told her about J. C., even though I'd told her only about 2 percent of it, scared the living hell out of her.

Because she knew Mike, telling her I'd introduced them to each other was the best thing I could do. I knew she would worry about me more than I needed her to, though. I'd already done that to her far too many times before. It seemed it would happen again.

On the bright side, it seemed the medication being prescribed to my mom was fully working. She asked about J. C. more. I could see she was taking on some unnecessary feelings because of the situation. It was as if she dwelled on the thought of something bad happening to me.

Things cooled off for a few weeks after the midnight call from J. C., but I had a bad feeling it was the calm before the storm. I knew the storm was coming; I just didn't know when. It would be unavoidable.

Things all happen for a reason. They wouldn't happen if they didn't.

33

Once It's Rolling, It's Tough to Stop

One of the things Mike and I had talked to J. C. about was attending a twelve-step meeting of some sort when he was out of town for work. There were multiple reasons. One, attending a meeting in his downtime might keep him from doing the drugs he was doing on the road. Two, he was less likely to know someone there, so he wouldn't have to worry about being seen at a meeting there. Third, as the programs were considered by many, including Mike and me, to be spirituality-based, he might hear something he could use to help himself.

A few weeks later into spring, for the most part, things had calmed down. There wasn't any drama. It was nice. J. C. asked me if I would meet his mom.

His mom didn't believe the changes she had seen in him, and his wife apparently gave me some of the credit for his change. I was flattered by his offer. I agreed I would meet her. I wondered about the conversations he had with her about the changes he had made, his life, and, most of all, me.

As we were talking on the phone while he was out of town one day, he said he felt it was time for him to go to one of the meetings, and he asked if I would take him. I'd hoped he would go on his own for his own reasons. I chalked it up to wishful thinking.

I was stunned by his request. I'd suggested it for so long that my shock overtook the reluctant feeling I had about taking him.

Because it was now spring instead of fall, I had other concerns. It stayed lighter outside much later now. My going to pick him up meant anyone could see us together. But I couldn't say no to him or pass up the opportunity. I was proud of him for wanting to go.

He said he didn't want to go to one alone. That was why he didn't go when he was out of town. He said it would be too uncomfortable. He was being honest about how he felt.

His openness toward other things became more apparent. There wasn't much that bothered him, it seemed. He was specific about people I should look out for when I was downtown, either coming in or leaving the building we were in. Those conversations made me nervous and made me more aware of my surroundings.

Since the night of the pre–New Year's Eve call, he had been taking different routes to the places he normally went to. He was surprised no one had ever known he was coming to the clinic. He also wasn't sure he wasn't being followed. He said it happened.

As much as I wanted to, I didn't ask what had gone down the night he called me at midnight. If he wanted to talk about it, he would. I learned from Mike that one had to deal with what was happening in the present.

I learned why I never saw J. C. on Mondays when I was getting wings with Frank: that was the night when he and his associates met. The place where we had wings was maybe a three-minute walk from the trolley line to his house. The trolley stop was directly across from the restaurant. He'd mentioned that he went there every so often.

A week after J. C. brought up the idea of going to a meeting, we decided to go. I was to pick him up at his house at six thirty. The meeting started at seven. Based on my experiences with the meetings, I was pretty sure we'd see some things he might not be familiar with.

I told him he'd see many varieties of emotions, both men and women, a wide range of age groups, and likely someone he knew. He was going to see people who were struggling and people who'd had some slipups. He might also see people in a worse place than he was right now.

I wanted him to see success too—people who were doing whatever it took and not doing what they'd done before. I hoped he could see himself being that way and avoid the repeated cycles.

The following week, he came into my group and told me directly to my face he would be at his house and ready to go at six thirty. One woman heard him say it and also heard my reply to him, which was as direct as I'd ever been with him: "You'd better be, or I'll kill you myself." We both laughed.

She was surprised to hear our conversation. "You and him are going to a meeting together?"

I nodded, leaned toward her to keep the conversation between the two of us if I could, and said in a soft voice, "You wouldn't believe what I've been through with him. This is quite an accomplishment."

The expression on her face was one of disbelief. She didn't understand. Not many did other than Donna and Mike.

That evening, I pulled up to his home, expecting him to be ready. It was a warm day; the temperature was in the mideighties. I didn't see anyone watching me walk up to his house. I went to the front door and knocked. I could feel the heat coming off the house. I waited about thirty seconds and then knocked again. No one answered. About thirty seconds later, his wife finally came to the door. Before I could even say hello, she said, "He's up at the courts, playing basketball. You can pick him up there, he said."

I stared at her for a moment, taking in her words. "What? Where is the court at?" I knew it wouldn't be right to be upset with her.

She saw I wasn't happy that he wasn't there and ready to go, as he'd said he would be. She stepped out of the house and pointed to the road across the street from where I'd come in. "Just go up there and make a left, and it'll loop all the way around to the top. He'll be there. I'm positive."

I tried to disguise my anger by laughing and saying, "He's killing me."

She laughed too. "You're not telling me something I don't know."

I shook my head and turned around to leave the porch. "I'll see you when I bring him back later."

Before she went inside, she said, "Thank you. He told me that he's told you a lot."

I was surprised to hear that from her. I stopped and looked back at her. "He's told me a lot all right. I don't think it's everything, though. He's a good guy. He just needs to keep doing what he's doing. I know he's trying."

She smiled and said, "He is trying. We're all happy about that."

I got back in my car and cussed him out for a minute as I turned around, but I couldn't stay mad at him, especially after seeing his wife's expression. I made the two turns and found myself on the road she'd been talking about.

I had passed that road many times but never been on it before. I had no idea where it led or what was at the end of it, other than now knowing there was a basketball court around there somewhere.

I drove up the road, which went up a steep hill, and came to a stop sign. I turned on my left blinker to signal that I was turning. It was the only turn available to make. At the stop sign was a car with three young-looking black men in it. We all made eye contact for a split second before I turned left. Immediately, they pulled behind me. The speed limit was marked at twenty-five miles per hour. I noticed their car was directly behind me now, on my back bumper. My heart sank in my chest. There wasn't any way I was going to speed up. I tried not to look in my rearview mirror too much, but I could see one man reaching around for something.

There were houses on both sides of the street, with cars lining each side the whole way up. The houses were older, and most of them looked as if they needed some type of work in one way or another. The road was about a quarter-mile long. It looped up and around to the right, as J. C.'s wife had said.

By the time I made it to where the road banked to the right, I saw that not only was the car in my mirror close to me, but now the three men inside it were saying stuff to me. I was invading their territory, it seemed. I asked myself, "Where the hell is J. C., and where the hell is this basketball court?"

I kept driving to the top of the road, and I noticed it leveled off some. As I drove farther, the road descended downward, and to my left was a basketball court with people playing on it. The car behind me was still locked onto my bumper.

Pulling up toward the court, I could see J. C. taking a shot from around the free-throw line. He pumped his fist as the ball dropped through the net. I signaled with my turn signal that I was turning off to the right, but there was no way the car behind me could have seen the signal because of how close it was.

As I pulled over, the car behind me stopped. Everyone on the court looked over toward us. A huge feeling of relief came over me when J. C. noticed me and called out, "Mr. Jack!"

He came around the fence. I saw him coming and stepped out of my car. We did the normal handshake and half hug we always did. The men in the car that had followed me earlier watched and then slowly pulled away. I looked at J. C. as they pulled by, staring at us.

Without hesitation, he said, "Don't worry; they're okay."

I smiled in relief. "Was it their job to scare the shit out of me the entire way here?"

He laughed. He thought I was making a joke. I was serious.

I saw on the court the man he'd helped with the TV a while back.

"Do we have a few more minutes, or do we gotta go?" J. C. asked.

I shook my head. "Nah, we have to roll. I don't want to be late. You know how I am about being late."

He laughed. "Yeah, I do." Then he yelled over to the guys on the court, "I gotta roll! I'll catch you later on!"

We got in my car and drove down the hill to the stop sign where one had to turn left. There again were the three young men in the car that had tailed me all the way around. At the sign, everyone in the car stared at the two us leaving together. My eyes locked onto the driver as I drove back down the hill.

When we got to the meeting, we were a couple minutes early. J. C. knew I had a thing about timeliness from my court experience. "Hey, Mr. Jack, we're not late, huh?"

I looked over to see him smiling. "No, we're not. It's all good," I replied. I was now calm compared to how I had been ten minutes ago.

After getting out, I stopped him at the front of my car. "I don't care if you speak in there. If you don't, that's fine. I do want you to listen. I want you to listen to who says what. You're going to see people in different places in their recovery. There will be some with opinions different from yours about things. It's okay. There may be people you like and ones you don't like. There will be people who are angry and ones who are happy with how life is right now. Please listen. Don't speak badly about anyone. We'll talk after."

As expected, we both knew people inside. A guy I knew was friends with Mike. I immediately introduced him to J. C., and it went as I'd imagined. As with Mike, I just let them talk. They spoke for a few minutes before the meeting started.

There were seven people at our table. There were easily twelve tables, plus people lining the border of the room. It was a big meeting. After the normal routines of the meeting, those in attendance broke into four separate groups.

I hoped J. C. would just listen and not speak, but that wasn't him. I was wrong to think that way. He was who he was. He spoke when it came to him. Although it didn't make much sense to anyone other than maybe me, I could see he felt he was a part of it.

The more I listened to others, the more I watched J. C. processing the experience. J. C. was a pretty good read on people. He used the skill in many ways to achieve what he wanted or needed or to deceive others in life. He was using it again. He was listening.

On the way home, I found that his perception of things wasn't far off from mine when we discussed the hour we'd spent there. He'd noticed some things that I could see hit him a little more than I'd expected. One was a guy he knew. "He looks a lot better now than I remember." He didn't say how he knew him, though.

It was around dusk when we left the meeting. It took some time to get out of the parking lot with so many people there. While we were sitting there, I asked J. C., "When do you get your license back?" I assumed his license was suspended. As long as I'd known him, he'd always taken public transportation or gotten a ride.

I couldn't believe his reply: "I'm not sure. It's been so long now that I don't even know what I need to do to get it back or when I do."

In disbelief, I said, "You're kidding me, right?"

He laughed, having expected my reply. "Nope, I've learned to adjust. You should know how that is."

He was right. I'd had to adjust to a few things. The similarities we had were more than I knew in a lot of ways. As we neared his home, I brought up one more thing I wanted him to think about. I didn't want an answer until he'd thought about it at least a little bit.

"In your wildest dreams, when we first met, could you have imagined we'd have the relationship we do today? What we've gone through individually and also together. All the conversations we've had and all the stuff that's gone down. Do you think it was supposed to happen, or do you think it was just dumb luck that has us sitting here right now?"

Before he could reply, I said, "I've thought about it, and I can't figure it out. So I'm asking you to think about it. I also want to talk about what happened tonight and what you got out of it too."

I waited to ask the questions till we were close to his house. I turned onto his street as I finished asking. He said, "Wow, Mr. Jack, I don't know."

I stopped him right there. "Think about it. We'll talk. Tell your wife thanks for the directions earlier." I shook his hand and told him we'd talk tomorrow.

34

The Beginning of the End

The following Monday, Frank and I met for wings. In the past, I'd talked to Frank about some of the stuff that had happened throughout the course of the new job but not everything. I'd mentioned J. C. to him a few times.

He always asked how things were going at the clinic. He knew I considered it a challenge. I thought it'd be okay to let him know the latest update on how things had turned out as of late without having him worrying about me too.

That evening, we both pulled up at the same time, and we walked into the place together and sat at the bar. We preferred to sit at the bar. The service was better. Most times, the same woman was working. Her shift started when we walked in around six o'clock each week.

The bartender loved Frank. Everyone did; he was a nice guy. She gave me a hard time but was only joking around. I gave it back to her pretty well when I could.

Every time we went in, the TV was on a sports channel of some sort. That evening was different, though; the news was on. I could see that the bartender was handling a table for the waitress, and she had been unable to change the TV channel. It was the perfect time to make a comment to let her know we had come in. I tapped Frank on the arm. "There must be some new help tonight, Frank; this bartender doesn't even have the right station on TV. This place is going downhill quick. Don't you think, Frank?"

Frank laughed, and the bartender's eyes locked onto the two of us.

"Oh! Hi, Frank. I'll be right with you. The guy next to you gets nothing." She rolled her eyes and then smiled. The people at the table she was waiting on laughed upon hearing what I had said. While waiting for her, I focused on the news coverage on the television.

The news featured a live report at a murder scene. The murder had happened earlier in the day. The name of the man murdered was what caught my attention: it was the name J. C. had given to me a couple weeks back. The man had been killed execution-style, and the killing was believed to be gang-related.

Frank had been watching the story along with me. He said, "Wow, that is just horrible. I'm not surprised that happened where it did. There's always something like that going on over that way."

I didn't say anything at first. I was frozen for a moment.

I reached into my wallet, pulled the piece of paper out, and looked at it. "What was the guy's name again, Frank?"

He pointed to the screen and read the name out loud.

I then handed him the piece of paper.

His face turned pale as he said, "Why do you have his name on that piece of paper? How would you even be associated with this guy?"

He asked more questions that I didn't answer right away. I was replaying the conversation from the call I'd received at midnight months back. Then I wondered if I would later be talking to a man who had murdered someone earlier in the day. I was pretty sure he was in town; I just wasn't sure if he was working or not. Had J. C. been involved in the murder in any way?

Frank was giving me a look I'd never seen before. "What is going on with things? Seriously."

I started to explain things in a relaxed voice to calm the moment down, but it didn't work. Frank saw through it. "You have the name of a gang member in your wallet, and he turned up dead execution-style. It's on the news. That's not normal. What's going on?"

The bartender came over and changed the channel. She gave us each a glass of ice water. "You guys want the same thing this week?" She grabbed a pen, preparing to write our orders down, already knowing them.

We both said yes, and she was gone. I was glad she was doing the waitress job too that night.

Trying to explain the situation to him was tough, but I explained it the best I could. Frank repeated over and over, "You're in too deep. Quit the job. Leave it behind you. Find something else. There is too much going on there for you to be involved any more than what you are. You could get killed."

My reply each time was "No one knows who I am." I didn't dare tell him about picking up J. C. at the basketball court. He would've flipped out about that.

Frank was not one to sugarcoat anything when something didn't feel right. I liked that about him. He was concerned about my safety. Like Mike, Frank was someone I trusted very much. I could tell him anything. I didn't feel good about not being completely honest with him.

Years back, I'd dragged Frank with me to meet the man who used a deck of cards to see what was going to happen. Basically everything he'd told Frank had come true. Frank knew I'd gone to some other people who did similar types of things too. Frank didn't go see any of them; it wasn't for him. But he was curious about some of them and what they told me.

I told him I was going to call one of those people. Maybe I could get some help that way. If the person felt it was that bad, I'd consider getting out of it right then and there.

Taking in the information I'd seen on the television, the paper with the guy's name on it, and the circumstances under which I'd received it, I couldn't deny I was in over my head now. I kept thinking about how far J. C. had come. I just couldn't get myself to walk away from him.

With Frank sitting next to me, I texted a woman who did work with tarot cards. I'd met her a few years back. She was awesome at what she did, and I trusted her to help me. Twenty minutes later, she replied. I arranged to meet her Saturday morning.

Frank looked at me, stunned. "I can't believe you. Quit the job. Get away from this guy." He didn't understand that I couldn't do it.

I told Frank, "I'll be okay."

When we left the restaurant, he said, "I hope it's safe to be seen with you. I'll talk to you during the week."

J. C. called me on my way home. He said he wasn't aware of what had happened. He couldn't believe what I told him about what I'd seen on the news. I believed him. He hadn't lied to me so far, so I didn't want to think he was doing it now.

He said his company would be out of town for the next few days. He'd be back Friday night. He again brought up the idea of my meeting his mom. I could hear Frank telling me to get away over and over: "Get out. Walk away." I told J. C. we would talk when he returned.

J. C. and I spoke every day, as usual. He said he was slipping away to talk to me. He said people asked him who he was talking to, because he said it was obvious when he was talking to his wife.

Saturday came. I was looking forward to catching up with the woman who did the tarot cards. She could also connect to other dimensions, as some of the others I'd met in the past could. Her skills with the tarot cards were unmatched. Learning to read the cards and interpret their meanings had taken years of teaching from people she'd known. I didn't understand how she did it, but I trusted the information she gave me.

It had been a while since I'd seen her last, but she remembered everything that had happened to me. She asked me not to tell her anything; we would talk about things after she revealed the cards. One by one, she studied them as she put them down. After the last one, she explained each one individually.

I had said nothing about anything, and the first words from her mouth were "I've got the feeling you need to leave your job or something to do with it. What are you doing now?"

I told her about the situation without holding any information back. I'll never forget the look on her face. She had a hard time believing I was still working there after all I'd told her.

I explained to her about the job, the people, and, lastly, J. C. She pointed to each card again and explained the seriousness of each one. She paused and then asked, "Is he in the hospital right now?"

I thought that was an odd question out of left field. Ten minutes later, I got a text from J. C. He said he was back in town, but he was in the hospital. I looked at her, and she smiled. How had she done that? She somehow had known it.

I explained more about him, and she said, "You need to quit the job. Today."

I tried to explain that it was okay, and I was fine.

She looked at me as if I were crazy. "Hey, you came to me and asked me what I could tell you about the situation you're in." She pointed down at the cards and circled around them with her finger. "I'm very serious. If you don't quit that job right now, something bad will happen. I'm not kidding you at all. The universe is warning you. It doesn't want you there anymore. The next warning will be more serious than the last one and so on."

Although she'd been right about things in the past, I still couldn't believe her.

She said some specific things about other parts of my life and then told me again to quit the job and let other things happen because they would. She knew I wasn't quitting. When I left, she said, "The best of luck if you don't quit. Realize you've done all you can do. It's up to him now."

I texted J. C. and asked why he was in the hospital. He said his wife had had back surgery. To me, that meant he wasn't in trouble, so why should I have believed I was?

The surgery was a good indicator his wife was going to have access to opiates again. I could only hope the situation didn't get out of hand.

The next week, I went into work, and it started a little roughly. A man who'd been kicked out the past week came storming in, demanding to have a prescription filled. He had two other guys with him, and they all were high on something. His wife had been arrested last week for shoplifting, and they were going to lose their child to child services.

He blasted through the door. One of the guys slid in behind him, while the other stood in the doorway. It became bad scene quickly. There was a nurse in the office, and two other female clients were in the waiting room. They were all terrified. The man was yelling threats all around. I thought I was going to end up physically fighting them.

I played it over in my mind as quickly as I could amid the yelling. I thought if I could knock the first one back, I could get the other out of the doorway. The last one was the one I was worried about. I couldn't account for him. I didn't know if the guys had weapons either. I anticipated that at least one of them, if not all of them, had something.

The nurse said she was calling the cops. The man replied, "They won't get here in time."

My heart sank. I wasn't letting any of them past me now. Rage came over me. "You'll be here when they get here, because I'll be holding you down myself! I don't care about you two. You two are just following this clown's lead."

The two other men eventually stepped back. I kept my eyes locked on the man I knew. "You'll end up just like your wife."

The three of them made the decision to get out of there. I tried to keep cool when it was over, but the atmosphere in the clinic was insane. That afternoon, I was in the elevator, when a fight broke out. I ended up taking an elbow to the jaw while trying to break it up. I ended up shoving one guy out the door onto a floor he didn't want to get off on to stop the altercation.

The next night, I worked until ten o'clock. I was told that would be my new schedule—noon to ten o'clock—on Tuesdays. Walking to my car in the middle of darkness through the city was not a great idea, even if the walk took only a little longer than five minutes. Plus, I had to do all the computer input work when I got home. The day didn't ever end.

On Wednesday, I was off, so nothing happened. On Thursday, my paycheck bounced. I was pissed off about that; it had never happened before. Donna apologized, saying it was fluke. Friday, though, was by far the worst day, worse than all of the others combined.

Friday morning, when I walked in, I saw a man from my original first group. I walked up behind him and tapped him on the shoulder. He swung around with an eight-inch knife, almost catching me in the stomach. Seeing it was me, he quickly apologized.

I couldn't believe how close of a call it had been. To top it off, we rode up the elevator together. I asked a nurse to check him, and she found the knife. He was dismissed for bringing a weapon into the office. He knew I was the one who'd told on him. I didn't care. God only knew what could've happened if the knife hadn't missed me.

Outside, after I left, I faced the final straw. In my talks with J. C.

over the past nine months, he'd told me about many different ways his group used younger people. I noticed a specific example as I was leaving on Friday.

I saw the guy who'd been driving the car behind me when I picked J. C. up at the basketball court. I was positive it was him. He was positioned as J. C. had described to me in one of our many conversations, across from the building I worked in.

He was signaling to a person in the backseat of the car. Why were they there? They knew what I looked like. They'd seen J. C. and me together. They were positioned so that I would have to walk through them to go to my car in the garage. They hadn't seen me yet, though. I slipped out and went the other way down the street.

I was terrified. I walked fast for two more blocks away from where I needed to go. I wondered if the third guy from the car was waiting for me near the garage. I was paranoid about everyone I passed.

When I got to the garage, I found my keys in the box near the pay station. Clayton and all the morning people were gone. I grabbed my keys from the box and got to my car. At that moment, I knew I wasn't coming back. I was done.

There was no good reason those two individuals would have been standing there outside my building. I wondered if they'd seen me. What if they had, and they followed me to my mom's home? I called her to see if she was okay. I just wanted to hear her voice. She was there. I didn't let on why I was calling; I just said I'd be there soon.

On my way back, I passed the bar I'd spent so many wasted years in and was surprised once more when I saw someone I knew walking inside. It was J. C.

What the hell was going on? I would not have believed all that was happening, except I was seeing it happen in front of me.

I didn't hear from J. C. at all over the weekend. Something was happening, and I wasn't comfortable with anything anymore. Worse, there was no one to tell. I couldn't tell anyone in my family. I had no proof of anything to go to the police if something happened either.

The next morning, I called Donna. I quit, effective immediately. She was concerned and asked about J. C. and if I was okay. I lied. I said I was fine. I told her I had a job offer out of state and couldn't pass it up.

I sat down with my mom and one of my sisters and explained the situation in detail. They were terrified when I was done. I said I needed to fall off the face of the earth for a little while. My car was in my mom's name, and my phone would go under my sister's name.

I canceled my plans to get wings with Frank on Monday. I knew he knew something wasn't right, but I didn't tell him anything about what had happened. I told him I'd quit my job. What happened next made everything that had happened in the past week seem mild.

I finally received a call from J. C. He sounded drunk to begin with. He was being punched by people. I could hear it happening. "Hey, Mr. Jack, how are you doing?" he asked, slurring.

"Are you okay?" I asked him. It was as if he were trying to defend himself and still talk on the phone.

"Yeah, I'm okay. I'm just out with the boys. We're having some drinks and some wings at the place up the street from my house."

I knew I'd just dodged a problem by canceling with Frank. There was no way I wouldn't have gotten hurt or worse by being there that night. I thanked God I'd decided to cancel. Something inside me had said, *Don't go.*

J. C. barely made sense for the rest of the conversation we tried to have. I didn't ask him any questions, but I tried to answer his. A few minutes into the conversation, I heard him get hit hard enough to drop the phone. It was a seriously punishing blow, based on the exasperated moan he let out.

Another person then picked up the phone and started talking to me. "Mr. Jack, we've heard about you. You and J. C. have been talking for some time now, I understand. We know who you are, and we'll find out where you're at soon enough. I'm looking forward to meeting you in person very soon."

I heard J. C. get hit or kicked another time. I heard him scramble to get back on the phone. "Mr. Jack, I'll call you tomorrow."

I couldn't believe what had just happened.

35

Learning to Hide in Plain Sight

On Tuesday, J. C. called me around two thirty in the afternoon. I had come to the conclusion that it would probably be the last time we spoke. He sounded terrible, as if he were in pain. He got straight to the point of addressing what I had heard happen last night.

"Some stuff has gone down lately, Mr. Jack. I didn't have anything to do with that guy dying, though. I wasn't anywhere near there. I was working. I'm not even sure who was involved. I didn't expect that to happen. That's the truth."

I appreciated that he answered my first question before I asked it. He then said, "You being seen with me at the basketball court—well, some people didn't understand that. They thought you and me were doing something completely different. Crazy as it sounds, now people think I want out to start something with you."

I knew the mess probably wouldn't have happened if he'd met me at his house that day, as planned, but he hadn't. This was the result of it. Unfortunately, the whole situation had taken a direction that had been possible at any time.

I was relieved he'd said he wasn't involved with the man being killed. I knew what I would have had to do if he'd told me he had been involved. However, the relief I felt went away as he continued.

He said he'd told whoever was above him that he wanted to leave and get out of the group. It was obvious they didn't believe him. The situation was now worse than he had ever intended it to be. More importantly, as he'd always told me, "You don't to ask to leave. You're in for good."

It turned out that in wanting to leave, J. C. wasn't alone. Some people who'd been playing basketball with him that day wanted out too. "People I know are thinking we're starting our own thing. The others guys wanting out—well, they look like they're coming with me. With us. That's why everyone is pissed off. They don't know the whole story. It's my fault."

I couldn't believe what he was saying. "If that's what they believe, then it doesn't matter what either one of us would say. That's messed up, man. I can't believe they didn't take you out last night." I was getting upset. "Tell me this then, J. C. I saw you Friday. I passed my old stomping grounds only to see you walking in there. What's that all about?"

He didn't know I'd seen him. He wasn't ready for that question. "Oh. Well, I've known that place a long time. I did some business there in the past. Business that probably ended up—well, that may have fallen into your hands. So I'm sorry about that. It's all coming down there now too, and nobody wants me to talk to nobody."

I'd heard from someone I knew who was still active in my old ways that something had happened recently. Things like that had happened many times before, but no one ever got in trouble. From what I'd heard, it sounded as if someone might this time.

"Hey, J. C., don't end up doing time for anyone. If you have to save yourself for you and your family, you do it. You're trying to make changes for yourself and for your family. You can't afford to go to prison for anyone.

"J. C., if you hadn't joined that group early in life, you probably would have been killed by them as an enemy of them. That was your means of survival. You survived. Now you've got the opportunity to try to make some of the things you did worth it by doing the right thing now. Decisions like these can affect you for the rest of your life. You know the difference between what is right and wrong. I know that."

He was quiet for a few seconds. I heard him breathing into the phone. I pictured his expression. It was an easy decision; he just had to go through with it. The hard part was facing the unknown reactions of others and what would happen because of it.

When I'd decided to change, it had only mattered if I went through with it. There was fear that went along with the change. I second-guessed the decision all the time. I questioned the who, how, where, when, and why, and most of all, I wondered what would happen. What would life be like?

Unfortunately, I was involved there too. My intentions had only ever been to help. I'd hoped to be an influence the way others had helped me. However, the way it was playing out, the situation had gotten more out of hand than either one of us could've imagined.

"This is why I'm gonna miss talking to you, Mr. Jack."

Right then, I knew this was it. He knew it too. Over the next hour, we talked about all the good things we had in common and the things we'd learned from each other. We spoke about the good and not so good.

He made it clear that I needed to stay under the radar. He was positive someone would be looking for me. He told me not to get a job for a while if I didn't need to. He was specific about how his group found people. They were organized.

I learned from him about trying to be one step ahead and having an awareness of my surroundings. I had watched his actions every time he walked into the office and group. He was programmed to be alert. Now I had to be.

We talked about our families for a little bit after that. Neither of us had had a father figure, and we talked about the result that absence had played in our lives. We talked about our moms. In our own ways, we had put them through much more than they deserved.

The conversation we both knew would be our last was slowly coming to an end. I thanked him for all he'd helped with. He didn't understand at first. I explained it to him.

"J. C., you taught me more than you know. The gift you gave me was allowing me to help you. I received help from people who had doubts about me. They stuck with me through it. In my opinion, you've probably come further than me. You've got the ability to do more and go beyond even what you think. Sometimes you can't see it until you step away from it and look at it in another light. You'll see the change. You'll be amazed by what has happened."

His words to me were just as kind about my not giving up on him and pressuring him without pressuring him. I'd made him think in a different way about change and about himself. He now looked at things differently than he once had.

We knew that neither one of us was safe for the near future. We agreed that we hoped we'd see each other somewhere somehow and that we'd both be healthy and well when we did. Saying goodbye felt like closing another chapter in life.

After the call, I explained everything to my mom the best I could. I showed her the paper on which I had written the name from the night of the call. I pulled up the name on the internet and showed her the story. Explaining it further was easier for me after that, but it was a lot for her to take in. It led her to ask a familiar question I'd heard before: "Well, what's next?" Admitting I didn't know was all I could say. Admitting I was afraid was easy.

I said, "I've come to the conclusion that I don't exactly lead the prototypical normal life, but I don't think I'm meant to either. I don't think that's why I'm here."

We talked more that afternoon about all that had happened. What I told her didn't make it better, but I had to tell her. My mom was a person of religious faith. Her beliefs had gotten her through many tough times. I had a feeling she was going into that mode again.

My plan for disappearing came into focus that evening. I was going to eat my words once again. I would spend my time at any local library that had an adjacent police station connected to it. I'd move to a different one every day. Because of my past, I knew where all of them were. It was the last place anyone would have looked for me.

I had to also explain the situation to the rest of my family, and there was no enjoyment in it. It was difficult for them to understand. Their reactions were all pretty much the same: disbelief that I'd put myself in that position. They all had their own lives to live. They were concerned about my issues' effect on my mom. None were happy that I was making her worry.

One person who did understand was Mike. He was the only one who'd met J. C. and who was able to understand any of it.

It was June at the time. I saw how blessed I was to have set aside some cash from my landscaping business to finance myself for a little while. I knew that money wasn't going to last forever, though.

I was now paranoid about everything I did and everywhere I went. I wondered, *How long will this feeling go on? A month? Three? Six? A year? Longer than that?* I watched the news a lot. I never heard J. C.'s name.

Frank and I found another place to get wings. It wasn't near the restaurant we had gone to before. He asked if I was okay every week. I said I was, but I was nervous to get back into a job or something new until I felt safe. J. C. had made it clear how easily a person could be found.

I ended up going to a coffee shop during the mornings and tried to just blend in after the first few months of going to libraries adjacent to police stations. I started to write on my computer.

The more I wrote, the more I enjoyed it. I was nearing what I thought was the end of my project. I again found that things could suddenly change in an instant, whether or not I liked it.

My finances were running low from not working. I knew I had to do something eventually, and maybe writing was an option or a lead to something else. Then, one morning, my computer died. I took it to a store, and they told me there was nothing they could do. I had to accept it. It was old. It had locked up. I hadn't seen it coming. The worst part was that I thought I had backed up my work, but I hadn't.

I was crushed. *This can't be happening. This is a horrible joke.* I asked myself what in the world I was doing wrong. I thought I'd done the right thing the entire time. Nothing was working out the way I had hoped it might.

The combination of all the things that had happened had me questioning life on every level possible. I was angry at and about everything. It was a nightmare. My level of frustration with things had reached a new high.

As always, Mike saw something I didn't. Talking to Mike helped again. He hadn't always understood me or everything I'd thrown at him, but he usually had me look at things from a new angle I hadn't seen.

As I complained that life was falling in on me again, he had heard enough. "Hey, maybe the ending hasn't played out yet. Maybe you'll see it happen; maybe you won't. Maybe it's time to get on. You're stuck, and you're angry, neither of which is helping you."

The calendar was passing by, and I didn't even notice. It had been eighteen months since everything had gone down. I was the way he'd described. I was repelling good things from happening. It stunk that he was right. I didn't want to admit it. I had to get through that predicament and get on with life. I just wanted to know it was okay to do so.

One cold winter day, I got that answer finally.

As I did every day, I played the lottery. There was a supermarket where I played regularly. It was a sunny, bright day, and I walked across the parking lot with my head down and tucked into my jacket to shield myself from the cold wind blowing. While approaching the building, I looked from side to side to make sure no cars were coming. I noticed a man in a big white ski jacket standing next to a cement pillar, shielding himself from the wind. He looked to be waiting for someone. His head was down in his jacket, as mine had been earlier.

I couldn't believe my eyes when I walked over to him. It was J. C.

I said sharply to him, "Hey!" I didn't have any other words in me.

His eyes lit up, and he smiled from ear to ear. "Mr. Jack! Oh my God!"

We shook hands and gave each other a half hug, as we had done in the past. We both felt disbelief that we were standing in front of each other.

Each of us asked the other how he was doing, stunned. He said he was out of the group and considered nonactive. He was free of everything, including drugs. He was clean, and his wife was too. He explained to me how everything had happened. He was glad I was safe. He said, "They were coming after you because of me. When I met the guy who was later killed, I was trying to buy my way out. I'm not sure what happened with him or who even got him.

"The guys you saw at the basketball court that day all wanted the same thing as me: to get out. Those guys in the car saw you and me together, and they told some people about seeing us. That's when they thought you and me were gonna do our thing. That's when things started to get out of hand."

He then said, "You must've hid well, Mr. Jack. They were looking for you for a while. I know that. I was afraid to contact you. I'm sorry about that. I really am."

When I told him where I went to hide out, he was impressed and said, "Oh, that's good. I don't think they would ever think about going there. That's smart."

He also asked about Mike. He said meeting him was probably one of the biggest turning points of our time together. I'd known that already.

As we talked for around ten minutes, neither one of us noticed the weather or how cold it was. We were both just happy we had met again. It was a relief to see him. At that moment in time, I finally felt free. Life was okay again. Mike had been right: I'd gotten an ending—finally.

J. C. asked me to apologize to my family for him. "I'm sure there's some stuff you probably didn't deserve to go through because of me."

He was right; I hadn't deserved to go through what I had. But if I didn't forgive him, none of what had happened would have been worth it. I saw my part in all of it now. Our meeting that day was both healing and a relief.

I gave him a hug and said I had to go. The last thing he said was "Thanks, Mr. Jack, for everything."

I walked away toward my car. Halfway there, I paused, and then I walked back over toward him. As I neared him, I asked one last request of him: "Please just call me Jack. That's what my friends call me." I laughed as I said it.

He laughed too. "Nope, you're Mr. Jack."

We shook hands, and I walked inside the store, remembering why I'd gone there to start with. I had almost forgotten to buy my lottery ticket.

I went in and played a couple bucks down for the evening draw. I was on top of the world all of a sudden. When leaving the store, I saw that J. C. was gone. I was happy he'd been there. Seeing him was what I'd needed.

Walking to my car, I felt as if I had won the lottery already. In many ways, I had. I called Mike and told him who I'd just run into. He couldn't believe it either. While I was talking with Mike, my phone beeped: someone else was calling. It was J. C. I asked Mike to hold on.

"Mr. Jack, my brother picked me up. I wish you could've met him. I told him all about you. I forgot to tell you one more thing: I spoke in a few secondary schools to young kids about staying out of gangs and that life. It felt good to do that. I took your advice too: I saved myself. You may see something happen soon enough. Take it easy, Mr. Jack."

I was blown away by what he'd said. I returned to the phone call with Mike, and he couldn't believe what I told him.

I told my family about running into J. C. They were happy for me, but they'd never understand the whole thing. I had to be okay with that.

In the spring, I took a job with a temp company, and within a month, I was hired on full-time. It turned out to be decent money, but I also felt as if I were in a babysitting position. I stayed on until just before winter came again. During my time working there, I ran into and started seeing the same woman I'd been seeing the past.

Again, neither she nor my family understood my leaving that company. Nobody could understand what it felt like to go door to door unannounced. Many times, homeowners weren't receptive. A man working with me had a gun pulled on him when I was forty feet away from him. I knew that job wasn't for me. It was a temporary job, and leaving it wasn't a career choice I'd be kicking myself over later on in life.

Experiencing something and telling someone about it are two different things. It's different when it happens to you. In a way, things were repeating themselves in my life. I had to do what was best for me.

When I started seeing the woman from my past again, we agreed we wouldn't tell our families we were seeing each other until we felt we were on stable ground to build a future together. I disliked the idea of not being honest with my family, but I understood the fears and added pressure their knowledge might cause my relationship with her. The only person I told was Mike. He understood the connection she and I had. He was neither for nor against it. He told me, "You'll find total happiness, or you'll end up moving on."

I ended up getting a job in a sporting goods store. I worked in the shoe department. The place sold every type of shoe you could imagine: tennis, basketball, court, cleats of all kinds, leisure, boots, kids', men's, and women's. There were more than sixteen hundred different types at any one time.

Things went okay there. With my mom's health much better than it had been in the past years, I moved into an apartment. I had time to myself; plus, I could continue the relationship that somehow had been interrupted in various ways in the past.

My brother helped me move in, which I enjoyed. He and I had come a long way. The way I had lived my life in the past had damaged our relationship. That was all it was—the past. Things had come to be a thousand times better. Changing my life's direction had shown me how wrong I was with him. He was a hell of a guy. I'd been so busy with myself for the past few years that I hadn't been in any of my family members' lives much.

While we were moving my things into my new place, my brother said he had heard some news about the bar I used to go to. He said the place was going to be torn down. I knew it had shut down a while back. I had my guess as to why. I started to put two and two together and figured maybe that was what J. C. had meant.

Little by little, the story came out from people I ran into here and there. One woman I knew from my past had the whole story. The police had found some illegal things going on there. She said one person had gone to prison. Everything made sense; it was true.

About six months later, I ran into the person who'd gone to prison. The person actually said hello to me. I saw that the person wasn't driving an expensive car, as before. The person was now driving a beat-up twenty-year-old car. Duct tape held the passenger door together.

I hoped J. C. had chosen to do the right thing as much as to save himself and his family. Sometimes things seem like they'll never happen. His change had been worth the wait.

Knowing that individual would have easily let J. C. go to jail, I looked at it as karma. J. C. was making changes, and none of them were easy for him or those around him. If he'd caught a break, well, then good for him. In my opinion, he deserved it. Some might disagree with my opinion.

I never spoke to J. C. again after that winter day. I don't need to. Through a bit of investigating, I found out from sources that he moved a thousand miles away. He's in control of his own life today. From what I've been told, he's well. I wish him the best.

36

Last Chapter

Never admitting the truth to yourself is one of the worst things you can do. People do it all the time. Because I'm human like everyone else, I can do it with the best of them. It's called making a mistake. Some mistakes are larger than others, and some have greater impacts and repercussions.

People pleasing is something else I know I do. It's debatable what people pleasing might be. It's mostly done from the position of fear. Maybe it's reverse manipulation—controlling people or keeping everyone happy and preventing the natural occurrences we or others would have to encounter as a result.

After a few weeks of my agreeing not to tell our families about our relationship, the woman I was seeing involved her parents in our lives again. I knew if I told my family about her, I'd face resistance from them, so I didn't tell them. I preferred not to face that.

I place no blame on anyone but myself. I could've done something and been truthful. I chose not to. That was a lesson I hadn't learned yet, I guess. It was a mistake not to be honest with myself and others, regardless of how they chose to see it.

I interacted with my family, but I never said I was involved with her again. As with everything, there were different ways to look at it. It was my life, and I could live it the way I wanted, so any other opinion didn't matter. I had a feeling I knew what my family's thoughts about it would have been. The relationship had failed to work out many times before, so why would it work now? The result was usually a painful lesson somewhere down the line, as history had proven.

That said, I had continually told my family and friends the past would be different each time we got back together. It would be for a while, and then things would fall away.

For almost a year, I kept the relationship a secret, and things went smoothly for me. I was coming up on another sobriety anniversary. My family was proud of my accomplishment. I was part of my family again. All the relationships had been rebuilt.

My brother called me a week before my anniversary. He offered to take me out to dinner. I said no. I lied about what I was doing and declined his offer. I felt terrible about what I'd just done. I felt sick to my stomach that I'd lied to him. Being dishonest was difficult now for me.

The day before my anniversary, I was at work. I noticed I was getting a call from my mom. My mom never called unless something was really good or really bad. I'd also spoken to her earlier in the day, so I knew something was up for sure.

I'd just gone on break, so I had my phone in my hand. I was walking into a store to get something to eat. The words she said stopped me from moving in any direction. I froze.

"Jack, he's gone. Your brother is gone. The police are at his house." She then said she'd call me right back. "I'll call you back in a minute. They're calling me right now."

I thought to myself, *This isn't happening.* No one around me knew of the news I had just received. I walked quickly back toward the store where I worked, staring at my phone, waiting for my mom to call back and explain what was going on.

My phone lit up again with a call from my mom. I heard the pain in her voice. "Yeah, he's gone. He had a heart attack."

I was stunned. "What are you talking about? Wait. What? There's no way."

There was silence for a few seconds. Her voice cracked. "It's true."

I said, "Okay, I'm leaving here now."

I found a manager and relayed the news I'd just gotten. My emotions started to take over, and my eyes welled with tears. The manager told me to just go.

My brother was only fifty years old, way too young to be gone. The news spread quickly to family from my mom. No one could believe what had happened. He'd spoken to one of my sisters just the night before.

A part of each person in my family died that moment. The next few days were brutal. Arrangements were made for a funeral—arrangements no one had expected to be making. The funeral would be on Saturday, with a one-day viewing from two o'clock until eight o'clock.

Everyone had a terrible time accepting that he was gone. My mom, who had buried two husbands and many others, was now saying goodbye to her oldest son. I'd seen my mom cry only a handful of times in my whole life. Crying was something she just didn't do. This was by far the worst loss she would have to experience.

My entire family was devastated by the loss, which no one had been prepared for. All I could think about was lying to him the last time we'd spoken. It tore me up inside. That was not the way I would have wanted my last conversation with him to go. I couldn't tell anyone that either.

A couple days before his viewing, my sister put a post on social media about the tragic and untimely passing of our brother. There wasn't enough time to put an obituary in the newspaper. My family agreed it would be easier on my mom to do it in one day. There was no easy way, though.

When Saturday came, people were at the funeral home all day nonstop. The day, as difficult as it was, seemed to go by quickly. More than two hundred people signed the guest book. Friends, coworkers, and people he'd known throughout his life came. My sisters' friends came, and my mom's friends came. Mike and Frank both came. There was so much support for my family; it was amazing.

The only person not there was the woman I was seeing. With four days in between his passing and the viewing, there was plenty of time for us to come to a decision about whether or not to tell my family. We had some long discussions and concluded that it might be too much to make such a reveal at the time. We both agreed on it, but I still wanted her to come. She didn't, though.

The day after the funeral, I came clean to my family that I'd been seeing her. My family asked why she hadn't been at the funeral then. That didn't go over well with them. For starters, I'd lied about seeing her, and some were disappointed she hadn't been there. They felt that if she cared about me, she would have been there regardless. That was kind of how I felt too.

The following Sunday, I went to dinner with her and her family. When I walked in, her dad came up to me said he was sorry to hear the news of my brother. What he said next made me look at things in a different light.

He said, "You know I would have come if I would've known."

After I left, I thought about what he'd said: *If I would've known.* It replayed in my head over and over. Had she not told her parents my brother had died? She spoke with her mom every day. I knew that for a fact. Her dad and I had gotten along great since we met, despite all she and I had been through, so I believed he would have come.

I wondered if our previous breakups had been something telling me she wasn't the one. Maybe it just wasn't meant to be.

She was a beautiful woman inside and out. I loved her. I was sure she loved me. But that hadn't stopped issues from separating us time and again. I thought about what had happened and the things I'd accomplished without her. I was happy. She did plenty well without me in her life. Life went on for each of us. When it was good, it was great, but when it wasn't, it wasn't. I just felt it wasn't meant to be.

About a week later, I planned to tell her I needed a break. It was time to move on from the relationship—this time permanently, though.

After telling her as politely as I could, I never looked back. I had to close the chapter. I had no anger, resentment, or negative feelings toward her. It was over.

I was grateful for it. Everything had run its course. That didn't mean I didn't care for her and all she and I had had together, because it wasn't that way at all. I just felt it was time.

A few weeks after that, another thing happened that I wasn't ready for: I found out my brother had a life insurance policy in my name. I was sure he'd never expected it to be used, but it was enough to get me going in another direction. It gave me the opportunity to leave my job. It took a couple more weeks, but the time finally came.

I went to the bank and spoke with a woman about paying off some existing debt I owed and doing something with what was left of the money.

The woman asked me about what I did and things like that. Not thinking much of it, I said I had written a book. "It took me to the craziest, scariest place I'd ever been."

She asked, "Well, what made you write it then?"

Sometimes when I brought up my reason for writing the book, it didn't go over well, but that day was different. When I told her about the two women, she said that she personally had some hesitations about seeing someone who could connect with the dead, but she also knew a woman who could do it. She said her friend was amazing at it.

I felt I was there to meet her and meet the other woman through her to connect with my brother.

A week later, I went back to the bank. The woman contacted her friend, who agreed to see me. I was excited about it but nervous too.

The regret of lying to my brother the last time I'd spoken to him weighed heavily on me. I hoped maybe trying to contact him could help me somehow help my family with what they were going through. Like me, they were all having a difficult time with his passing.

I asked a friend of mine, a girl I used to work with, to come with me. She agreed to go with me but admitted that she was a little nervous too.

It was the first time I hadn't had any doubts about meeting a person with those abilities. I had a good feeling about the endorsement of the woman from the bank. I also had a feeling this was supposed to happen. It had been six months since my brother's passing.

The night we met the woman, I let my friend go first. She spent an hour with the woman. When her time ended, she came into the room with a smile that said volumes without her saying a word. When she finally spoke, she said, "Wow, that was awesome! Your turn."

I went into the room. There were candles, statues of angels, and all kinds of things in the room. The energy of the room was calm, peaceful, and serene. The woman explained who she was, the gifts she had, and how they came to her from within. I explained the past few months and some of the things from my past. She saw how difficult it had been for me. "Well," she said, "your dad and your grandmother on his side are here." She paused for a couple seconds. "Your brother is here too."

I felt a tear roll down my face.

She continued. "He's fine. In fact, he's great. They all are. They don't like seeing you and your family like this, so you have to tell them he's okay. You have to understand that he was only meant to be here for that long. He did what he wanted to, and quite honestly, he did it really well." She smiled as she conveyed the kind words.

I nodded and agreed. "Yes, he did. At his funeral, I saw and heard about him from all the people who came. He touched a lot of people's lives in many ways. He taught me a lot after I got myself back together." I could hardly speak, and my voice cracked as I thought of him.

She smiled to console me. "Yeah, he saw you there. He was there." She paused for a moment and then floored me with her next statement. "He also saw all you went through to get yourself back from where you were at. He also knows what you did with J. C." She then asked, "Who was this J. C.? What happened with him?"

I smiled but said nothing. I hadn't mentioned anything about that, and she'd hit it directly with his name.

"Your brother is right next to you now. He's really proud of you. Nothing you've done has been easy. He thought you were crazy to visit people who do this sort of stuff, but he's glad now that you're crazy enough to still do it." She laughed. "I guess he's talking about seeing people like me. Oh, they're all laughing too now!"

I felt a warmth surround me that I had never felt before, and I asked her what it was.

"Your grandmother just gave you a hug," she said.

I told her she could do it again if she wanted to. Over the next hour, I felt the energy continually flow over me.

I received a tremendous amount of information to share with my family. She told me, "Don't worry; just do it. It'll work out."

I had no doubts. I was confident I just needed to do what was asked. I'd been told that before.

As many times as I'd gone to see someone who could see beyond, connecting with my dad and exchanging some type of communication with him never got old. He was the person on that side of the family whom I knew the least and the person I most wanted to know more about. Based on what has been shared with me, he's with me more than I realize, which he probably is.

My friend and I both had amazing and much-needed experiences that evening. We talked about it a little bit after we left.

It was soon November. Ten days after I met the clairvoyant woman, I went to a mass for my brother with my mom. My mom had read the time wrong, and we were an hour early. We went to get a cup of coffee to kill the hour. I told her everything. She then told my sisters the next day. My brother had asked me to tell them to please not be sad anymore.

Over the next few weeks, my brother made his presence known to my sisters. Knowing he was there didn't make them miss him less, but they weren't as sad about his loss as they had been before. Time would hopefully heal the pain eventually.

Talking about things with my mom was more difficult than talking with my other family members. I explained to her what the woman had told me, but my explanation didn't answer everything the way she wanted to hear it. I'd been told my paternal grandmother had met my brother when he passed over. Upon learning that, my mom was visibly upset. I hated seeing my mom cry, especially knowing I'd just caused it.

I didn't understand and asked her why she was crying.

She looked back fifty years to answer. She said that every time she and my dad had visited my grandparents, my grandmother had swooped my brother away all to her herself. *That's what grandparents do*, I thought. My mom didn't take it that way.

She continued to cry as she said, "She got him again, just like she always did." It upset her. I didn't know what to tell her.

I told my younger sister about it, and she pulled my mom aside a week later. My mom told her the same thing. My sister, though, made better sense out it. She turned the tables on my mom.

My sister asked, "What do you think she thought about you taking her son? You took him, and you kept him. How do you think she felt about that?"

My mom's face dropped. She'd never considered that. She had only seen it one way—her way. After fifty years, she was embarrassed. She'd found forgiveness. It had also come back to her.

To me, it made sense for my grandmother to welcome my brother to wherever they were, as my mom wasn't able to do it. My grandmother loved him. Love is the basis of everything there and here. It is the basis of who we are as human beings and why we exist.

The experience of my mom's realization showed plenty. Anyone can experience something important at any age. My sister and I were grateful my mom was capable of forgiving and moving forward. We knew we all were blessed that she was healthy and fully restored.

The way it happened was amazing, considering all the factors that went into it. My sister and I, at different points, had to help my mom find it. My visit with my brother helped the healing process.

For a period of time before that, I'd been upset about all the things that had happened to me. Few, if any, could really understand what all had occurred—with the exception of Mike, that is. He was there at my lowest point. Mike was the only person I could introduce J. C. to. He was the only person I knew who could help me help J. C.

I love my family and appreciate all they've done for me. We're all different. We don't always agree, but that's okay. Our differences don't stop love from being within the dynamic of who we are and how we see life. All the experiences we've had individually and together have created who we are, how we think, and how we see people and things in life.

Having the conversation with my brother and being able to communicate as if he were sitting next to me ranks second only to the day I met my dad in the same way. My regret about lying to him and not going to dinner had me feeling horrible. I knew he knew that. He eased the situation by relaying to me that he hadn't known it would be our last opportunity to see each other. If he had known, he would have done many things differently too.

Sitting there that evening with him, I wished I had changed my life earlier than I had. But I hadn't. The change had happened when it did and in the way it did for a reason, as other things had. He had no bad feelings toward me, only love. In fact, he was even prouder of me after learning more from wherever he was.

The experience reinforced to me that everything we do is seen, whether we believe it or not. Some might think talking to those who've passed is not possible, but I do. The feeling I left there with that night enabled me to help my family. It was the right time for it to happen.

Weeks after everything went down, I came to terms with things myself. The regret I'd been carrying lifted. I still miss my brother very much. When I'm alone, I speak to him as if he's right there. I kind of think he still is. I remember what I learned from him in both good and difficult times.

With all that's happened, I'm happy I made the changes I did. I know what I like and what I don't. I'm like everyone else in many ways. We have good days and not-as-good days. We make mistakes. We react to everything we encounter, big or small. We judge things based on our perceptions and beliefs. We can both assume and take things for granted. We don't always understand, so we ask questions. We can create as much as we can destroy. We have limits but are unlimited.

We like feeling good as much as not feeling bad. We like to be in control. We can be influenced, and we can influence. We can learn and teach. We give, and we take. We can be honest, and we can lie. We can make dreams come true, and we can crush them—our own and others'. We can love or hate anything or anyone, including ourselves. We can blame and be blamed. We can forgive and be forgiven. We also know the difference between right and wrong. We usually conceal a behavior when it's wrong, which is a pretty good sign. We can be respectful and be ignorant. We can be anything.

More often than not, we gravitate toward like-minded individuals for all the reasons above. There are exceptions to that; it can be said that opposites attract. We all grow and develop from the people, places, and things we come in contact with either directly or indirectly. That means we can have or form an opinion on anything if we want to take the time to.

We can have experiences that last for a moment or an entire lifetime. They can change our physical, mental, and emotional states to higher or lower extremes. We can experience the feeling of having it all or losing it all.

Life-changing moments can happen for anyone at any time. Sometimes we might not even notice they are happening for us or against us. They just happen.

One phrase I learned along the way—and still hate—is "Time takes time." Having it explained to me and thinking about it further made me dislike it even more—mainly because it's true. Process it anyway you please. To me, it's like this: I can't rush it. I can't make it stop. What time teaches is different for everyone. It can be slow, painful, agonizing, and unwanted. It can be wonderful, enlightening, and enjoyable. It can provide valuable lessons on all levels. It can offer knowledge that was previously unattainable, simply because it is time for that knowledge to be known. It can also go by quickly.

This applies to the beginning of time and all the debates that come from that. It's proven in what we've learned and accomplished throughout time as a whole and as individuals. The frustrations, tragedies, and enjoyments time allows us to experience are different for all of us.

Time is constant. We might feel we are fighting it; we might feel we are waiting on it. It might seem as if we're losing it. We can feel as if time will never end. We might feel that a particular time is right or wrong for where we are or what we want. Sometimes time pushes us, and sometimes it slows or even stops us.

What controls time or allows time is different for everyone. How we see time is our choice. Our belief in it or fear of it comes down to the free will of the people we are inside. What we do in the time we have is ours to experience with what we have to experience it with. Time takes time.

Time is a teacher too. It's called history. We can learn from it.

Knowledge, perspective, and experience can change any of us and cause growth on multiple levels, enhancing us. We should not judge or see life based on possessions or the physical. We should focus on the positive impacts and influences around us.

I've learned that some important lessons can come from the least likely places and least likely people. Many of us are living proof that these lessons happen every day.

As much as we are the same, though, we are different. It's supposed to be that way. We are all here together for that reason. Our individual identities and uniqueness are the gifts we all have to offer. By having, learning, refining, and using our skills, talents, and abilities within, we can find purpose and reason.

The people I've met who sense, see, or connect to different levels or dimensions are all gifted with talents of their own. Some, like me, are fascinated by the ability they possess and where it came from. Some are skeptical based on fear or doubt. It's all okay.

All of them, at some point in time, helped me. They made me aware of things or asked me to look at myself to see my own things to work on. They are all spiritual people. They aren't all alike. But why would they be? They are their own unique individuals, as everyone else is.

People have questioned or judged such people and their abilities throughout time, but the same is true for almost any other person in any other field of life.

Many religions and the stories within them speak of people being able to do these things, so why would it not be possible in today's world?

Whatever allows us to live and evolve isn't as far away as we might think. It's here with us; it's watching. It's near to us. It gives us life. It gives us what we need in order to sustain, grow, be, and experience more. Sometimes it's so subtle that we might not even notice. It provides new ideas too.

What we do with what we have in the time we have to do it is different for everyone because of the many factors we are meant to experience and the people we are meant to experience them with.

Somewhere inside each of us is our purpose for being here. Perhaps there's something we must do, overcome, or assist with. Perhaps our purpose is just to live the life we choose. Finding and experiencing one's purpose could be easy or difficult, depending on all the things that happen in a person's life.

On a planet of seven billion people, it's plain to see we might not all be here for the same reason, purpose, or experience. What if that is the reason we are all here—to have individual experiences and also be one as the planet we exist on?

We must treat each other as equals because we are all the same. We should treat each other equally one to one, male to female, race to race, country to country, religion to religion, and so on.

Life constantly brings tragedy and joy all over the world. Some experiences we can control; some we can't. We might not agree on everything, and people will view certain solutions differently. We might consider certain things right or wrong.

In my own experience, I found that when I was doing something wrong, I almost always tried to hide it because I knew it was wrong. Other times, though, I did something wrong because of my own ignorance.

When I changed my thinking and actions, I found I still made mistakes. I didn't have to hide them, though. My intentions changed next. Making changes wasn't easy all the time. When I was trying to do the right things, I had little to hide. I was just being me. I was being my authentic self. I wasn't sure who that was until I allowed that person to come to forth.

Had I not taken on what I did, none of it would've happened, including what happened for me on May 26, 2004. Maybe it just had to be. Many things happened. Each small step I took led to the next one and so on.

I had to come to see and understand how I was part of my own problem and what I could and couldn't control. I became willing to change.

My disease doesn't discriminate based on gender, race, or religion. I overcame it just as others before me did and even more ahead of me will.

In changing, I learned there are no coincidences; things happen for a reason. I'm grateful for it all. Free will is the deciding factor more often than not.

The way I see it now is like this: yesterday I was, today I am, and tomorrow is just that.

Printed and bound by PG in the USA